I0761641

FIRST DO NO HARM

ALSO BY S. J. ROZAN

Paper Son

The Art of Violence

Family Business

The Mayors of New York

FIRST DO NO HARM

A LYDIA CHIN / BILL SMITH MYSTERY

S. J. ROZAN

PEGASUS CRIME
NEW YORK LONDON

FIRST DO NO HARM

Pegasus Crime is an imprint of
Pegasus Books, Ltd.
148 West 37th Street, 13th Floor
New York, NY 10018

First Pegasus Books cloth edition January 2026

Interior design by Maria Fernandez

Library of Congress Cataloging-in-Publication Data is available.

ISBN: 979-8-89710-032-3

10 9 8 7 6 5 4 3 2

Printed in the United States of America
Distributed by Simon & Schuster
www.pegasusbooks.com

For Tom, Guy, and the great JL.

Dammit, fellas.

FIRST DO NO HARM

CHAPTER ONE

I've had the dream for as long as I can remember. I'm perched on a dizzying edge, staring at the ground far below. It's twilight: not quite dark, but nothing is distinct. I have to jump because it's the only way to get where I'm going and I absolutely have to get there. But when I step off, into the empty air, will I be able to control the fall? My heart pounds. A flash of ice races up my spine.

I step.

And that weightless second after I do, that moment when the question's still unanswered—that's why I do it, every time. Yes, I need to get there, wherever *there* is. But I know as I'm doing it that need is not the reason.

That dream's not, and never has been, a nightmare.

◆

It was the same now. That moment on the edge. But not quite the same: I was awake and could've backed out of this one. There was another way to get down. Like in the dreams, I couldn't make out what was below, but not because it was dark. The July morning was bright, the sky was a glorious blue, and the ground was far, far away, at the bottom of two and a half miles of empty air. And there wasn't anywhere I needed to get to. I could've chosen not to step out of the open airplane door.

Except my brother pushed me.

Technically, he didn't push. We were attached, me in front, sitting with our legs dangling out of the plane, and he jumped. But just before he did, I was about to. He pushed but I'd have pulled. I wanted that moment. And I got it.

Weightless, wind rushing, blue around, sun flashing, green below, that giddy moment lasting and lasting and stretching on, way longer than the dream, until a sudden tug and then silence, no rushing, just floating, down, sideways, sailing along above an abstract of greens and browns that slowly resolved into buildings, roads, fields. A truck, some cars, a Quonset hut. A dust cloud above a dirt strip.

"Now," I heard in my ear.

Laughing, I tucked up my knees.

Elliott stuck the landing.

He was the skydiver, after all.

◆

Back in the hut I was still laughing as I asked, "Can we go again?"

"Not today." Elliott grinned as he slipped his glasses back on. "I knew you'd love it."

"Don't tell Ma you took me."

"She'll know anyhow." He folded and tagged the parachute, the harnesses. He was right. My brothers and I have spent a lot of time over our lives trying to hide things from our mother. It rarely works.

Elliott passed the gear across the counter to a bearded, muscled guy who, I imagined, was just waiting for his shift to end so he could go jump.

"So when can—" I stopped as Elliott's phone played "Confusionality" by Doctor Django and his Nurses. He checked the screen and answered, stepping away. I strolled around the room, looking over the photos of shrieking free-fallers, floating formations, and a set of flyers in wingsuits. How had I waited this long to take Elliott up on his offer to join in?

My brother slipped his phone back into his cargo shorts and turned. I was about to repeat my half-asked question when he cut me off with one of his own.

"You know a good criminal lawyer?"

CHAPTER TWO

My brother needs a lawyer," I told Bill over the phone from the skydiving hut.

"Your brother is a lawyer. Unless it's a different brother, in which case *his* brother is a lawyer."

"It's Elliott, he needs a criminal lawyer, and it's for a friend."

"That's what they all say. What happened?"

"The friend was found at the hospital in the company of a dead body."

"Did he make it dead?"

"No."

"That's what they all say. New York City? Long Island, upstate, New Jersey?"

"That's as far as your reach extends?"

"God no. You need Nebraska? The Leeward Islands?"

"Just testing. Manhattan."

"The guy's in custody?"

"Yes, and he'd rather not be."

"That's what they all say."

◆

Bill called me back five minutes later. By then Elliot and I were in his car drinking tea as he zoomed us out of the Sussex County airport and raced toward the George Washington Bridge. Drinking tea, that's what the Chin family does when we're stressed. Also, when we're calm. Or hungry, stuffed, happy, sad, sleepy, or wide awake.

"Leo can't do it himself," Bill reported. "But he has a bad-tempered young woman with a chip on her shoulder he recommends."

Leo would be Leo Kirschenbaum, Bill's longtime attorney. Any recommendation of his was worth taking. "Sounds lovely."

"Not according to Leo. But she may be what your guy needs." He gave me the details.

"Juanita Cohen," I told Elliott, putting down my phone and picking up his. He raised an eyebrow at the mismatched name but said nothing. "You want me to call her?"

"Yes, thanks, and put it on speaker."

I tapped in his password. My brothers and I all know each other's, and our mother's, too. Hers is "phone."

"Cohen." A woman's voice, sounding harried, growled out of Elliott's sound system after three rings. "Talk loud, I'm on the street."

"Hi, Ms. Cohen. This is Dr. Elliott Chin. I'm calling because—"

"Because some asshole got himself arrested because he was stupid enough to sit beside a body waiting for the police to show up. That you?"

"Not me—"

"No, I mean, that's the case and you're paying the bills? Leo told me."

"For now."

"All I need. What's his name and where is he?"

"Jordy Kazarian. Manhattan Detention Center."

"I'll call you when I've seen him." Cohen was gone.

"Wow," Elliott said. "I don't think I've ever heard anyone slam down a cell phone before." A horn blared as a blue BMW roared past us. "Sorry." He slowed the car down. "I guess I'm a little upset. About Jordy. I'm driving like a maniac."

"Elliott? You always drive like a maniac. And that guy was just trying to prove his gas Beemer can beat your electric Porsche. You may be upset about your friend Jordy but it's also just barely possible you're upset because someone got murdered at your hospital."

"Well, but . . . I mean, people die in the ER all the time. It's been a long time since I've been upset about a patient dying."

I doubted that but didn't say so. "Murdered is different and this wasn't a patient. She was a nurse, a colleague. Did you know her?"

"Sophia Scott. We'd met. We ran into each other every now and then. But I didn't really know her."

"And how come, if she was killed yesterday, you didn't know about it until now? I'd think murdered is different enough that the news would burn up the wires."

"It will now. Jordy says Admin put a clamp on it. I guess they were able to keep it on until the arrest. You can see why they did it—not the kind of thing you want people to know happens in your hospital." He was silent for a few moments, then said, "I feel like . . ." He trailed off.

"Like you should have been able to do something? Like you always feel? Elliott, you barely knew her and you weren't there. And why am I even saying that? I can't talk you out of feeling that way. So tell me this—who's Jordy, why does him getting busted upset you, and why were you the guy he called?"

For a minute, Elliott didn't answer. He acted like he was concentrating on his driving, but he drives like he runs the ER at River Valley Downstate Medical Center: fast, smooth, on the edge but never rattled, no matter how big, wild, or dire the situation. By long-trained, finely honed, and by now deeply trusted instinct. I gave him time. It wasn't the road he was thinking about, or a jerk in a Beemer that was bothering him.

"Jordy's a diener. At the hospital," he finally said.

"What's a diener?"

"Morgue assistant. Prepares patients for autopsies, maintains the equipment, things like that."

"You still call them patients when they're dead?"

He glanced over at me. "Why not?"

"Because it's kind of weird. To us living patients. So why'd he call you? Instead of his family or something?"

"His mother was the only person in his family who'd have anything to do with him. She's gone now. No point in calling his father, I guarantee."

"How do you know?"

"He's River Valley's chief of medicine."

"Oddly cozy, both of them at the same hospital. So you know him?"

"Too well. There's another one, too, Jordy's brother. Also a doctor."

"Yet Jordy called you."

Elliott looked almost embarrassed. "I saved Jordy's life once."

"Oh no. Seriously, bro? So now you're supposed to be responsible for him forever?"

"No, it's not like that. It's just, he thinks I know what to do in situations. He comes to me for advice. That kind of thing."

"Ah. Situations." I nodded sagely, which was lost on Elliott because he was watching the road. "Like you're, I don't know, some kind of older brother?"

I have four older brothers, but only the oldest two—Ted and Elliott—ever really acted like older brothers. The next brother down from them, Andrew, has always been my buddy. As kids he was my partner in whatever childhood crimes we got up to. Our mother disapproved of our carrying on but we constantly cracked our father up, and at least when we got grounded it was together. The brother closest in age to me is Tim, and from the day I was born he thought it was his job to boss me around and make me as boring as he was.

After our father died when I was thirteen, Ted, as the eldest, did his best, but he was born the absent-minded professor he is, professionally, today. Elliott, by contrast, was always there, present, paying attention. Helping out. It was Elliott who tried, whenever he could, to accompany Ma to my school plays and track meets, Elliott who vetted my boyfriends—and also Elliott who made sure I understood birth control.

Becoming a doctor, I've always suspected, was Elliott's way of being an older brother to the world.

"How did you save Jordy's life?" I asked now. "I mean, actually or metaphorically?"

"Actually. The first time I met him was about five years ago when he turned up in the ER, OD'd on a drug cocktail. At one point his heart stopped. I got him going again."

"God, Elliott, just like that guy's daughter last spring. Have you thought about starting a religion? At least a website. Rise from the Dead dot com."

My brother threw me a quick glance. "It happens in the ER every day, Lyd. People flatline, we bring them back. It's in the playbook."

"Yeah, well, seeing your brother's face plastered all over the news doesn't happen every day. Or your son's. Ma was so unbearable about you Tim got jealous."

Elliott flushed. "That guy" last spring had been one of the glitterati, a private equity king named Seymour Larson. Met Gala, City Ballet Ball, Landmarks Conservancy Board. Giant yacht, private jet, fleet of Bentleys. Endowed chair here, library wing there, concert hall somewhere else. Wherever A-listers were found and photographed for the rest of us to envy you'd see Larson, smiling, holding a drink, light bouncing off his pale bald head. His glamorous wife would be standing beside him, and somewhere in the young-people part of the glitzy crowd would be his dazzling daughter. Beautiful people leading their best lives.

Until the daughter, Hartley, was delivered by screaming ambulance to Elliott's ER with her skin turning blue and vomit all over her Paolina Russo shantung blouse.

When you save the life of a celebrity you become one yourself. This happens especially if the celebrity's dad, far from trying to hush the whole thing up, gives interviews praising the ER staff and Dr. Chin in particular while he decries bloodsucking drug dealers who prey on young people whose judgment is still poor. The papers, news sites, and local TV all had the story, and they all had photos of Elliott: in stained hospital scrubs in the ER, in action; in a clean white coat over the stained scrubs outside the ER, with Larson; and in a suit and tie in the fancy river-view conference room at the top of the hospital's administration tower, between Larson and Elizabeth Gordon-Platt. Gordon-Platt was chief administrator of the hospital, the widow of a former parks commissioner, and a member of Seymour Larson's social circle.

Hartley, after she was released from River Valley, was shipped off to rehab, Do Not Pass Go.

The police commissioner announced a new war on drugs.

Larson, in each photo, managed to look both jubilant and grateful. Gordon-Platt, in the one in the panorama conference room, smiled like a cat who'd eaten a whole cage full of canaries and had just been told there were more.

Elliott, in all those photos, looked uncomfortable and impatient. His fifteen minutes of fame deeply embarrassed him, in no small part because of the relentless teasing of his brothers and sister and the ceaseless crowing of his mother. And here I was starting up again. Why, shame on me. I moved on.

"So Jordy's a user?"

"Not anymore," Elliott said, with what I hoped was gratitude for my forbearance but was probably more like the relief you feel when a mosquito you haven't been able to swat finally flies away. "He was self-medicating against the trauma of being in med school."

"Remembering you in med school, I'm not surprised. But morgue assistants have to go to med school?"

"No. Jordy thought *he* did, though. He was on the way to becoming a doctor. He hated it but he's from a family of doctors—grandfather, father, older brother—so it never occurred to him he had a choice."

"Not his mom?"

"She was a social worker. Jordy says she put his dad through med school, then they broke up."

"You mean then he ditched her because he didn't need her anymore."

Elliott looked over at me, then back to the road. "I wasn't there."

"Jumping to conclusions, guilty as charged, but seriously, I'll bet you dinner his second wife's young, blonde, and curvy."

"How do you know there's a second wife?"

"There always is. Anyway, Jordy. When did he drop out of med school?"

"After his OD. He said what happened in the ER was like a wake-up call."

"A wake-up-the-dead call."

"He said being dead and coming back made him think the dead might be more interesting than the living. He quit school and applied for diener jobs. River Valley offered him a job right away, because he was already overqualified. I think they thought DeBreng—Jordy's dad—would be happy."

"But not?"

"He was mortified. But what's he going to say, 'Fire my son, he's a loser'?"

"And they took Jordy even though he had a drug problem?"

"One of the drugs he'd taken he had a scrip for," Elliott said.

I looked over at my brother. "And that was the one you put in the record?"

"I had no way to be sure what else he'd taken. He was only guessing, himself. The one with the scrip could easily have been the one that almost killed him. Anyone can forget if they took their meds and double dose. People make mistakes all the time."

They sure do, I thought. I looked out the window to see a blue BMW getting a ticket at the side of the road.

◆

Back in New York, Elliott dropped me on the west side and headed home across Central Park. I was still buzzing from the jump so I subwayed to the dojo on White Street to work off some adrenaline. An hour and a half later, after I'd helped lead a beginners' class through some basic moves and served as sparring partner for some more advanced students and then worked on some combinations of my own, I hit the showers. I came out feeling ready to take on the world. When I checked my phone, I found a text from Bill: CALL ME.

"Hey," I said, following instructions. "What's up?"

"You were. I forgot to ask before, how was the jump?"

"Oh my God, it was amazing! You should come with me next time."

"The Navy offered me that opportunity. You're harder to resist than Uncle Sam, but marshalling all my willpower, I still say no."

"You don't know what you're missing." I slipped into my George Takei T-shirt.

"You missed something, too. Between when I talked to you and now, I got an interesting phone call. A lawyer wants us to work on a case."

"Well, great, but I'm waiting for the interesting part. Isn't that pretty much what we do?"

"We haven't worked for this lawyer before. It's Juanita Cohen."

I stopped, one high-top in hand. "You're kidding. It's not the case I called you about? My brother's friend the diener?"

"The guy's a diener?"

"You know what that is?"

"Of course. That makes it even more interesting. Yes, that case. Cohen called Leo to recommend a PI and he suggested us."

"Is that some kind of conflict of interest?"

"Only if Leo's getting kickbacks. Which of course he's not because that's illegal."

"Oh. Bet he gets some nice whiskey at Christmas, though."

"Brandy, and Hanukkah. Meeting at one thirty. You want to come?"

"You bet. Where?"

"Your office."

CHAPTER THREE

My office, because Bill doesn't have one and Juanita Cohen's law firm was small and some other meeting was going on at their place.

"What if I'd said no?" I asked. "Like if I had some other case I was working?"

"Working on a case I don't know about? Cheating on me? I'd have been heartbroken and I'd have met them at Shorty's."

Shorty's Bar, downstairs from Bill's apartment on Laight Street. He does occasionally meet clients there, but mostly not for the first time.

But I didn't have any other cases, and I was intrigued. At two o'clock, in brown slacks, a blazer, and a sedate tan linen blouse, I was ready to welcome Bill, Juanita Cohen, and Jordy Kazarian to my office in the back room of the Golden Adventure Travel Agency on Canal Street.

I'd organized two extra chairs from the travel ladies and I had the hot water ready for tea or coffee. As arranged, Bill, in his usual black jeans, T-shirt, and denim jacket, met the clients outside. This would preclude them from having to find my doorbell, which is numbered but not named. It saves a lot of face in Chinatown for anyone who's spotted in this doorway to be able to say they were looking for a price on a Yangtze River cruise.

Bill knocked and opened my office door, standing aside for Cohen and Kazarian. Both of them glanced around as they entered, taking in my scroll paintings, my license, and my wheezing air conditioner in the single barred window that looks onto the air shaft. I took the opportunity to size them up, too. Cohen was about my height, meaning an inch or two above five feet, thin, with her wiry dark hair clipped back from her face but escaping in tendrils. She carried a battered briefcase, wore a slack suit, a white shirt, and no makeup. My brother Andrew, ever the fashionisto, would have been mildly dismayed to see that with her gray suit her Oxfords were brown.

Jordy Kazarian was taller, maybe five nine or ten, with a red-cheeked round face, curly dark hair, and a bouncy step. Jeans, navy sweatshirt, Converses. Cohen, according to the research I'd done while I waited, was thirty-one. She looked ten years younger. Kazarian, who was twenty-six, just looked ten.

Kazarian nodded with satisfaction. "I like it. If you can't solve someone's case you can just shoo them over to the travel agency and help them disappear. Efficient use of resources. Hi, I'm Jordy. The client." He'd already met Bill outside; now he stuck out his hand to me.

"No, Jordy," Cohen said, also offering her hand. "I'm the client. You're mine, I'm theirs. Juanita Cohen. You're Lydia Chin."

I nodded in answer to this non-question and said, "Elliott Chin's sister. Before you ask."

"Oh, I know. Not questioning Leo's recommendations, but I looked you up."

"Due diligence." Jordy grinned at her. "See why I like you?"

"Told you that doesn't matter."

"Told *you* it couldn't hurt."

I offered coffee or tea. Coffee for everyone but me. I had decent coffee in the office because Bill brought it, just like I left tea at his apartment. I spooned some into the large French press—he brought that, too, and a small one for when it's just him—while Cohen and Jordy took seats across from me. Bill sat in his regular chair beside my desk.

"Leo says you're good," Cohen said.

Bill said, "He said that about you, too."

"And you guys are partners?"

Bill nodded.

"So I'd be hiring both of you." Her dark eyes assessed me.

"Yup," Bill said.

"Is that a conflict of interest?" I asked. It seemed to be the question of the day. "If Elliott's paying your bill, and you're paying mine?"

"He's not," said Jordy. "Dr. Chin guaranteed he'd pay so I'd get a lawyer, I mean not Legal Aid, because he didn't know if I had enough money. I talked to him just now. But I do have enough and I'm paying."

"And it wouldn't have been a conflict of interest," said Cohen. With the first hint of a smile I'd seen from her, she added, "Though it might have been interesting."

I poured the coffee and handed her the *Hamilton* mug. I put milk from the tiny fridge and a bowl of sugar packets on the desk and gave Jordy and Bill their coffees—the *Doctor Who* mug for Jordy, the Staten Island Ferry one for Bill. I sat with my jasmine tea in a bamboo-painted cup as Cohen said, "Okay, here's where we are. Jordy's out on an ROR—"

"Released on my own recognizance," Jordy filled in.

"I think they know that," Cohen said. "At least I hope so."

"We do," Bill affirmed.

"I got the charge knocked down to trespassing. But that might not last. We want to know what happened before he's re-arrested."

"I'd like to know what happened in the first place," I said. "You were arrested on a homicide charge in the company of a dead body and now they're calling it trespassing?"

"I—" said Jordy.

"No." Cohen stopped him. "We need a contract. Anything you say, if they're not working for me, they can be questioned on."

"Wouldn't it just be hearsay?" Jordy asked.

"Wouldn't stand up in court but one way or another it could come back to bite us. You have a standard contract?" She looked from Bill to me.

I glanced at Bill to make sure he wanted to go ahead with this. He nodded, so I pulled a contract out of the drawer in my desk. We all sat in silence as Cohen read through it with Jordy peering over her shoulder. She nodded a couple of times, crossed things out, filled other things in. When she got to the signature line, she looked up. "You're as good as Leo says, right?"

"Are you?"

Now she did smile. "From my experience," she said, "Leo doesn't exaggerate."

She signed, Bill and I read, initialed her cross-outs, and signed while she was filling in and signing a second copy. Then we signed that.

"Now?" Jordy asked his lawyer, stretching out the syllable.

"Now."

"Cool. So"—he turned to me and Bill—"you know I'm a diener at River Valley Downstate? You know what that is, a diener?" We both nodded. "Does it creep you out?"

"Not relevant, Jordy," Cohen said.

"Just wondering." He grinned.

"The meter's running," she said. "Theirs and mine."

"Okay, okay. So," he picked up his story, "I was working two shifts yesterday. Middle of the second one I was kind of tired and we had nothing going on in the morgue, so I went to the nap room."

"The hospital has a room for that?" I asked.

"Officially? No, no, no. That would be admitting people need naps when we work double or triple shifts. *That* would be admitting we work double and triple shifts regularly, not on any BS emergency basis. *That* would be admitting staffing levels are too low. That's the quiet part—once they say it out loud, my gawd, the public might find out! People would choose other hospitals! Which are just the same but they don't know that. Or we might go out on strike! Staffing and paychecks and health care, oh no! That's exactly what's going on with the nurses right now, you know. If they get what they're negotiating for—oh, the dominoes! Management is quaking in its Ferragamos."

"You a union organizer?" Bill asked.

"Nah, just a rank-and-file member. Eleven ninety-nine," Jordy said.

"What's that mean?" I asked.

"Non-professional staffers' union. Everyone but nurses, doctors, and management," Jordy said. "And while we're talking about doctors, your brother was one of only four doctors with enough balls to sign a letter in support of the nurses." He grinned. "The other three with balls are women."

Cohen broke in. "Hey, can we stick to the point? Vote union, rah rah, but we're not here to do labor law." She flashed him the kind of look that when it came from my mother used to make me point at Tim and say, *He started it.*

"Yeah, okay," said Jordy cheerfully. "Where were we? Ah! So no, it's not an official nap room. But everyone knows. It's in the east basement." He added that last bit as though it clarified things.

"East basement?" Bill asked.

"Closed. Kaput. Off-limits. Eight years ago, in that hurricane? Most of the east basement flooded. Before my time but, oy, what a mess! It could flood again, especially with the river rising—you know, climate change, end of the world, that stuff—and the hospital has plenty of basement, acres of it. So that area's shut down."

"But you nap there?" I asked. "Isn't it all, I don't know, moldy and stinky? I mean, because of the flood?"

"The flood didn't hit quite all of it. There's a part that didn't flood but it would've been too hard to section it off, and no reason to. They just shut it all down."

"Oh. So that part, that's where the nap room is?"

"Staff and management seem to have different ideas about what 'shut down' means," said Cohen. "That's the 'trespassing.'"

"So why the original homicide charge, and why drop it?" I asked.

"They rushed it. The evidence is all circumstantial. Jordy was there, she OD'd, he used to be a user, they think he knew her, so on. And the only prints on the syringe were his."

"I pulled it out, for God's sake. And she was wearing gloves."

"Shooting up, but wearing gloves?" I asked.

"Old sterile habits die hard."

I looked at Bill. He said, "I guess maybe. Did you actually know her?"

"No. But they don't believe me and how can I prove it?"

Cohen said, "We were lucky enough to get a judge who thinks upstanding citizens with regular employment shouldn't have to sit in jail on circumstantial evidence. But the police are looking for more and I'm pretty sure they're going to re-arrest him as soon as they think they have it." She gave us a tight-lipped smile. "The detective is pissed off."

I jotted down some notes while Jordy slurped his coffee. "Go ahead," I said to him.

"So I was napping," he went on, "and I woke up, got myself together to go back to work, opened the door, and there she was, this nurse on the floor in the hall with a syringe in her arm."

"All right," Bill said, "we need to be really detailed here. First, were you on anything? Something to keep you awake through a double shift? Something to help you sleep?"

"Not me. A drug-free diener I am, I am. Dr. Chin told you how we met? That was the old me. No more of that, just natural highs. Except this." He lifted his mug. "I do live on this. This, fyi, is way better than the sludge we make in the morgue."

I wasn't sure how I felt about that compliment, and I was sure I didn't want to know how or where they made their sludge in the morgue.

"So you weren't high," Bill said. "What woke you?"

"You mean, a noise or something? I don't know."

"Had you set an alarm?"

"No. I had my phone. If they needed me, they'd call. But they didn't. Not sure why I woke."

"How long had you been there?" I asked.

"About an hour."

"So you woke up and . . ."

"Got myself together, opened the door to leave, and there she was."

"Where?"

"A few feet to the right of the door."

"How did you know she was a nurse?" Bill asked.

"She was in uniform. Nurses green, orderlies purple, security blue, techs gray. Supervisors pink, serves them right."

"And you're sure you didn't know her?"

"Totally. Down where I work, we don't see the medical staff much. Once a patient gets to us, they're beyond all that."

"But that's a theory of the other side," Cohen said. "That they not only knew each other, maybe they were having an affair and Jordy killed her. Or at least, he was helping her shoot up and then, when she OD'd, he panicked, shoved her out of the room, but then decided he'd better play innocent, so he called the cops."

"Which is nuts on many levels. For one thing, besides not knowing her," Jordy said, "I bat for the other team." He waggled his eyebrows. "If I was ever curious about that side of the river, I'd start with someone I actually knew and liked. Also, that's the nap room. Strict rules against it."

"Whose rules?"

"Everyone's." He shrugged, drained his coffee. "Hookup room's down the hall."

CHAPTER FOUR

"There's an official hookup room." I didn't ask it as a question, just to verify that I'd heard correctly what Jordy Kazarian had said.

"Well, again, not official-official." Jordy set his empty mug on my desk. "But everyone knows."

"There's a sign-up sheet."

Bill nodded thoughtfully, as though approving of the reasonableness of that.

"Somehow," I said, "I'm thinking the State won't be impressed with an 'of course we weren't hooking up, it's against the rules in the nap room' defense."

"You can count on it," Cohen said. "Or the 'I'm gay, she's not my type' one, either."

"Okay," said Bill, "so you woke up, went out to the hall, and there she was. You didn't know her and you saw the syringe still in her arm. Then what?"

"I pulled it out but I could see she was too still. When you're unconscious your eyelids flutter, your veins and arteries pulse, your chest moves no matter how shallow your breathing is. Tiny things, but I spend my days with dead people. I recognized her. She was one of mine."

"What did you do?"

"I felt for her carotid in case I was wrong. She was warm but there was nothing."

"You touched the body?"

"I touched a sleeping woman to make sure she was a body." He folded his hands calmly.

"See if," Cohen corrected. "When you talk to anyone, the police or anyone, say 'see if.' Not 'make sure.'"

"Ah. Gotcha. She's subtle, huh?" He pointed his thumb at Cohen. "So when I saw she was, dead I mean, I called Security, and then 911."

"All right," I said. "Tell us who she was and what killed her."

"Her name was Sophia Scott," Cohen answered. "She died of an overdose, fentanyl and heroin, but she wasn't a known user and the whole setup was odd."

"Odd, how?"

"She was—"

The street doorbell buzzed. Everyone turned with me as I checked the video screen. It showed a large man leaning his fist on the doorframe and scowling right into the camera.

"Oh, my sweet Aunt Fanny," breathed Jordy. "It's my father."

As the scowling man pulled back, we could see another man behind who'd been eclipsed by him. "Oh, double no," Jordy said. "And my brother."

I exchanged a glance with Bill as the man on the video screen jabbed the doorbell again. Dark-haired, square-jawed, he wore a navy suit, white shirt, and navy tie, all of which nicely set off the crimson glow of anger in his cheeks. The other fellow was dressed in a similar getup except his tie was a paler blue. From what I could see of his face he was also scowling.

"What should I do?" I asked Jordy. "You want me to let them in?"

The man jammed the buzzer again and yelled into the speaker. I hadn't pressed the "listen" button, so his words were silent but his intention was clear.

"We can pretend no one's here," said Jordy. "We could all hide under the desk."

"I'll go out and suggest they go away." Bill stood.

Jordy sighed as the man on the screen took out his cell phone. "It's not worth it," he said. "He'll just—"

My phone rang. I answered and put it on speaker.

"This is Dr. Irwin DeBreng and I know you have my son in there." His voice barked into the air; he made no mention of the other son, whom he had out there. I turned the speaker volume down. "If he doesn't come out in sixty seconds I'll consider it a hostage situation and call the police. I'm—"

"Jesus Christ, Dad!" Jordy leaned over to my phone. "Such a drama queen. You're scaring the neighbors. Just come in." He looked at me. I buzzed the door open.

Bill went into the hall to beckon to DeBreng and DeBreng so they wouldn't burst in the first door they saw and terrorize the travel ladies. DeBreng the Elder pushed past Bill into my office. He looked even bigger—and madder, and sweatier—than he had on the screen. DeBreng the Younger also wore a perspiration sheen, and a look that said he had far better things to do this fine summer morning than hang out in a barely cool backroom office on the low-rent end of Canal Street. Gazing at him, I was astonished at how alike he and Jordy were: curly hair (his cropped tightly, like an angry black halo), blue eyes (darker than Jordy's), high round cheekbones (glowing scarlet), dimpled chin (deeper than Jordy's). His sullen expression, though, pretty much differentiated the two of them into tragedy and comedy.

DeBreng Senior glanced around, located his errant son, and said, "Come on, Jordan, let's go."

"Not going," said Jordy.

DeBreng Junior shot his brother a look that darkened the whole room. Senior had already turned to leave. He frowned as though what he'd heard made no sense. Turning back, he scanned the room again, seeming to register the rest of us for the first time. "Who are you people?" With a scowl he jabbed a finger. "You're the lawyer. Juanita Cohen." He put verbal quotes around "lawyer" and spoke with a sneer, as though the mismatched nature of Cohen's name made it, and her, clearly not serious. "Your office told me where to find you. But they didn't say who *you* were. Who're you?" The finger went back and forth between me and Bill.

I stood and said, "I'm Lydia Chin. This is my partner, Bill Smith, and this is my office. Would you gentlemen like coffee?"

"No. Who are you? What kind of office? Why is Jordan here?"

"Jordy's my client," said Cohen, in the strained tones of someone doing her best to control an explosive temper. That might have been reality, or it might have been a courtroom trick. "Chin and Smith are private investigators. They work for me."

"Private—oh, what bullshit! What the hell do you need private investigators for, Jordan?" He suddenly swung on me. "Chin? You're not—"

"I am. Elliott Chin's sister."

DeBreng ground his teeth. "For crap's sake! That's a conflict of interest. Jordan—"

"Dad? You're the doctors." His finger also went back and forth, from father to brother. "She's the lawyer." He pointed at Cohen. "And she says it's not."

"Then she's a crappy lawyer. You need a real one. I called Frank Maxwell. Let's go."

Jordy let out a theatrical sigh. "Oh, Dad, I know you hate it, but you're not in charge here. I *have* a real lawyer. A criminal defense lawyer, not your golf buddy. My criminal defense lawyer says I need private investigators. These are private investigators. So we're here. And you're leaving."

"Oh, Jordy, for God's sake," said his brother. His voice, which we were hearing for the first time, was surprisingly deep and unsurprisingly exasperated. "Would you knock off the playground heroics? You didn't play hooky from school. You killed—you got arrested for killing someone."

Jordy broke into a glowing grin, as though what he'd just heard was hilarious. "Thought so! Wow, that's family for you. You both think I did it, right? Right, Dad? Frank Maxwell's going to tell me to take a plea, isn't that the plan? So I can go to prison, out of sight, out of mind, and you can go back to rising through the medical world super-strata and pulling Brad behind you."

Junior said, "Oh, fuck you!" He might have gone on but Senior was sputtering.

"What the—you can't—" Senior managed to get out.

"Talk to you like that? I know. You've told me many times. Now please, would you go? The meter's running."

"The—" DeBreng Senior took a few deep breaths. In a calmer voice he said, "Jordan, please, for once in your life don't be a goddamn idiot. I'm trying to help you. This isn't some high school graffiti escapade or another dumb-ass get-rich-quick scheme where you can throw your grandfather's money away. This is a crime. Your whole future, even such as it is now—"

"And there it is." Jordy checked his watch. "Record time, two minutes and fifty-two seconds. Jordy Kazarian doesn't want to be a doctor and all the evils of the world flow from that."

"Jordan! Stop it. Your future—"

"For fuck's sake!" Jordy threw up his hands. "The only future you ever gave a shit about was the doctor one. Since then, crickets. Him"—pointing at brother Brad—"he actually never gave a shit at all. Which was fine with me. Now suddenly you two show up, desperate to help. Horseshit, Pops. Like everything else, this is all about how it makes you look." He sat back in his chair. "I almost wish I'd done it. God, how embarrassing—my son, the murderer! That's even worse than a diener. Sorry. Unless—" He stabbed a finger into the air, looking struck by a new idea. "Unless it's not me, it's her? The nurse I didn't kill? Sophia Scott. That's why you're so mad? You were doing her. And you're afraid I was, too. But wouldn't you be proud if I were? Because at least I'd be a real man, and not—oh no—a faggot. But I thought you didn't do nurses anymore. In Admin it's all secretaries and receptionists and personal assistants. Very personal, I'll bet. How come you haven't been MeTooed yet, Dad?"

I blinked, feeling knocked back by this cheerfully delivered volley of sarcasm and bitterness. I glanced at Cohen; she seemed impressed. Bill's look was one of measured approval. He hadn't liked his father, either.

DeBreng Junior was silent, though his eyes popped and his mouth was working, as if he was trying to prime the pump so some words would gush out. DeBreng Senior, face white with rage, pulled himself up military straight. "Come with me now, Jordan, or you're on your own."

"Which is more or less where I've been telling you I want to be."

In three strides Senior was across my office. He yanked open the door. Turning, he said, "You'll regret this, Jordan," and flushed magenta: Jordy had said the same words in the same tone along with him. He stalked out.

DeBreng Junior turned to his brother. "He means it, Jordan. If you don't do this his way he'll wash his hands of the whole thing. He won't dig you out of this hole."

"I never asked him to dig me out of any holes. He only ever did it because of what they'd say at the country club if he left me to rot in one. But this time, this time, Brad, I'm going to dig myself out. He can go to hell. And speaking of going." He cocked his head at the still-open door.

Brother Brad, face purple, slammed the door shut.

CHAPTER FIVE

Whew," I said. "That was exciting." Muscles and jawlines eased around the room. I could've sworn I saw the furniture relax.

"With Dad, things are always exciting. Dad and Brad. Quite the childhood in our house." Jordy resettled, resting an ankle on his thigh. "Okay, let's keep going."

"You sure you don't want a minute?" I asked. "Maybe another cup of coffee?"

"If I took a minute every time dear old dad stomped on me, I'd have years saved up. But more coffee, totally." He held out his mug. "It's a good thing no one told him how great this coffee is. Dad's a giant coffee connoisseur. He'd have stayed." His affability was back, but I sensed a brittleness to it now.

I clicked the kettle on. "Anyone else?" Bill yes, Cohen no. "Okay," I said. "Be right back." I took the French press into the bathroom and rinsed it out, came back and spooned coffee into it. By then the kettle was ready and I poured the water. I brought the press to the desk and set the timer. Jordy opened his mouth but I lifted a finger. He was going to get his minute whether he wanted it or not. When the timer went off, I pushed down the plunger and poured Jordy and Bill their coffee.

"Kazarian," I said. "Your mother's name?"

"It was the least I could do. There are two Doctors DeBreng at River Valley, plus dear departed Grandpa, who was head of orthopedics in his day. I thought if the loser in the morgue had a different name they'd all forget about me."

"Your dad obviously hasn't."

"Not for lack of trying."

"Or your brother either."

"Oh, for poor Brad it's even harder. You have to feel bad for the guy. He had to put up with his loser little brother looking just like him and being in the same school as he was for so-o-o-o long. Then when I wasn't anymore it was because I got kicked out. So embarrassing."

I thought of my brother Tim. I'd embarrassed him all through our childhood, sometimes with Andrew, sometimes alone. Yet there was no question in my mind that if either of us ever needed him, he'd be there. And if either of us got arrested for murder and said we didn't do it, a pile of proof as high as the moon wouldn't convince him we had.

"All right," I said now. "The dramatic interlude being over, we can proceed. You were about to tell us what was odd about the situation with Sophia Scott. Assuming we're still on this case." I looked to Cohen, who looked to Jordy.

"You want me to fire them?" she asked him. "Assuming *I'm* still on the case?"

"What, you people all think I was blowing smoke? That as soon as Dr. DeThang left I'd fire you because he said to?" Jordy looked offended.

"No," said Cohen. "It's just good to have clarification."

"As a matter of principle I try never to do what he says, so nobody's fired. Kumbaya. Now the nurse?" Jordy held up his hands as though he were about to conduct an orchestra. Cohen rolled her eyes but she nodded.

He dropped his hands and continued. "So, putting aside the fact I had nothing to do with it, still, shooting up right outside the nap room is kind of a very stupid thing to do."

"Because you might get caught?"

"Users shoot up alone, or with other users. Not in a hallway on the other side of a door where random sleeping citizens might wake up and try to do you a favor and save your life."

Like my brother did for you, I thought.

"Is there a shoot-up room?" Bill asked.

"You're tripping."

"It's a reasonable question," I said. "There's everything else."

"Well, if there is, I don't know about it. The impaired staff is mostly on pills. You can take those anywhere. Some people may be shooting up, too, but if they do that, it's an after-hours off-campus activity."

I stared. "Do I have to tell you how alarming that statement is?"

"Yeah, reality's a bummer." Jordy shrugged with sympathy though he didn't seem particularly bummed.

"That didn't cut any ice with the police, though, I'll bet," Bill said. "That no one would shoot up in there or near there."

"Totally not. Kinda like me being gay. They have no imagination, do they?"

"They're paid not to. What else was weird?" Bill asked.

"The tie-off. It was clumsy. It's the first thing you learn how to do. Any nurse would've gotten that right."

"Tell them about the needle," Cohen said.

"Right, the needle. It was a 25G. If your shit is pretty pure—like, not brown tar—you'd use a 28G. Or an insulin needle, even."

"And hers was? Pure?" Bill asked.

"Residue says yes," said Cohen. "Except of course the fentanyl. But that doesn't change the needle."

"What do the numbers mean?" I asked.

"Needle gauge. Higher the number, smaller the gauge."

"What's the advantage?"

"Smaller puncture. Less chance of infection. Less chance of missing the vein. A nurse would know that stuff also."

"She would," Bill said, "but the police theory is she didn't inject herself, you did. Isn't that what you said?" He looked to Cohen for confirmation.

"Yeah," said Jordy, "but whatever, I'd know it too. For one thing I'm a goddamn diener, I know my veins and arteries. And also, remember, I used to be a bad boy. If I did the injection, I'd have done it right."

"Ah. But you couldn't sell them that, either, I bet," Bill said. "'I used to be a junkie, obviously I didn't do it, I'd have done it right.'"

"Yeah, no." Jordy shook his shaggy head.

"Boy," I said. "A lot of stuff here going unsold." I finished my tea and asked Cohen, "Were there other people in the nap room also?"

"Yes, two. At least, when Jordy woke." She nodded to him.

Jordy said, "One was another nurse I didn't know."

"Etta Thomson," said Cohen. "Neonatal ICU."

I got a shiver from the idea of a nurse for the tiniest unwell babies working a double shift, but Bill just asked, "You have her info?"

"Yes, and also for the other one, an orderly named Enrico Buenavista."

"I know Enrico," Jordy said. "Been to ball games together. Mets," he added.

"At what point did they each wake up?"

"Enrico, when the Mets finally got a hit. Okay, sorry. When I made the call to 911. The door was still open. He stuck his head up to tell me to shut up. Phone calls, talking, strictly prohibited in the nap room. Then he saw I was in the hall and the body. Thomson didn't wake up until security came. She must have been really out."

"Security got there before the police?"

"Their office is in the basement. Not over there, but close."

"Did they touch anything?"

"Just her, to make—to see if she was dead."

I thought maybe Cohen would pat Jordy on the head and say, "Good boy," but she didn't.

"Okay." I glanced from one to the other. "Anything else we need to know?"

"I didn't do it," said Jordy.

"That's where we started."

"Just making sure."

Juanita Cohen texted both me and Bill her list of witnesses and contacts. "Who's the detective on the case?" I asked.

"Helena Church at the 23rd Precinct. Motherly looking but don't be fooled."

"You know her?" I asked Bill. He knows half the NYPD.

"No," he said. "But I always like to meet new people."

Cohen texted us Detective Church's contact information.

"What else was found at the crime scene?" Bill asked. "Her handbag? Wallet? Phone?"

"Just her phone. Her bag and wallet were in her locker."

"Did you touch the phone?" he asked Jordy.

"I didn't see it."

"It was in her pocket," Cohen said.

"And I wouldn't have," Jordy said. "I may be crazy, but et cetera, et cetera."

"The phone's interesting, though," said Cohen. "Something for you to follow up on. Nothing from Jordy, of course, but about a dozen texts from a prepaid burner. 'Same time, same place.' Always with a date. All within the last three months."

"How do you know?" I asked. "The cops told you?"

"They don't have to tell me much, yet. But the detective is convinced the burner is Jordy's and kept asking him about it. Before I got there."

"I kept my lip zipped." Jordy mimed zipping his lip. "But I did ask her, 'Gee, all these texts I didn't send, what did they say?' I might have given her the impression my memory's not great. I thought what they said might be something my lawyer would want to know when I got one."

"You should've just shut up," Cohen said. "And from now on you won't say gesundheit to a cop who sneezes unless I'm there. You'll leave the strategy to me."

"Oui, mon capitaine!" Jordy straightened up and gave a crisp salute. With a grin, he said, "I was right, though, wasn't I? You did want to know."

"I could've found out without you acting like an idiot child."

"We'll look into it," I said, as she glared at him. To Jordy: "Let me ask you something else. What did your father mean about dumb-ass get-rich-quick schemes, and your grandfather's money?"

Jordy sighed. "They might have been dumb-ass but they weren't about getting rich quick. Or at all. Grandpa left me and Brad each a small pile. Some of my friends needed money for startups. You know us millennials, everyone's got a startup. I invested in a couple of companies. Twice they flopped. Those times I lost. Two other times, as it happened, they succeeded and I made a little, actually more than I lost. Dad doesn't remember those when he's telling me what a jerk I am, which is always."

"What about your brother?"

"What about him? He's a jerk too but Dad doesn't know that. Oh, you mean, did he invest, too? Hah! The minute Brad got Grandpa's check he put it into treasury bonds or something zero-thrill like that and I think it's still there, cashable in thirty years. He's like Dad. Why do you think they're both orthopedists, and Gramps was too? Nothing in medicine is predictable, but orthopedics is one of the closest. They come in after the crisis is over, the car crash or whatever, and fix whatever's fixable. You might never be like you were but you'll be better than before they got their surgical gloves on you and you'll be oh so grateful. They get called heroes and they work regular hours. Then they go home to Scarsdale."

"Both of them?"

"They live around the block from each other."

I thought about the sizzle and rush of joy I'd felt free-falling with Elliott that morning. And how sad it would be to dislike your brother so much.

Our client, the lawyer, and her client, the suspect, left on mutual promises: We'd update Cohen at the end of the day, and she'd let us know if anything changed in Jordy's legal situation. Jordy, for his part, was advised to go home and lie low. He said he would.

"Seriously," Cohen said. "You better believe the NYPD has eyes on you."

"Cops? Watching moi? Are they cute? Am I allowed to take out a beach chair and watch them back? Kidding!" he said when he saw her face. "I guess I'll just go home and binge *Six Feet Under*."

CHAPTER SIX

Bill began making a couple of calls to set up meetings. I had some to make, too. The first was to Elliott.

"Lyd," he said. "So soon. What's up?"

"Can we go again now?"

He laughed. "Next week. Is that it?"

"No. That lawyer, Juanita Cohen? She was just here. In my office. With Jordy Kazarian. She needs PIs on his case and she hired us."

A beat. "She did? Is that okay? Not a conflict of interest?"

"Question of the hour, but everybody says no. Anyway, I just thought you ought to know."

He didn't answer.

"Ell? Something wrong?"

"No. No, not wrong. Just . . ."

"Spill, big bro."

He sighed. "Seymour Larson? He wants to give the hospital a lot of money." Another pause. "With my name on it."

"Your name? Like on a new wing or something?"

"That's what he wants, yes. A whole new ER pavilion. But I don't like it."

"Oh, come on. This is great! You saved his daughter, he wants to pay it forward. Let him."

"We don't need a new pavilion. A couple of new pieces of equipment, sure. But River Valley needs more nurses and the nurses need a raise. We need new elevators in the towers. For God's sake, we obviously need a better security system for the east basement. Everyone always wants to endow a building. No one wants to pay the water bill."

"'The Elliott Chin Emergency Pavilion' sounds a lot better than 'The Elliott Chin Water Bill Fund,'" I pointed out.

"First of all, it'll be 'The Elliott Chin Emergency Pavilion Made Possible by a Generous Gift from Seymour and Anita Larson.' And I don't really want the Elliott Chin anything."

"Yeah," I said. "I know. But what are you saying? It complicates things to have your sister involved in this case?"

"Give me a minute to think things through. For one thing the . . . I mean, Scott's death has already complicated things, to put it mildly. People are canceling elective surgeries right and left. They're asking ambulances to take them to other hospitals. Admin is having a cow."

"Well, it kind of makes sense. Murder makes people nervous."

"Thank you, Captain Obvious. Even Larson's PR people told him to hold off until the story fades away, and they seriously need the good PR."

"They do? Why?"

"Don't you remember the black eye he got just before all that stuff with Hartley? He tried to buy that software startup that didn't want to be bought? They fought him off and found a white knight, but he ended up looking like an unfeeling, rapacious, predatory SOB."

"I thought they all were, those guys, and it didn't bother them."

"That's not his persona. He's supposed to be the good guy of Wall Street."

"Is there such a thing?"

"No. It's a sales pitch like everything else those people do. But it works for him. Rich people and retirement funds and anyone else can tell themselves they're not being unfeeling, rapacious, predatory SOBs, they're making money with Santa Claus."

"So he needs this donation to polish his image."

"And so does the hospital for the same reason. They're desperately hoping I'll just shut up so they can accept the money and announce the good news. You know, steer public attention away from the murder, and incidentally from their labor troubles. Did you see the press release the nurses' union issued about the murder?"

"No, when?"

"About an hour ago. I'll send it to you. Talking about what a tragedy it is, but how while this is a unique calamity, nurses do face danger every day as they work to keep patients safe. Like that. Public sentiment in the nurses' favor is the last thing Admin needs right now. Hospitals never look good when nurses go on strike."

"You think they will?"

"If they don't get what they want I think they should."

"Jordy told me you signed a pro-nurse letter." The light dawned. "Oh, Ell. You're in trouble again, aren't you?"

Elliott had ducked disciplinary hearings, navigated negative performance reviews, and generally failed to endear himself to his bosses his whole career. They'd kept him and, with gritted teeth, promoted him because while doctors serve at the pleasure of management and my brother gave management no pleasure, he was immensely popular with patients and staff. Patients were his first priority and the medical staff who served and trained under him were his second. After that, the non-medical staff. Then came the urgent care clinic north of the hospital—in other words, East Harlem—which he founded and where he donated time so people without paperwork could get treated—in other words, undocumented immigrants. The hospital itself, the giant corporate entity that owned all the real estate and raised all the money and was run largely by non-medical professionals, came last.

I could actually hear his grin over the phone. "It's worse than you think, and way better. I actually wrote the pro-nurse letter. Admin knows that. They were after my butt and then Larson, who knows nothing about the nurses, comes along with this pile of cash. So they couldn't touch me. And then I rejected it. I wish you'd seen the steam blowing out of their ears. That's where we were when the murder happened. Now they have two problems. One, they want this investigation to get wrapped up as fast as possible and for everyone to forget about it, especially if the nurses are going to go out. And two, they're afraid that while Larson's people have the thing on pause, I'll try to talk Larson out of the new building and into something much harder to cut a ribbon on. And I do plan on doing that, by the way. So they're all jittery wanting the murder solved soonest. Also . . ."

"Also what?"

"Well, if they have these two big image problems, a murder and a possible strike, and there's nothing Admin can do about the murder, that puts pressure on them to settle with the nurses, doesn't it?"

"I'm getting a headache. I can't even play chess."

"Not my fault. I tried to teach you."

"What you want, what would it look like?"

"An endowment fund. The Elliott Chin Endowment if he has to. A pot of money for nurses' overtime, maintenance, recurring bills. I don't care. It's just, the capital budget is huge and the operating and maintenance budgets always limp along. Because people like Larson want their names on buildings."

"Okay, so, you're a hero because Larson wants to give a new building, but you're a bum because you don't want it, but you might end up a hero if he gives the money for something else, and meanwhile the nurses might go on strike and you support that, and so should Bill and I take Jordy's case or not?"

Elliott laughed. "When you put it like that, go ahead and take it."

"Why?

"Because you guys are the best, and Jordy deserves the best."

"Be serious, Ell."

"I am being serious. A hospital employee was killed and deserves justice, but a hospital employee is being blamed and he deserves justice, too. The best way to get it for both of them is to find out what really happened. If Jordy did it, which I doubt, but if he did, you'll find that. Otherwise, you'll track down who did."

"You have a lot of faith, bro."

"I know you."

"Don't make me blush."

"You're blushing? Quick, switch to FaceTime."

"Very funny."

"Tell me, how's Jordy?"

"So cheerful that you'd think the state was offering him a trip to Bermuda and not Greenhaven. Is he always like that?"

"He was a little shook up this morning when he called, but basically, yeah."

"Have you met his dad?"

"He was there, too? Dr. DeBreng? With Jordy?" I could hear Elliott's surprise.

"Not exactly with. He came crashing in halfway through and issued demands."

"Ah, okay. Yeah, that's what he does. I've crossed swords with him once or twice. What demands?"

"That Jordy fire us all and come with him to meet with his 'real' lawyer. How come you've crossed swords?"

"He's chief of medicine. He thinks I run an inefficient department."

"Do you?"

"Yes."

"You do?"

"The short version is, he wants them in and out fast, I want them not coming back. He wants them admitted so the ER is cleared, I want them to go home to their own beds. Different philosophies. It affects how you triage, how long each doc and nurse spend with each patient, how many specialists you call for. Neither way's wrong, but as long as I'm in charge of this department, it runs my way."

Bill signaled he was going out for a smoke. I nodded, and as he left I asked my brother, "What's his objection?"

"DeBreng takes his fiscal responsibility seriously. He thinks my budget's too big and by now he takes it personally when I get what I want year after year. So I take it Jordy didn't fire you?"

"Jordy told DeBreng which stop to get off at."

"That's my boy."

"That's why he's so cheerful, right? Because he's finally out from under his father's thumb?"

My brother laughed. "I'm emergency medicine. Psychiatry's down the hall. Yes, take the case."

"Okay, but if it gets to be a problem—"

"It won't."

"Says you, but okay. And you're sure we can't go jump again right now?"

"One of us is working."

"I thought this was your day off. Oh, shit. You mean me."

CHAPTER SEVEN

After we clicked off I called my cousin Linus Wong, founder and president of Wong Security Services ("Protecting People Like You from People Like Us"), a two-person cyber firm operating out of Linus's parents' garage in Flushing, Queens.

"Cuz!" Linus shouted into the phone after two rings. As usual, he had the phone on speaker, so he could do eight other things while we talked. The Ying Yang Twins blasted from the sound system. The music volume dropped and he demanded, "What's buzzin', cousin?"

"Bees," I said. "How're you doing? Is Trella there?" Linus's girlfriend, Trella Bartoli, was the firm's other member, its CEO and CFO.

"Hey, Lydia," Trella called. "I'm here. You close enough for coffee? We have a new Sumatran super-dark roast." Coffee was Wong Security's principal fuel and Trella was the executive in charge of it.

"No, I'm in my office. This is a professional call. I want to hire you. If you're not too busy."

"Too busy for you?" Linus said. "My mom would kill me. Wassup?"

Linus's mother and mine, also cousins, disapproved of the career paths their offspring had chosen. Not all their offspring; my four brothers and

Linus's older sister were golden. Linus and I were the problem children. However, they'd long ago come to the mom-logic conclusion that if we worked together we could at least look out for each other. Given some of the stuff that had happened on some of our cases, my silent reaction to that theory was *if you only knew*, but we were both still in one piece and didn't enlighten them.

"I need background on some people. A diener at River Valley Downstate named Jordy Kazarian—"

"What's a diener?"

"Morgue attendant."

"No kidding? Like Igor?" He pronounced it EYE-gor. "Cool. In fact, icy. Who else?"

"A nurse there named Sophia Scott. Deceased."

"Recently?"

"Yes."

"And Eyegor did it?"

"Says he didn't."

"Do we believe him?"

"Not telling. Don't want to tilt your thinking one way or the other."

"Tilt!" he yelled. "That's from old pinball games, you know," he added helpfully.

"Thanks for that."

"No worries. Who else?"

"That's it for now. If we dig up anyone else, I'll call you."

"Dig up! From the morgue!"

"If they're in the morgue, they're not buried yet," I pointed out. "Well, wait. Give me Dr. Irwin DeBreng, too."

"Who's he?"

"The diener's father."

"Doctor. Same hospital?"

"Yes. He's chief of medicine."

"That's why Eyegor works there?"

"Not why, in spite of."

"Screwy family dynamics, say no more, not our department. We'll sniff around and report. Speaking of sniffing, Woof says hi."

"Hi, Woof," I said to the big yellow dog no doubt spread out on his rug in the middle of the tech-laden office, thumping his tail.

"Okay, cuz, we're on it. And hey! With three you get a bonus! Want to try out our new undetectable fountain pen voice-activated recorder?"

"Next time I come by. Thanks, Linus. Call me when you have something."

"You know it. Peace."

"Peace," I responded, though in the garage office of Wong Security, peace was in short supply.

◆

I met Bill out on Canal Street and we took the 4 train uptown. La Lechonera on 103rd Street was a knockout of herbs and roast-meat smells. Catchy Latino music filled the air. Bill probably knew the genre. More than half the tables stood empty, the lunch rush being over.

A thick-set middle-aged woman with indifferently styled dark blonde hair and splotchy cheeks waved us over to a Formica table where she sat over a mostly empty paper cup of coffee. Her navy sport jacket didn't do much to conceal the gun at her hip. I'd googled her so we knew what to expect, and the familiarity with which she greeted us made me sure she'd done the same.

"Best café con leche in town," she said as I slid onto a plastic chair. "I'd get some if I were you. Detective Helena Church."

"Bill Smith. This is Lydia Chin. I'm getting some."

"Bring me another," she called after Bill as he went to the counter.

Helena Church gave me a closed-lip smile and tapped her wrinkled fingers on her cup. Bill came back with two frothy coffees, and a can of club soda for me. Church looked at me and said, "Really? You don't know what you're missing." She sipped the foam off her new coffee.

"Detective—" Bill started.

"Yeah. Kazarian. I can't give you anything. You've been in the business a while, so you know that. You've also been in trouble before—you more than you"—Bill, then me—"so I guess you don't always listen. Well, listen. You will not screw around in my case. That lawyer—Cohen?—already left me standing with my thumb up my ass, circumstantial this, circumstantial that, and I didn't exactly appreciate it. Next time I arrest that weirdo I'll have all the evidence I need."

"And if you don't?" I asked.

She stared straight at me. "I won't arrest him until I do. If you two fuck with me, though, I'll arrest *you* on any pretext I can find. Nobody screws around in my cases. Got it? Thanks for the coffee."

Cup in hand, she stood and left.

CHAPTER EIGHT

Have you noticed," I asked Bill, "the number of people today who have not been charmed by us? Doctors DeBreng One and Two, Detective Church, even Juanita Cohen seemed like she wasn't quite convinced."

"I think Jordy likes us."

"For a homicide suspect, that guy is unnaturally cheerful."

"Probably because he's not in med school anymore. I bet Woof wagged his tail when you called Linus."

"Yeah, but I bet he wished it was you." Woof's bounding, spinning greeting whenever he saw me was the one he gave every human who crossed his path. With Bill, though, he had a special bond, brought about by an earlier case in which—along with Linus, Trella, and my oldest friend NYPD Detective Mary Kee—Woof and Bill had saved my life.

I checked my watch. "How about we try the two other witnesses? Enrico Buenavista and Etta Thomson? Maybe we can charm them. Then we can try the security chief, McGraw."

"You're the boss."

"Actually, no, you're the boss. Cohen called you."

"Because I called Leo because you called me. You're the boss."

So, being the boss, I assigned Bill to call Enrico Buenavista while I took on Etta Thomson.

Cohen had said each had taken a day or two off, after they woke up from their naps to find Sophia Scott dead on the floor. But that was then. We found each on duty this afternoon and willing to speak to us.

"Well," I said, "I guess waking up in a room near a dead body doesn't require all that much recovery time when you're a medical professional."

"Maybe none. The days off were probably to get over being grilled by Church. They're the next two built-in suspects if Jordy doesn't pan out."

◆

The buildings of River Valley Downstate Medical Center alternately sprawled, hulked, or soared on two square blocks of Manhattan's Upper East Side, a quick walk from La Lechonera. What most people think of when they hear "hospital"—that is, the towers that hold patient rooms—shot up from the center of the site to dominate the skyline. The emergency room entrance was labeled with huge red signs and pointing arrows, but we weren't going there, and besides, I already knew where that was, Elliott having worked at River Valley for close to ten years now. The main pedestrian doors, a sort of afterthought on the wide curving driveway, took a little more looking but eventually revealed themselves. Everything else—medical school, clinics, operating rooms, pharmacy, testing and research labs, pathology, the morgue, administrative offices, delivery bays, storage, facilities offices—occupied low-to-medium structures added to the original 1890 brick hospital building over the years and therefore sandwiched in wherever space allowed, with no actual plan.

The atrium, though cold, was light and airy, with triple-height ceilings and big windows giving onto a planted interior courtyard. We told a sweet young man at the visitors desk we were there to see Etta Thomson;

he checked to see that she'd phoned down about us. Then he gave us stick-on IDs with grainy photos. He directed us to the elevator. Bill got off at the sixth floor, where Buenavista was working, and I went to nine to find Thomson in the Neonatal ICU. I texted her from the elevator lobby as we'd arranged.

Be right there, she texted back. I was kind of glad she was coming out to the elevator lobby. I wasn't ready for all those tiny babies and their tubes and beeping machines.

"Right there" turned out to be close to ten minutes. I was scrolling through my email when the double doors swung open and a wiry light-skinned Black woman burst through. "Lydia? Etta. I apologize. Had to get my babies covered." She smiled.

"No problem. This won't take long. I just have a few questions. As I said on the phone, I'm an investigator working for Jordy Kazarian's lawyer."

"I thought they dropped the charges."

"Word travels fast."

"Honey, this is a hospital. Gossip we haven't heard isn't worth hearing."

Now it was me who smiled. "Well, you're almost right. They reduced it to trespassing. But we're trying to find out what actually happened."

She chewed on her bottom lip. "I can't help you, I'm afraid. I was asleep until Quick Draw arrived. Captain McGraw, I mean, head of security. I sleep like a log, that's a blessing." Her look was apologetic.

"For a nurse I'm sure it is," I said. "So nothing seemed out of the ordinary to you, when you got there and settled in?"

"No, everything seemed normal." Thomson tilted her head. "Only thing off, when I woke up, I mean, besides Sophia being dead, was her being down there in the first place."

"What do you mean?"

"Sophia never used the nap room. Why would she? She never worked a double shift unless the world was coming to an end."

"Really? I'm a little surprised that was allowed. It doesn't seem fair to the other nurses."

"You can't force a nurse to work overtime. It's in our contract. And there's plenty of people who want to work it. You're saving for a house, for your kids' college, for a little vacation. Or your bestie needs a day off. Everyone works a few extra shifts now and then."

"Except Sophia Scott."

"Well, she's not—wasn't—the only one. But nobody likes a diva."

"Did you know her well?"

Thomson shook her head. "Not well, no. We overlapped because my babies, when they get better, sometimes they spend time in OB/GYN with their mamas before they go home. Or if they have a problem down there after delivery the baby might come to us. So we know each other, the OB/GYN nurses and us."

"Is there anything you can tell me about her that might help? Friends, enemies, anyone she was seeing?"

"I don't know who her friends were. Or her enemies, come to that, though like I said, she was a diva. But you don't kill someone because they don't work overtime, do you? I think she had a boyfriend but I don't know who."

The swinging doors opened and a tall Black man came out. Thomson beamed at him. "He's doing beautifully," she said. "Is your wife still in there?"

He nodded. "She's holding him now. I have to go to work. Thank you for everything."

"No, thank little Nathan. He's a fighter." Thomson turned to me. "I need to get back. Can I help with anything else?"

"If you think of something, call anytime." She already had my number but I gave her a card anyway. "Thanks."

She nodded, smiled again at the man, and bustled back through the doors. The elevator opened and the man and I got on, collecting other passengers as we descended. At the lobby I turned to him. "Good luck to little Nathan," I said.

"Why, thanks." He gave a surprised smile. Then he disappeared into the afternoon.

CHAPTER NINE

Bill came down a few minutes later. "Well," I said to him as we stood in the atrium, "I seem to have charmed Etta Thomson. How did you do with Buenavista?"

"Whatever the he-man version of that is. I told him Jordy said he was a Mets fan and we both shook our heads sadly, and instantly bonded."

"One of you is a cheap date. Did he have anything interesting to say?"

"Only that he's sure Jordy didn't do it and he didn't hear or see anything until he heard Jordy calling 911."

"Nothing about Scott?"

"He didn't know her. If they ever met it would've been in passing on some unit but he's sure they never worked together. Why? What did Thomson say?"

"That she was surprised Scott was anywhere near the nap room, since she never worked double shifts."

"Really? That's interesting."

"And that Scott had a boyfriend but she didn't know who." I thought for a minute. "I'm still the boss?"

"Eternally."

"Then I say, let's go talk to that security chief. McGraw?"

"Okay, but it'll bring our average down. No one has ever charmed a security chief."

Bill, who'd talked to McGraw from my office while I was on the phone with Elliott, called him again from the atrium. McGraw gave highly specific directions to his basement office, which told me his visitors got lost all the time. We had to go back to the sweet desk guy for different badges, and then we started to follow the red line on the shiny vinyl floor. Not far from the lobby, it led us around a corner where the ceilings lowered, windows vanished, and the too-bright fluorescent lights and sharp smell of antiseptic kicked in. A series of bends gave away the fact that this chilly corridor was taking us from shoehorned structure to shoehorned structure. We bypassed a couple of elevator banks before the red line delivered us to the one we needed. These elevators, like the others, had a camera at their doors and here someone was apparently watching us. The B2 lock was turned to "Off" but once we were in and the doors were closed, the elevator started down.

The B2 basement corridors were pipe-hung, low-ceilinged, and cramped by concrete-block walls. "I'm half expecting to see cobwebbed skeletons in the corners," I told Bill as we walked. "People who tried to find the security office without directions."

"You would, except they dust them off and give them to the anatomy professors."

Two more corners, and we found ourselves facing a double steel door. A gray plaque beside it said SECURITY and a smaller one, JAMES MCGRAW, CHIEF. The camera above the doorway was less elegant than the ones upstairs. Rectangular and utilitarian, it perched like a crow. My taps were answered by a buzz.

The door opened into a surprisingly large, though by now unsurprisingly cold, room where file cabinets bordered white block walls hung with framed plans of the hospital campus. An open door on the right led to a large briefing room full of chairs in uneven rows. Windows in its far wall showed another corridor and the door there stood open, too. On the left a glass door, this one closed, and a large window revealed a room of multiple video screens watched by eight men. In front of us a young Black woman with glittery fingernails—and a sweater—sat at a monitor-topped reception desk. For a person who spent her whole working day underground, I reflected, she had a lot to look at. She smiled but she didn't need to announce us because a fourth door, to the inner office behind her, was also open, and a man stood filling it.

"Smith? Ms. Chin? Jim McGraw," he said. "Come on in." The security chief wore a blue uniform like the hospital guards and carried a few extra pounds around the middle. He had a bristly blond mustache and the kind of colorless hair that's the halfway stage between blond and gray. Dark circles under his eyes were almost startling in his pale face. I supposed spending every day down here in B2 would make you pasty. The circles, I'd have bet, were either caused by, or made much worse by, the murder, on his watch, of Sophia Scott.

He waved us to square metal chairs with vinyl seats in a shade generally called olive, though I'm not sure I'd eat an olive that color. A bookshelf on one wall held user manuals for various alarm, CCTV, and electronic lock systems; thick three-ring binders in different colors; and texts on risk assessment and security management. Behind the chief's metal desk the wall was occupied by certificates of completion of this course and that. Alone on the wall on our left was a large cartoon drawing of a horse in a hat, holding a six-shooter in one hoof.

The chief, as he sat, caught me looking at the drawing. "Quick Draw McGraw," he said. "Gift from the precinct when I left the NYPD."

"Where's his sidekick? Baba Looey?" Bill asked.

"Yeah, well, I work alone. So what can I do for you?"

"Sophia Scott," Bill said. "We work for Jordy Kazarian's lawyer."

McGraw shifted his bulk in his chair. "Big fucking mess. Excuse my French," he said in my general direction.

"Don't worry about it, I don't speak French," I said. "Why is it a mess?"

He stared. "The girl is dead!"

"True, but 'mess' isn't usually the first word that comes to mind when someone's dead." Also, I wanted to add, Sophia Scott had been thirty-six. She wasn't a girl. I kept quiet, though.

McGraw heaved out an elongated breath. Finally: "My guy. Delgado. Didn't know a fucking thing about that 'nap room.'" He made air quotes and this time didn't excuse his language. "Never took him for a fuck-off but shit. Dammit. Guy never went in there."

"In there, where? The nap room?"

"The whole goddamn east basement! The shut-down area. I have six guys assigned to that level, in shifts. A lot of area to cover but too bad. That's supposed to be part of it, the east basement, even though it's off-limits. Once a shift, once a goddamn shift, whoever's on is supposed to go in, take a spin around. Is that too much to ask?"

"But Delgado didn't?"

"None of them did! Do you believe it? They had some sort of, I don't know, agreement. Area's out of bounds, they figured screw it. No one has to bother. I mean, what the fuck?"

"Aren't there time clocks?" Bill asked.

McGraw picked up a pencil, threw it down again. "Five years ago the hospital upgraded all the security systems. The guards check in electronically now. New video setup, cameras everywhere, all kinds of fancy-ass locks. Blew the fuck out of my budget. You think they gave me enough to cover it? Cheap bastards. Don't know where the money goes but it sure as hell doesn't come here. So I did the only thing that made sense. I left the east basement how it was. Didn't install anything new there.

Facilities signed off on not upgrading it. But it's still part of the job, guys just need to stick their heads in once a shift. Dammit!"

He sat back in his chair, scowling. Neither Bill nor I spoke.

"Wasn't just me, you know." He gave Bill a hard stare, as though Bill had said something and the something was judgmental. "I submitted a budget for the whole job. Management said no. I said, okay, here's a couple proposals how to do the job within the budget you want me to use. They called in a consultant, a fancy-ass security firm. The Michael Group, you know them? Could've just added what they paid them to my budget, but no-o-o-o, management loves its consultants. Prick in a three-piece suit came here, George somebody. No, George was his last name. Darius Georges, yeah that's right. I gave him the grand tour, the whole damn hospital. He reviews my report. The option he picks ends up being the one I recommended—cut out the east basement. Ten thousand bucks later, Jesus. So that's what we did."

He picked up the pencil again and turned it. Seeming to get himself back in hand, he said, "Fired all six of them. As soon as I found out. Such bullshit. But it's on me. Hospital's going to haul me to a disciplinary review. They should. I wouldn't blame them if they canned my ass. I should offer to resign. If I had balls I would, but I like this job. Hoping there's a way I can keep it." He looked again at Bill. "And a fat lot of good any of that shit does you, huh? About Kazarian."

"Everything helps paint the picture," I said.

"Paint the . . ." McGraw snorted. He offered Bill a commiserating glance. Bill smiled back.

"Says he didn't do it, I hear," McGraw said to Bill.

"We hear the same."

"Do you know him?" I asked. It was better than sitting there silently like a good little patronized girl. "Jordy Kazarian?"

"Why would I know him? My job's to keep them safe. I don't care who they are." While I was thinking, *You didn't really do your job, then, did you?* he added, "I guess I know a couple of the ER docs. ER nurses, too. They need a little strongarm help sometimes. Sometimes when they call for it, I go up there myself. I like to keep my hand in." He said this to Bill, though I'd asked the question. But then he turned to me, frowning. "One of the docs is named Chin. That guy, Jesus, he hates when I have to do the physical stuff. Ran up against him once or twice. Might be the ER head, I think. Any—" He stopped abruptly, maybe remembering some DEI training the NYPD had made him suffer through.

I put him out of his misery. "My brother."

The look that crossed McGraw's face was one I recognized from childhood: *That's* how the kid / the twerp / the *girl* got in here. On the Little League team, the Robotics Club, the Go Club. Some things I was good at, some bad, but either way it was usually assumed I was there trailing after one of my older brothers.

"Can we see the crime scene?" Bill asked. He has good radar for when I might be about to blow my top. After all this time he'd better.

McGraw shrugged. "Why not?" He lifted himself from his chair and preceded us into the outer office. "Back soon," he told the young woman, and led us down the hall.

CHAPTER TEN

Back to the elevator, and down one floor, to B3. Exit, go left, more turns and twists; any member of the hospital staff who went through all this to get a nap, I thought, must be really tired. As we walked I wondered how many people actually did work double and triple shifts. I remembered that routine, from when Elliott was in medical school, but the excuse then was that it was *training*: A doctor had to get used to making decisions under pressure, had to be able to work effectively when exhausted. I was suspicious then—it seemed more like a cross between hazing and exploiting low-paid labor than anything that could really be useful in the make-a-man/woman-out-of-you way—but it was a rationale. From what Jordy had said, the nurses, orderlies, dieners, and whoever else used the nap room worked extra shifts routinely not because it was a valuable part of their education but because there wasn't enough staff.

If that was true, I wondered, why wasn't there?

McGraw pushed through a pair of double doors with big NO ACCESS signs on them. We came into a dimmer corridor, lit by bare overhead fluorescent tubes.

“Is this the east basement?” I asked. “Why isn’t that door locked?”

“Ever hear of an exit door? In case some asshole ends up down here, law says he has to be able to escape from a fire or whatever shit. From either side.” McGraw’s tone said two things: That was a stupid question, and it just might be okay with him if the asshole got burned to a crisp.

Another corner, and we found ourselves in a hallway where further progress was deterred by a crisscross of yellow crime scene tape. McGraw pulled the tape down without a pause. Bill and I looked at each other and walked after him. He stopped about five feet to the left of a nondescript steel door.

“That’s where she was.” He pointed to the floor. Indicating the door itself, he said, “That’s the goddamn nap room.”

I stood with Bill surveying the hallway, which disappeared into gloom.

“That enough?” McGraw asked.

“I’d like to go in. The nap room,” I said.

McGraw scowled but he pressed the door lever and stepped inside.

The NYPD, I saw, had left the light on.

The famous nap room: in front of us, two rows of three cubicles each, formed by waist-high steel bookshelves, bare except for a few blankets and pillows here and there. Each cubicle held a cot on a rectangle of carpet. I could just about envision the pizza party that got all this stuff moved in here.

The light left on was a single low-wattage fluorescent strip near the door. All the other ceiling fixtures were empty, bulb snatched, no doubt, to make napping easier. The enforced darkness would account for the emptiness of the bookshelves.

“Jordy was sleeping there?” I pointed to the cot in the front left cubicle.

“Says he was. When I got here he was sitting out on the floor by the body.”

"You were first?" I knew what Jordy had said and I'd read the NYPD paperwork Cohen had given us but I wanted to hear what McGraw would say.

"You know I was" was his answer. "I mean, if you're any goddamn good you read the NYPD paperwork."

I ignored Bill's slight smile. "Was the door locked?"

"No. You have some kind of thing about locks?"

"Yes, I'm interested in security," I said innocently. "So, when you got here . . . ?"

McGraw's eyes flared. He turned, pointed, and spoke in the same monotone I imagined he used to give evidence in court. "She was on the floor out there. Kazarian was sitting by the body. I asked if he'd touched her. He said just to pull the needle out and make sure she was dead."

See if, I heard Cohen's scratchy voice in my head. "Did you also? Touch her?"

"In case he was wrong. But he wasn't."

"Did you know her?" Bill asked.

"I told you, no."

"No, you said you didn't know *him.*"

"I said I hardly know any of them. They're just my job. Better than retail, I told myself when I took it. Useful, you know? Something worth protecting. Shit. This place." He shook his head.

"But you didn't?" Bill persisted.

"Didn't what? Know her? No, I goddamn didn't. Okay?"

"Okay," I said. "Can we look around?"

He waved a hand. "Knock yourselves out." He leaned on the doorway and folded his arms, to wait until we were knocked out.

Bill and I wandered the dim room. Our inspection didn't take long. Each cot was equipped with a thin hospital pillow and blanket. I started to wonder how often those things got washed, but it occurred to me there was probably a naproom rule about bringing new linens and dropping the ones you used into the nearest laundry cart when you were done.

"Damn," I said to Bill as we stood in the back cubicle. "This place is depressing."

"I've slept in worse."

Side-eyeing him, I said, "That's not an endorsement. Of this place, or of you, either." I snapped photos with my phone. "And you better have been good-copping McGraw with all those little agreeable smiles while he was patronizing and insulting me."

"Of course I was. I was trying to charm him."

"A security chief?"

"Just call me Don Quixote."

We made our way to the door, where McGraw was checking his phone. "You done?" he growled without looking up.

"Done here. Could we see the rest of the east basement?"

McGraw snapped his head to me like I was insane. "No you fucking can't. Off-limits. Closed. No trespassing. You know those words?"

I had a tremendous urge to reply, "No speakee Engrish," but I bit my tongue.

Bill said, "We're in the off-limits area already. It would help us a lot to know how the killer might have gotten in here."

"Too bad. I have to go do a shift-change briefing and then I have to interview a roomful of assholes to replace the assholes I canned. If everything goes perfect, I won't get my sorry butt home until nine. I sure as hell have no more time for you. And no way I'm letting you wander around down here alone. Besides, who says Kazarian isn't the killer? Besides Kazarian? Let's go." He waited for us to leave the room and made sure the door was locked behind us. As he turned, a torn piece of yellow tape floated across his face. He ripped it down. I looked left and right while we walked behind him through the cramped corridor. Other doors, other hallways. Everything dim and lonely-looking.

"What about the hookup room?" I asked.

McGraw stopped. "The fucking what?"

"No one hooks up in the nap room. There's a separate room for that."

"What kind of bullshit—where is it?"

"We were told 'down the hall.' We thought you'd know. It has a sign-up sheet," I added, to be helpful.

"Jesus Christ," he said, but it was all he said. He shook his head and started walking again. We passed doors labeled things like ELECTRICAL CLOSET and FIRE PUMP.

"These mechanical rooms," Bill said. "Are they—"

"No. So much of this shit shorted out, flooded out, or rusted out because of the hurricane that they relocated all the mechanical rooms onto higher floors. Just abandoned all the equipment, even if it wasn't ruined. Cheaper than moving it. This hospital, it's all about cheaper." He pushed through the NO ACCESS double doors and we followed him back to the elevator. He pressed his key card to the Up button. A few moments later the bell dinged and the elevator doors slid open. We all stepped in, the doors closed, and as they opened again on B2 McGraw got out and said, "Have a nice day."

CHAPTER ELEVEN

You get the feeling he didn't mean that?" I asked Bill as the elevator rose. "About the nice day?"

"Hey, he's in a bad position. A woman died, he had to fire six men, and his job's on the line. I'd be crabby too."

"You? When you're usually such a ray of sunshine? So ignoring your penchant for defending and excusing rude, condescending ex-cops, how are we going to get into the rest of that basement?"

"I'd hardly call it a penchant." We stepped from the elevator to find our old friend the red line waiting for us. "It's just a right I exercise every now and then. Because if I were ever rude and condescending I'd want someone to defend me."

"I can't imagine a time when that would happen."

"Me being rude, or someone defending me? Normally, to get access to someplace near a crime scene I'd ask the cop on the case."

"Church." I nodded. "That'll work."

"Careful," Bill said. "Sarcasm is close to rudeness and I've already defended my quota of rude people today. Okay, how about we go to the expert?"

"Which would be who?"

"Whom."

"Oh, shut up."

"Jordy. Aren't Pathology and the morgue in the basement somewhere? I'm betting there's a much faster route to the nap room—and the hookup room, and whatever other rooms they have down there—than this." He circled a hand at the corridor and the red line.

"You mean, if you don't want to detour to see Quick Draw?"

"And who would want to do that?"

"Whom."

"No, who—oh, right, shut up."

If returning to the too-bright corridors of the ground floor had been like surfacing from a murky ocean, walking out into the late-day muggy sunshine from the air-conditioned lobby was like stepping into a hot bath directly from the windswept tundra.

"Wow," I said. "That feels good. I didn't realize how freezing I was. Why are hospitals always so cold?"

"To get to the other side. Are you going to call Jordy, or you want me to?"

"I will. But I'm calling Cohen first." Some lawyers don't mind if their PI talks directly to the client as work proceeds on a case. Some go ballistic. I had a hunch I knew which type Cohen was, and I was right.

"We need to talk to Jordy," I told her. "Is it okay to talk without you, or you want to be there?"

"Absolutely not okay. He's the definition of 'loose cannon.' I need to hear every word he says to you."

Cohen set up a conference call with Jordy, me, and Bill. Five minutes later Bill and I, side by side on one of the benches that lined the curving hospital driveway, heard Jordy's cheery "Hey, counselor!" bouncing through our earbuds. "Who're the other phone numbers?"

Cohen said, “Lydia and Bill. They have some questions for you.”

“Hi, Jordy,” I said. “How’re you doing?”

“Fine. I’m lying around reading Proust. Should I not admit that? Does it sound too geeky?”

“Which translation?” Bill asked.

“The Moncrieff. It’s flowery but I hear it’s the best.”

“It is the best. It—”

“Hello?” said Cohen. “How does it help our case for you to know what Jordy’s reading?”

“Wait, I know this one,” said Jordy. “‘The meter’s running.’ You’d better ask your questions before my lawyer fires me.”

“Or sends you a bill for every minute I’m on this phone listening to inanity,” said Cohen.

Jeez, I thought. The guy’s barely out of jail, his father’s cut him off, he’s not supposed to leave his apartment, and people think he killed somebody. I thought it would be polite to ask how he is before we start doing business.

Sighing inside, I said, “We were wondering how you get to the nap room from the morgue.”

“You mean, my exact route? Stairs and corridors?”

“We just got out of a meeting with the security chief. McGraw. He took us to the crime scene but he wouldn’t let us see the rest of the east basement. We think you probably don’t use the same route he took us on, and if we knew—”

“Stop,” said Cohen. “Jordy, just tell them how you get there. Lydia, do *not* say another word about why you’re asking.”

I exchanged glances with Bill and took my notebook out. Jordy began giving directions. I wrote them down. I asked which was the hookup room and he told me. “Any other rooms we need to know about?”

"If there are, I don't know about them either. But I only go there to nap. For all I know there's a door that leads to the Holodeck on the *Enterprise*."

"Christ!" muttered Cohen.

Quickly, I said, "What about other people, coming from, say, upstairs? Would everyone take the same route?"

"You'd probably come a different way from Facilities or Supplies or the loading dock, that stuff, but not so many of those guys work double shifts. I've never seen any of them in the nap room. Everyone else from upstairs, the nurses and all, they might take different elevators or whatever but they'd end up in that Corridor D I just told you about. I mean, some of the medical departments, like say the ones on the top floors of Donnelly Tower, that's the blue one, they're just too far away, so if that's where you're working you wouldn't go at all."

"What about people from administration?" Bill asked.

"I'm not sure how they'd get down there but they wouldn't have any reason to. Eight-hour days, forty-hour weeks, see ya. That's staff. Management, they don't work at all."

"Spoken like a union guy whose father is management," Bill said.

"Truth is truth. If it makes Dr. Irwin DeBoring look bad, that's an added benefit."

"Okay," I said. "If anything else comes up we'll call you."

"You mean you'll call me, of course," Cohen said.

"Of course." When we hung up, I asked Bill, "Do you think she knows we might try a little B&E?"

"Yes, and she doesn't care, as long as she and Jordy can both say they didn't know. When—"

My phone interrupted him with "Bad Boys."

"Hey," I said, answering. "What's up, Linus?"

"Got Sophia Scott for you. Want me to Dropbox?"

"Please. Anything interesting?" I put the phone on speaker and Bill leaned in.

"Yes. We're not the first."

"Who's not the first what?"

"Wong Security is not the first to stick our noses into Sophia Scott's life."

"What do you mean?"

"A month ago somebody did pretty much what we're doing. Looked around in here."

"How do you know?"

"Unless you're really good, you leave footprints." I detected a smug note in his voice.

"Which you're not doing."

"Of course not."

"Of course not. Can you tell who they were?"

"No, nor what they were looking for."

"Was there anything interesting to find?"

"Hard to know what's interesting. I'll send it, but here's the TLDR. Birth name, Kanellopolous. It means cinnamon seller, I looked it up. From outside Chicago. Left there after high school, went to nursing school in Florida, came to New York, been here since. Met Ronald Scott in Florida, Pediatrician. Marriage lasted three years, no kids, no-fault divorce. He lives in Seattle now—where he's from—new wife, two kids."

"Hey, Linus, it's me," Bill said. "Any contact between them lately?"

"Yo, Bill. Not that I could see from here, but it wouldn't be in an overview. I could try for her phone records. I know some guys—"

"No," I said. One of the rules I have with Linus is, when he works for me, he doesn't break the law.

When he works for other people, I can only hope he doesn't get caught.

"How long was she at River Valley Downstate and where was she before?" Bill asked.

"Nine years, and Montefiore. Used to work in the OR, now OB/GYN. Had an RN and an MSN." My cousin the techie loved rattling off initials.

"Anything sketchy?"

"One arrest, in high school. Graduation night, partying with some other kids. I guess that's why they call it high school."

"But you wouldn't know," I said.

"You know I wouldn't. Gotta stay sharp. Me and Trella, we get our highs naturally. Plus, I didn't have a graduation night."

Whether the joy of hacking into computer systems or building surveillance devices could actually be called a "natural" high was debatable, but I was just glad he and Trella were clean. The graduation thing was true. Linus had been tossed out of two high schools. After the second, he talked his parents into letting him take the GED, scored above 195 on each of the four parts, and just to make them happy, took the SAT. His combined score was 1576. ("Two hundred years better than George Washington!") Then he announced his intention of starting an electronic security business in their garage.

I said, "Arrested for partying?"

"Started with a noise complaint. Whole lotta shrieking going on. Police found drugs. Mar-ee-wha-na and a couple of Mollies. Picked up all four of them. The three girls, including Kanellopolous—you know how much fun it is to say that?—were minors. Held overnight, probably to scare them straight, then let go with a stern warning. The fourth, a guy, was a major. Two of the girls said they didn't know where the drugs came from but Kanellopolous dropped the dime, told them he was the candyman. He served a year."

"Bad luck."

"Hey," Trella spoke up. "I say this with the greatest respect, Lydia and Bill, because I know you have friends among the po-lice"—which

Trella, from an Italian family in East Harlem, did not—"but being over eighteen wasn't the guy's only bad luck in that case. He was Black. The girls all were White."

"Oh," I said. "Okay, I get it."

"Yeah," said Linus. "Anyway, Kanellopolous left for Florida that week."

"And nothing since? No contact with that guy, for example?"

"Negatory, cuz. So pure you could use her as hand sanitizer. No more drugs, no guns or porn. No criminal record in the fifty states or Puerto Rico, US possessions, or military bases. Ex-hubby either."

"Very thorough."

"Premier-tier double-platinum service for you. Of course, I *could* check to see if there's anything shady in her hospital personnel file."

"If you haven't yet it's because that would be illegal, right?" I said. "So no."

"Come on! You have any idea how easy a hospital is? The other guys did it."

"Wait. How do you know that?"

"Oops."

"Oh, Linus. You did it already, didn't you?"

"I was annoyed. With the other guys. I thought maybe I could track them from the point where they had to, you know—"

"I don't want to know. And I don't want you to do it again. Clear?"

"Yes, cuz." He sounded abashed but I'd have bet he was suppressing a grin.

"Seriously. I'm just trying to keep you guys out of jail."

"And we appreciate it, Lydia!" called Trella from across the room. I didn't for a minute think I could count on her to keep Linus on the straight and narrow—or to stay on it herself—but it was good of her to acknowledge my attempt.

"Well," I said with a sigh, "since you did it, did you find anything?"

"Funny you should ask. Passed over twice for promotion because she wasn't 'management material.'"

"What does that mean?"

"Says here, 'Not good with people. Competent nursing but patients and colleagues complain about attitude.'"

"Hmm. Anything else?"

"Yeah. She was on the nurses' union negotiating committee."

"For the new contract? So they don't strike?"

"Union Strong!" I heard Trella yell. That Italian family contained a multitude of Teamsters.

"Correcto," said Linus. "You want us to dig into that?"

"Why not? See if you can find who else is on the committee and how the negotiations are going. And, Linus—"

"I know! Legally only! Anyhow, the committee member list is already part of the Dropbox file. Like I said, premier-tier double-platinum. You think maybe there's like, union corruption and stuff?"

"I don't think anything. This is the information-gathering phase."

"Righty-o. Sending the Dropbox link. Your other two, Eyegor and Dr. DeBreng, are cooking. Legally only! Did you know there are two Dr. DeBrengs at that hospital? You wanted Irwin, right?"

"I did know. The other one is Son of Irwin and you know what, do him, too."

"You got it. Chill."

"Chill, legally only!" I answered, but he was gone.

CHAPTER TWELVE

I settled back on the bench and crossed my arms. I could see a puzzle-piece of sky squeezed between the canopy over the driveway and the high-rises across the avenue. The morning's glorious blue had faded to a pearly heat haze. Traffic honked and pedestrians knotted up at street corners. An ambulance came screaming down the emergency room driveway. I wondered if I could talk Elliott into going skydiving again tomorrow.

"On reflection," Bill said, his arms resting on the back of the bench, "if Quick Draw is interviewing new security guards this evening and then hauling his sorry ass home around nine, it might be a great time for us to spelunk in the east basement."

"Spelunk. You're a show-off, you know that? Did you really read that translation of Proust Jordy's reading?"

"And the new one, too. Well, a couple of books of the new one. It's like reading a new translation of the Bible. Once you have that beautiful language in your head, nothing else works for you."

"I'll take your word for it. You're right about the east basement, though. He pretty much told us it's got no security and he won't be around." My phone dinged with the arrival of an email. "Here's Linus's Dropbox link."

I thumbed open what Linus had sent but before I could go through it, Bill said, "If we're going to sit around staring at our phones, how about we do it at a café like everyone else in New York? Plus I'm starving."

Caffeine and food being not a bad idea at all, I agreed and headed us toward a Puerto Rican place nearby, where Elliott and I have grabbed café con leche a couple of times. I liked it because of the yellow walls, mounted photos of coffee and tea plantations, mismatched comfy chairs, and yellow Formica tables. Elliott liked it because the coffee was great and it was just far enough from the hospital that not many doctors went there.

"Too cheery for you?" I asked Bill as we pushed open the door. The air conditioner wheezed like the one in my office, but unlike mine it actually cooled the air.

"How will I stay my usual glum self if you take me to places like this?" he answered.

"You'll just have to work at it." We ordered and settled in to read Sophia Scott's file.

"Well," I said, halfway through my Darjeeling, "Linus seems to have called it. Whatever reason there might have been to kill this woman, it's not here. Let's try the ex, see if she had enemies, that kind of thing."

"Church will have done that already." Bill sat back, finishing off his second empanada. "If she's still so hot for Jordy, the ex won't have had much to offer."

"Unless she's not hot for Jordy because she's found the owner of the burner phone."

He shook his head. "We'd be off the case already, or at least on pause. If Church turned in another direction, Cohen wouldn't waste a minute before she stopped the meter from running."

He was right.

"We can follow up with the ex later," he said, "but how about this—these people on the nurses' negotiating committee. They'd know Scott pretty well. I'm betting Church isn't looking at that angle at all."

I lifted my mug to him, having already devoured my cheese and avocado on seven-grain bread. "Have I ever mentioned that I think you're pretty smart?"

"'Smart-ass,' I believe is what I've heard."

"That too."

We divided Linus's sixteen-person list and started making calls. A couple of times I had to leave messages, but most people on my half of the list answered. No one I talked to had anything unpleasant to say about Scott, but I detected a note of not speaking ill of the dead. "Professional," "efficient," "skilled." Okay. A drug user, an accidental OD? If so, a total surprise. That seemed to be the consensus. I asked who her friends had been; no one seemed to know. Finally one woman, an ICU nurse named Sharon Ives with a high, melodic voice, offered more. "I admit I was surprised when she volunteered for the negotiating committee."

"How so?"

"She'd never shown much interest in the union. She was a member, everyone is, but committees, info meetings, even holiday parties, she never came. I never saw her at anything social, and I don't think she even worked much overtime. A just-do-your-shift-and-go-home type. But you know, people get fed up. I've been organizing for years and I've seen it before—one too many late-night bedpans and a two percent raise, and something blows."

Based on the conversations I'd been having, that was new, and surprised me. "Really? It's just, what I've been hearing is what you said—she did her shift and that was it. I'm trying to get a bead on who she was. So you're saying she turned into kind of a firebrand?"

"No, nothing like that. She didn't go out of her way to educate herself on the issues, and since negotiations started, she's been basically the most conservative voice. Like she really wants us to take the offer, settle, no strike. I guess after a few sessions she didn't think the offer would get any better."

"Is that the general view?"

"Absolutely not. It has to get better. Safe staffing, decent health care—health care, this is a hospital!—a reasonable salary increase—you know we've only had a two and then a three percent increase since COVID? The hospital has plenty of money. We're asking them to spend a tiny bit of it on the people patients see and depend on most."

That sounded a little rehearsed, like she'd given that speech before, but I couldn't argue with anything she was saying. "Good luck," I said, "and thanks."

Another thing I found was, on my half of the list I only had two people who knew Jordy, and they didn't seem convinced he could've killed Scott, but didn't seem convinced he couldn't, either.

"Agnostics," Bill said at one point when we'd both put down our phones to attack new mugs of tea and coffee. "The only one on my list who knew Jordy was exactly like that. They're great on juries, but not so great as character witnesses."

"Let's see if we can get Jordy off the hook before he needs juries and character witnesses."

"You know"—Bill put down his coffee—"he's very appealing, but he might be guilty."

"Yeah," I sighed, "I know. But I can do this work better if I believe he's not. And"—I locked onto his eyes—"I know you can too."

"Me? I'm just a cynic who believes the worst of everybody."

"And I'm just your partner who believes you're full of baloney. Finish your calls and let's figure out our next move."

Bill picked up his phone and tapped in the number of the next person on his list. I headed for the ladies' room. When I got back, Bill was scribbling in his notebook. He held up a hand to stop me from doing whatever I'd been planning to do. "Thanks," he said into the phone. "Yes, that's great. Half an hour, see you there."

I sat as he clicked off. "That was a nurse called Talia Venturino. She didn't want to talk about Scott on the phone. She wants to meet in person. She just got off her shift."

"Interesting. Meet where?"

"Central Park, over on the west side. A bench near Strawberry Fields."

Even more interesting. In my experience, people didn't want to meet PIs in a park so we could all enjoy the trees and grass. Largely, it was because they didn't want to be overheard.

CHAPTER THIRTEEN

Half an hour later Bill and I sat listening to a bearded guitarist offering an earnest, though unfortunate, rendition of "Imagine."

"Is it wrong of me," I asked, "to wish she'd chosen the *Alice in Wonderland* statue?"

"Or the Shakespeare Garden," Bill said, lighting a cigarette. The singer's voice rose to a wail on "*living for to-DAY.*" Bill added, "Or the restrooms."

"You know it's illegal to smoke in the park," I said.

He waved the cigarette. "With all the weed in the air no one will notice." I had to admit that was probably true.

As the singer launched into "Penny Lane," we were given a wave of the hand by a lanky woman walking up the park path in jeans and a T-shirt. She looked to be near sixty, with the fine-lined face of someone who spent a lot of time outdoors. Her big shoulders, muscled arms, and radiant athletic energy made me suddenly think getting older might not be so bad after all. I wondered if she was a swimmer.

"Hi," she said, stopping in front of us. "Mr. Smith?"

"Bill. This is my partner, Lydia Chin."

"Pleased to meet you. Talia Venturino." She plopped down on the bench beside me and leaned across me to Bill. "Bill? Stop smoking."

"Sorry." Bill ground his cigarette out. "Thanks for seeing us."

"I didn't mean stop smoking now while I'm here. Stop. End. Finish. Quit. It's going to kill you."

"Thanks," I said. "He's heard that before, but from a medical professional it might penetrate."

"I'll work on it," Bill said. "Can we move on?"

Venturino leaned back and looked up at the treetops. "You do that, work on it. Get the patch. Hypnosis. Twelve-step. Find something. Otherwise your partner here will be working alone. Okay, moving on." A pause and a sidelong glance at us. "You guys are working for Jordy Kazarian, is that what you said?"

"For his lawyer," I answered.

"But you've met him, right? God, he's weird, isn't he? Very nerdy but cheerful all the time. Dieners are all nerdy but he's the only one I've met who bounces. You know?"

"We do know."

"I have a hard time thinking of him as a killer. Do you guys think he killed Sophia?"

"He says he didn't."

Venturino squinted at me, then laughed. "You're as bad as a lawyer." She settled in, elbows on the back of the bench, and eyed the crowd around the singer. "I've been waiting for someone to ask me about Sophia, but no one has."

"By 'no one,' you mean the police?" Bill said.

"I guess a detective came, but he didn't talk to me, or anyone in the union, as far as I know."

"She," Bill said. "Helena Church is her name. And you think she should have?"

"Of course she should have. What kind of an investigation is that? Is that how you'd do it?"

"She's pretty sure she has a suspect."

"Cops are idiots." After that declaration Venturino paused and looked Bill over. He was never a cop, but he does sometimes have that unnerving hard-man look. Venturino turned away again and went on, "Sophia is—was on the negotiating committee for the new contract. I guess you know that. That's where you got my number." Stretching her neck again to look at Bill, she said, "How did you get that list, by the way?"

"Legally," I answered her.

She shifted her gaze to me, clearly waiting for more.

I said, "We have access to certain non-public databases. As licensed investigators." Which Wong Security used with my passwords as a private contractor employed by Chin and Smith Investigations. Which, I've been told, is probably defensible in court.

"Well, it's not a secret. The union membership has a right to know who's negotiating for them. There's even a Zoom link so any member can watch and listen in real time. Management didn't want that but we wouldn't come to the table without it." She smirked. In a smooth, quick move she swiveled on the bench, sitting on her hip so she was facing us. Maybe not a swimmer, a dancer? "Sophia wanted to settle. Every time they made a new offer she pushed to take it."

"That's what we've heard," I said. "But no one else agreed?"

"Some people. Not most of us. You ever negotiated a union contract?"

"No," I said. Bill shook his head.

"This is my second time. It's excruciating." She sighed. "It goes like this. They make an offer. We make a counteroffer. They say our demands are ridiculous! Unrealistic! We'd better come to our senses or forget it. Sometimes they actually get up and walk out. Dominance, you know? They're suits. Lawyers, MBAs. We're just nurses. Way down the food chain. Plus our committee is all women—straight and gay—and gay men. Half of us are BIPOC, some are immigrants. Them, five White men, a Black man, a White woman, and you better believe they're all straight, or at least you better believe they want you to believe they're all straight." She kicked at some dirt. "One of them, a sourpuss bald dweeb called Walsh, he's the one who leads the walkouts. He likes to bait us." She lifted her head to glance at Bill. "He smokes, too. You can smell it on his clothes." Swiveling to sit back again and look across the park, she said, "He's new, been at River Valley about nine months. I think he's sure we've already decided to strike no matter what so he's just trying to score points. Look tough to his new bosses." Venturino shook her head. "But the woman's the worst. Margaret Weldon, attorney at law. Hard to believe a woman can treat other women like that. 'You nurses don't understand. You have to see the bigger picture. The hospital has obligations. You're not the only calf pulling at the tit—'"

"She didn't really say that," I broke in.

Venturino smiled thinly. "She said 'udder.' Condescending bitch but her whole performance is for the men on their side of the table. Dancing for the master, you know? She 'let it slip' the other day"—air quotes—"that the hospital's already got an agreement with a travel nurse company in case of a strike. Like that's supposed to scare us. High Point Nursing, I think. Not the usual company but the usual one probably wanted too much money. God almighty, River Valley would cheap out on its own grandma's funeral."

Bill smiled and I asked, "What's a travel nurse company?"

"Just what it sounds like. A company that provides temporary nurses. You tell them how many nurses you need for how long, and they send them. In a disease outbreak, say, or something like a chemical plant explosion, a hospital might need more staff, or more specialist staff, than they have." She switched her gaze from the crowd to us. "They use them a lot during strikes. Ever been in a hospital during a strike? It'll be fully staffed. With nurses who're competent at nursing but don't know where the toilet paper's kept."

"Sounds like union busting," Bill said.

"We don't like it—or the nurses who do it—very much, but you can't leave the patients on their own." She looked at Bill like that should have been obvious. "The hospitals don't like it either. It costs them a lot of money, much more than we do because they're paying the nurses a premium and they're also paying the company that provides them."

"Doesn't it bother you that the hospital's so sure you're going to strike that they're already talking to this company?" I asked. "Wouldn't that mean they aren't planning to offer anything better and you can go ahead and strike for all they care?"

Venturino shook her head. "They have to be ready. If we're going to strike, we're required by law to give them a ten-day warning. They have to do the same thing, by the way, if they're going to lock us out."

"Does that happen often? A hospital locking out nurses?"

"They'd be crazy. If your nurses are willing to work past their own strike deadline, why wouldn't you let them? They all use it as a threat, but I've never heard of anyplace doing it."

"So you've given the ten-day warning? Is that why they're talking to this company?"

"We haven't—yet—but they'd be stupid to wait until we do. They need to be ready to replace nurses shift by shift if we go out. They're probably already paying High Point to have people on hold. You know what, I hope they are. The more it costs them to not just give us what we're asking for, the worse they look."

"Do the nurses ever walk out of the negotiations?"

She gave a sour smirk. "No. Only management does. Then two days later they do us a big favor and come back to the table with another offer. Like we didn't know they were going to do that and we should be grateful. It's so stupid." She sighed. "Four times now. Their offers don't get much better, they just move the money around. A bigger raise, but less health care. Health care, but no guarantee on staffing levels." She shook her head. "Jerks."

"It sounds very frustrating," I said.

"Ya think?"

"But what about Scott?"

"It started to seem—to me, I never talked to anyone else about it, though I guess other people might have picked up on it too—but I thought management knew more than they should have about our deliberations. Our priorities. What staffing levels we'd accept, what we were willing to leave out of the health care coverage, that kind of thing."

"You're talking about the difference between your demands and what you'd decided among yourselves you'd agree to?" Bill said.

"Their offers started tracking with those things." She looked from me to Bill. "It had to be we had a mole. Someone was reporting back to them."

"It sounds like it," I said. "And you think it was Scott."

"I know it was." Venturino flopped back again, pulling one long leg up to plant her sneakered foot on the bench. The singer lifted a water bottle. Tourists dropped dollars into the guitar case. If we were lucky he'd be taking a break. "I worked with her in Pediatrics for a while. I didn't like her."

"I thought she was in OB/GYN."

"When things are tight you can get temporarily reassigned. Even if it costs overtime. The hospital would rather do that than get travel nurses in those situations. It was a perfectly reasonable transfer but Sophia objected."

"But she went?"

"Oh, she went. I mean, she objected formally. She filed a protest of assignment. Her supervisor called mine, said he couldn't afford to be without her. It's not up to the supervisors, though. There's a rotation, and OB/GYN had plenty of nurses who could cover. So too bad. It was only a month, we had someone out with a broken leg, but my God, you'd have thought she was being shipped out to East Bumfuck." Venturino looked away again. "Like I said, I didn't like her. Not that I kill people I don't like. Place would be littered with bodies." A sudden bright smile, which faded. "But nursing, even if you don't like each other, you've got each other's backs. You know? Because of the patients. But Sophia was . . . On the unit, she pretty much carried her weight, but that's all. She didn't help, she didn't step up, she didn't work overtime. In fact, the opposite. She'd be late starting her shift, she'd make phone calls from patient rooms—she liked to see what she could get away with. If I were her supervisor, I'd have cut her off at the knees. People like that, they push because it's fun. If they get away with something, they push more next time. But Sophia never got written up on her own unit so she pulled the same shit on ours. That's not nursing."

"Interesting," I said. "That doesn't sound like someone who'd volunteer for a committee. Especially such an intensive one."

"No, it doesn't, does it? What she did do, she flirted with the doctors and sweet-talked the male nurses, the sales reps, the orderlies. She was hot, don't get me wrong. I could've gone for her myself, except she made it clear she didn't like women. And I don't just mean in bed. You know the type, right?" Her look was entirely for me, not Bill. "None of us knew that much about her personal life but it seemed like the come-ons were one thing, I mean kind of automatic, but for actual boyfriends she always punched above her weight. No nurses, certainly no orderlies. Doctors, supervisors, or outside guys she met at bars. One time a Wall Street guy but he didn't last."

"What happened to him?"

"I heard he went off with a supermodel."

I saw Bill's hand move toward his jacket pocket, where the cigarettes were, but Venturino caught the movement too and gave him the stink eye. He stopped.

"Anyone lately?" I asked.

"I don't know. Gossip was yes, a new guy, but I didn't care enough to go deeper. Ask your brother." She glanced sideways at me and laughed. "Oh God, look at your face! I didn't mean she was seeing him. The sainted Dr. Chin?" She put a hand to her mouth in mock horror. "Just ask him for doctors' lounge gossip."

I tried to ignore the heat in my cheeks. Bill grinned.

Venturino smirked another moment, then said, "So when she volunteered to do it, be on the committee, a lot of us were skeptical. But Sharon—Sharon Ives, have you talked to her?"

I nodded and Venturino went on, "She said we should give Sophia a chance. That maybe she'd, I don't know what, found Jesus?"

"Seriously?" said Bill.

"Come on." She snorted. "Sharon said people get fed up and maybe Sophia had changed."

"That's what she told me," I said.

Venturino shook her head. "People don't change. They just get more like themselves. Sophia was selfish. She got a kick out of getting away with things and probably always had. There was a rumor that back in high school she skipped out on a drug rap by selling out her boyfriend."

"We heard that, too."

"Is it true?"

"Likely." If Linus said so, it was true.

"Not surprised. Whatever she was on that committee for, it wasn't the union members. At negotiating meetings she'd undermine us when we were trying to show a united front. She'd be conciliatory with management, and by conciliatory I mean she kissed ass. She really, really didn't want a strike."

"Why?"

"Part of me thinks it was because everyone else did and she wanted to see how contrary she could be. But that's a lot of work for not much reward. So I don't really know. But it's not just my opinion. Ask Sharon, ask anyone on the committee. Sophia was pushing for a membership vote on the contract. This most recent offer sucks as bad as the other ones. But we need time to convince the members. They're getting tired of this but they're not ready to strike. They will be after another couple of rounds, but if we'd voted now we'd have lost. We'd all be stuck with a shitty contract for the next four years."

"So what happened?"

"I fed her bullshit." Venturino glanced at us, then turned back to watch the singer, who'd begun to belt out "When I'm Sixty-Four." "Jesus, Mary, and Joseph, he's awful," she said.

"Bullshit?" Bill asked.

"I gave her info from one of the subcommittees I'm on that she's not. What I told her wasn't true, and bang, it showed up in the next offer management made. In a garbled form, not in a way that would have worked, and undercutting us, but unmistakable. I did it again to make sure."

"And?" I asked.

She turned her gaze to me. "I'm sure."

I glanced at Bill, then said, "What did you do? Did you confront her?"

Venturino nodded. "I did. I told her to quit the committee. I said if she was still on it in twenty-four hours, I'd expose her double-crossing ass."

"When was this?"

"The day before she died."

CHAPTER FOURTEEN

Bill reached again for a cigarette, then dropped his hand, muttering, "Shit." That might have been for the cigarette, or maybe for what we'd just heard. "You threatened her the day before someone killed her, and it didn't occur to you to tell anyone this until just now?"

Venturino snapped her head toward him. "Of course it fucking occurred to me. I knew this is what would happen. 'You sure it was the day before, not the day of? How mad were you? How heated did it get? Did she threaten you back? Attack you? She did, didn't she? If it was self-defense, anyone can understand that. It's okay, just tell us.' Jesus. I'm only telling *you* because cops screw over innocent people all the time and I didn't want that to happen to Jordy. But fuck it." She stood. "Use it however you want. I'm out of here."

"No, wait," I said. "Please."

She'd started to stride off but she stopped. She spun to face me.

"You said those things," I said. "We didn't." I didn't add, *and you're not wrong.* "But this is kind of a shocker, you can see that, right? How did you expect us to react? Nobody's accusing you of anything. But this changes all the calculus and I wish we'd known. If she was a management mole, there are more people involved, more possible motives. You need to tell the police about this."

She gave me a good long look. "You tell them. If that detective wants to call me, she can, but I bet she won't. It would be a lot easier to say I'm making it up. That I had some beef with Sophia. Like you said, the cop has a suspect, no one liked Sophia, and I'm the only one who knows she was a rat."

"No," Bill said. "Whoever her management contact was, they know, too. And you may not have been the only one on the committee who knew."

Venturino stared daggers at him. "Tell me you're not saying a nurse killed her because she was selling us out. For Christ's sake, we bust our humps to save lives every goddamn minute of every goddamn day. We don't kill people."

"Someone did."

"Well, it wasn't a fucking nurse!"

"Do you have any idea," I said quickly, "who Scott's management contact might have been?"

She swung her gaze back to me. "No. None. Good luck to Jordy, but I'm leaving. I'm done here. I have to get to practice."

"Aha!" I said. "I knew you were a jock. What sport?"

She fixed me with a dark look, then suddenly smiled. "Fencing."

◆

"Well," Bill said as we watched Talia Venturino melt into the crowd. "We're doing better. At least one of us sort of charmed her. Is it okay if I have a cigarette now?"

"It's never okay if you have a cigarette, but it's even less okay when you get all crabby and twitchy. How about when this case is over you go away someplace by yourself and quit?"

"No chance." He slipped a cigarette between his lips and struck a match. "If I'm going to be miserable, believe me, so are you." He took a long pull. "We need to call Church, right?"

"Let me," I said. "Apparently my charm offensive is working."

"As opposed to my just plain offensive."

Because I was much too big a person to respond to that, and because he'd just about promised to quit smoking, I merely took out my phone and pressed the detective's number.

"Church. Who's this?"

"Lydia Chin."

"Who?"

"We met at La Lechonera."

"We did? Oh, yeah, you drank seltzer. Why're you calling? I told you guys I'm not giving you anything."

"I'm trying to give you something."

The singer moved into "Lucy in the Sky with Diamonds." That was it. I got up, tilted my head at Bill to join me, and walked away.

"Give me what?" said Church. "Because I have my captain all over my butt to clear this case fast and I have no time for bullshit."

"It's a motive."

A brief pause. "Whose?"

"I don't know. We just talked to a nurse on the union negotiating committee who said Sophia Scott was a management mole." The dappled path under the trees got blessedly quieter with each step away from Strawberry Fields. I gave Church a quick rundown of our talk with Venturino. I didn't mention her threat to out Scott; let Church discover that on her own, or not. As far as I was concerned it wasn't the important part. Bill strolled beside me, contentedly, if illegally, smoking.

"Why didn't I hear about this anywhere else?" Church demanded when I was done.

"You didn't ask. You were so set on Jordy—"

"Not your business. Give me this nurse's number."

I was tempted to say "Not your business," but it was, after all, why I'd called. "I'll text it to you. But it seems to me—"

"Yeah, well, not to me. Who kills people over union negotiations? More likely this nurse had some beef with the vic and she's trying to smear her now. Maybe she even did it herself. But I'll look into it, yeah. Send that text."

"Speaking of texts, did you find the owner of the burner phone yet?"

"How the hell do you know about that?"

"You told Jordy, for God's sake."

"I swear—"

"Okay, you didn't. That's all I asked."

I sent her Venturino's number and then put the phone back to my ear, to hear Church say, "Got it. Bye."

I slid the phone back in my pocket. Bill said, "Charmed?"

"Not a bit. She said people don't kill over union negotiations."

Bill shrugged. "Jimmy Hoffa's never been found."

CHAPTER FIFTEEN

Because I was the boss, I called Sophia Scott's supervisor. I told him who we were, who we were working for, and asked if he could give us a few minutes.

"You work for Kazarian?" he said. "The guy they arrested? What do you want from me?"

"There are just a few things to clear up."

A pause. "Yeah, okay." He sounded harried. "Can you come up now? I'm slammed but Jesus. I mean, for Sophia. If it'll help."

"We're on the west side. Twenty minutes?"

"Yeah, fine."

To meet Venturino we'd walked across the park. Now we let the MTA crosstown bus help us out. We made it to the hospital with two minutes to spare.

OB/GYN was on the eighth floor, which was a lucky number for the Chinese moms. I wondered if they'd done that on purpose—doubtful—and hoped the luck extended to everyone—possible, especially if you're superstitious, which of course I'm not. We stepped off the elevator into yet more bright lights reflecting off yet more polished floors. I heard yet more beeping, and sniffed yet more antiseptic scent.

"It might drive me nuts to work here all day, every day," I said to Bill as I texted Scott's supervisor.

"It would drive you nuts to work any one place all day, every day."

I smiled. Sometimes he's very right.

A stocky man strode around the corner of the nurses' station. His close-cropped red hair was echoed in the five o'clock shadow on his jaw. "Ms. Chin? Mr. Smith? Liam O'Brien." He wore pink scrubs with his badge clipped to the pocket. *Supervisors pink, serves them right*, I heard Jordy say. "Come this way. There's a room we can talk."

We followed him past doors with patients' names lettered on cards tucked into plastic slots. Some doors were open. One of the rooms was filled with flowers; another had balloons floating on the ceiling, proclaiming "It's a girl!" O'Brien opened a door to a small windowless room full of tissue boxes, copier paper, cartons of latex gloves, two armchairs, and the powerful smell of burned coffee.

"Secondary lounge," he said. "We make do. Want coffee?" He waved his hand at a portly glass pot holding what looked like something you could pave a road with. Even Bill turned the offer down. O'Brien shrugged and poured himself a cup. He added milk, which disappeared without effect into the murky depths.

"But," he said, as though Bill or I had spoken, "you're working for the diener they arrested?"

"Jordy Kazarian," I said. "Do you know him?"

"No. No reason I would. Frankly those guys creep me out. And Sophia—I mean, I don't know why I'm even talking to you."

"You think Kazarian is guilty?"

"Look, I know everyone deserves a defense, innocent until proven guilty, all that, but if you ask me, if there's anyone who could kill someone, it'd be a diener."

"Why?"

"Come on, you spend all day with dead people, it's got to, I don't know, rub off?" He sucked the top layer of coffee off the too-full cup. "Anyway, what do you want to know? We're shorthanded here and I need to get back."

"You haven't replaced Scott?"

"It's not just her. Another nurse quit the day after."

"The day after they found Scott, you mean?"

"He wanted a job in a place people don't get murdered. Can't blame him." He took a bigger gulp.

"Tell us about Scott," Bill said. "We're just trying to get a picture."

"Yeah, well, she was on this unit six years. Always professional, dependable. Going to be hard to replace. And, you know . . . six years . . ."

"You were friends?"

"I was her supervisor, so not really friends, but you see someone every day . . ." He trailed off again.

"Would you say she was cooperative?"

O'Brien gave Bill a sharp glance. "What do you mean?"

"I don't know that much about hospitals"—Bill opened his hands innocently—"but there must be times when you need people to step up, to fill in, take an extra shift or that kind of thing. Or am I wrong?"

O'Brien relaxed. "No, you're right. Yeah, Sophia always did whatever she was needed for."

"She worked overtime?"

"Everybody does."

"Why?" I asked.

"Why what?"

"Why do people need to work overtime? We've asked before and been told it's because there's just not enough staff. In your opinion, is that true?"

He nodded.

"Well, then, why don't they hire more? Isn't that one of the things the nurses' union is asking for? More staff?"

"It is but they won't get it. You know about 'just in time' inventory? Similar idea. Keep your staff lean, give them extra shifts when you have to. It's cheaper than staffing up for peak needs."

"Isn't overtime time and a half? Why is that cheaper than having an extra nurse or two on each unit?"

"It's not just salary. Each employee is also health care, withholding, retirement, all kinds of benefits."

"And each employee working overtime is also exhausted. They go to the basement to take naps so they can go on taking care of sick people."

"The hell are you, some kind of union activist? Don't take it out on me, I don't run this place."

Bill asked, "Are you a union member?"

"The nurses' union? No, supervisors' union's different."

"But you knew Sophia Scott had volunteered for the nurses' contract negotiating committee?"

"Sure. Why not? I didn't see that management was going to give up much—still don't—but you might as well try."

"She seemed to agree with you. She wanted the nurses to accept each offer as it came out. She was very much against a strike, we've been told."

"Anyone with any sense would be. March around in this heat for a while, lose a couple of weeks' pay, let your patients get their care from travel nurses, then come back to just about whatever the offer was the day you went out." He shrugged. "But look, what does any of that matter now anyway? Whoever killed her, this diener or whoever, I don't think it was because of the contract negotiations."

"Like I said, just trying to get a picture. I'm wondering, for example, what she would have been doing down in the east basement. You think she was headed for the nap room?"

"I have no idea. Did you ask your client?"

"He says he didn't know her," I said.

"What else is he going to say?"

Bill asked, "Did you ever see him up here?"

O'Brien's brows pulled together. "Maybe. I don't know. If he came up—you mean like to see her?—I wouldn't have noticed him, particularly. There are strangers on the unit all the time—techs, orderlies, nurses on some errand or other. As long as she was on a break or someone was covering for her, I wouldn't have a reason to pay attention."

"What about other people? Scott's friends? Boyfriends? Do you know if she was seeing anyone? Anyone else ever come up here to meet her?"

"I don't know anything about her personal life. If she was seeing someone, she didn't let it interfere with her work. All I know is, she was a good nurse." He drained his coffee. "Listen, I need to get back to work. If Kazarian didn't do it, then I hope you find who did, but I have a feeling you're wasting your time." He crumpled the coffee cup and tossed it into the trash, and held the door open for us.

◆

Down once more in the lobby, Bill said what I was thinking. "A good nurse. Did whatever she was needed for. Worked overtime."

"The first, we've heard before. The second is an outlier opinion," I answered. "The third is news."

"Unless Venturino's the outlier. Maybe she had some grudge, the way Church said, and Scott was much beloved."

"Come on. The nurses I spoke to, the ones on the committee, including that Sharon Ives, they all seemed to think the same thing."

"And it should be an easy thing to check. If for now we assume it's true and Scott might have been a competent nurse but she was kind of a slacker, the question becomes—"

"What was O'Brien hiding?" I finished.

"Took the words—"

"Right out of your mouth."

"Do you think he was—" Bill stopped but I didn't pick it up. "Hey, I thought you were reading my mind."

"I left. It was dark and spooky in there."

"Getting it on with her?" he finished.

"Haven't you ever heard of a euphemism?"

"That is one."

We headed outside while I thought. "No," I said. "He's hiding something but he wasn't giving off boyfriend vibes. He'd have been doing an if-that-son-of-a-bitch-killed-my-woman dance, he seemed like that kind of guy. No, it's something else."

"I wonder," Bill said, "if it's maybe the something that got her killed."

CHAPTER SIXTEEN

It's kind of unpleasant down here," I said. "Just for the record."

"Noted."

Bill and I, along with Security Officer Benita Juarez, were making our way along Corridor D as instructed by Jordy. We'd just navigated the stairs from the morgue. That we were in River Valley at all at this hour was due to a phone call I'd made while we fueled up at Earl's Beer and Cheese, a bar not far from the hospital with precisely the menu the name would imply.

"Hey, Ell," I'd said when my brother answered.

"Not until next week," he'd said. "And never at night."

"Damn. That was going to be my third question. The second was, what was the word in the doctor's lounge about Sophia Scott's romantic life?"

"Among the senior docs, a lot of garlic and silver crosses. The younger guys would think they could handle her but she went through them like Ma Zi Ren Wan through your GI tract."

"That's disgusting."

"But like Ma always promised, effective."

"Rumor was she had a new boyfriend. Do you know anything about that?"

"If she did, it wasn't a doctor. Word would have spread."

"All right, those were my third and second questions. My first was, how do Bill and I get into the hospital after visiting hours?"

He sighed. "Do you really have to?"

"Depends. Does your authority override River Valley's security chief?"

"Quick Draw? In my dreams. No one overrides him. Sometimes he might do favors for people he likes, but that's not me."

"Yeah, I heard you get steamed when he exercises his muscle in the ER."

"From who?"

"Whom, I think. From him."

"Glad he noticed. Restraining a patient is one thing. Cracking them over the head so we have to deal with a concussion along with a bad batch of coke—I can't have that kind of crap."

"I can't argue with that, but yes, we do need to see the basement. McGraw showed us the crime scene but he wouldn't let us have a look around anywhere else and—"

"Don't tell me."

"Why am I hearing that so much?"

"You don't need any of the medical departments, right?"

"I don't think so. Unless they're down there."

"Only Pathology."

"We need to locate the morgue, but we don't need to go in."

"And you mean tonight?"

"Tonight. Kind of now."

"I'll call you back."

While we waited, Bill called Dr. Ronald Scott, Sophia's ex-husband, in Seattle. He got the office voicemail and left a message. I ate a child's size mac-n-cheese, having not long ago had a sandwich. Bill, not slowed by his recent empanadas, worked his way through a giant taco. Couples flirted at the bar and Van Morrison's "Brown Eyed Girl" drifted through the air.

"This music is even before your time, right?" I asked Bill.

"Retro-hipster," he affirmed. "Food's good, though." By "good" Bill generally meant not just "tasty" but also "big" and "greasy." In this case, though, I agreed with him. We ate in silence, listening to a playlist of the greatest get-in-the-mood hits of the '60s and '70s. Finally my phone rang with Ella Fitzgerald singing "Someone to Watch Over Me." Elliott had put it there.

"Go to the main desk in the lobby," Elliott said. "You'll be met by a security guard who'll accompany you wherever you want to go on the basement levels. No, don't ask, you can't go alone. And it's lucky for you Quick Draw left already. You knew that, right?"

"I confess."

"His assistant chief, who's on nights, is Sergeant Lucas Montero. He's a downhill racer. We've gone a couple of times. I can't keep up but Janie whips his butt." My brother the skydiver was married to my sister-in-law the ski racer. The only reason their kids didn't wrestle alligators was, I suspected, because it wasn't nice for the alligators. "Quick Draw wrote up in the log that you guys came but he didn't leave any instructions about you, so Lucas is willing to pretend you're legit."

"We are legit."

"He's doing me a favor, Lyd, so don't get him in trouble."

"Oh, come on. Trouble? Me and Bill?"

"Yeah. Let me know if you come up with anything."

"I thought you didn't want to know."

"Bye."

So Bill and I had finished up, paid up, and gone up to River Valley Downstate. At the info desk we were met by Security Officer Benita

Juarez. Tall and thin, with sharp cheekbones in her light-brown freckled face, she told the desk guy to give us passes, waited until we'd pasted them on, and raised her eyebrows for instructions.

"Can we start at the morgue?" I asked. "We don't have to go in, just to locate it."

Although Juarez shrugged her bony shoulders, the corners of her mouth perked into a small smile. Maybe she thought ghouls who wanted to locate the morgue were funny. "Told to take you anywhere you want to go. Come on." She headed away from the lobby, turned a different corner from the one we'd taken earlier, and brought us to an elevator we hadn't seen before. "What you hoping to find?" she asked as she pressed her key card to the panel.

"I wouldn't say we're 'hoping,'" I said, though I sort of was. "Just in case there's anything the police missed. We're told they didn't search the whole east basement." I said that as a half question, to give her an opening to tell us what she knew.

But she just said, "Yeah, maybe. I didn't have basement duty then."

The elevator came, closed us in, and headed down. When it stopped, the doors opened onto a wide vinyl-floored hallway with bright fluorescents hung from low ceilings. It was cold and silent and smelled strongly of disinfectant.

"Morgue's this way." Juarez used her key card to swipe us through a pair of locked double doors labeled PATHOLOGY and into a new, wide corridor. Down here three gurneys could pass each other with room to spare. I hoped they never had to, but I guessed it was good to be prepared. A few steps on was another pair of doors to the right whose plaque read AUTOPSY.

"We don't—" I started but Juarez swiped us in.

A thin Black man and a large White woman, both in gray scrubs, sat at a stainless steel table. They looked up from their card game.

"Yo, Juarez," the man said.

"Yo."

"Not sure how to tell you," the woman said, "but these two are still alive."

"Private investigators," Juarez said. "Working for Jordy."

"No shit," said the man. "Great guy, Jordy. Didn't do it, right?"

"Says he didn't," Bill said. "We're here to see what's what."

"How can we help?" the woman asked. "I'm Valerie, this is Paul, by the way."

"Bill."

"Lydia. You guys are dieners, too? You work with Jordy?"

"Shifts are always changing around here." Paul spread his hands and grinned. "Usually it's not this dead."

I glanced from one to the other. "You don't really make dead jokes here."

"They do," said Juarez. "And you can't get them to stop."

Paul shrugged. "Kills the time."

"There's a large body of evidence proving that," Valerie said. "But Juarez doesn't dig it. She's too stiff."

"Gallows humor," said Paul. "I mean, we're just hanging around."

"Oh my God," I said. "Okay, as long as we're here, tell us this. Jordy said he was on his second shift and it was . . . dead . . . here so he went to take a nap. Is that normal?"

"Totally," Valerie said. "Especially when it's late." She waggled her eyebrows on "late," in case I'd missed it.

"You grab some sleep when you can," said Paul. "If there's a bus crash or something, we can get buried pretty quick."

Juarez snorted.

"You guys use it, too? The nap room?" Bill asked.

"I do, if we're working two shifts," Paul said. I waited for the joke, but it didn't come. "Valerie goes straight to the hookup room. She's a lady-killer." Ba-DUM, there it was.

"I am, but I don't go straight there. I don't do anything straight," Valerie said. Oh no, did this mean they were going to start making gay jokes now, too?

"Okay, thanks," I said. "One more thing. Do your bosses know about these rooms? The nap room and the hookup room?"

I included Juarez in my glance. She shrugged. "I guess they do now."

"Dr. Johnson always knew," Paul said. "It's fine with him as long as we get back fast if they need us. He thinks we shouldn't have to work double shifts in the first place."

"Why do you?"

"The budget. Management butchered it."

CHAPTER SEVENTEEN

When we left the morgue, Juarez asked jauntily, "Where to?"

"That's why it made you happy when I asked to come down here," I said. "Are they always like that?"

She grinned. "I love the morgue rounds when they're on. They crack me up."

"You mean," Bill said, "they slay you?"

"Oh, good, more!"

"No, no more," I said. "Those guys were enough. We're working here."

"Yeah," Bill said. "I guess the time for jokes has expired."

Juarez grinned, shaking her head happily. I gave Bill narrowed eyes and directed us along the path Jordy had laid out. As soon as we went through the next set of double doors, the light level got lower and the floor turned to bare concrete. While we walked I said to Juarez, "McGraw told us he didn't know anything about the nap room until Scott's death, or about the hookup room until we told him."

"I sure didn't, either."

"You guys don't use those rooms?"

"You mean, us guys, Security? Nah. For one thing, we don't work double shifts if McGraw can help it. He hates to pay overtime. And if it's true the basement guys had this agreement they wouldn't bother with the east basement, then I guess they didn't know either."

"So you think McGraw really didn't know?"

She pursed her lips and stared straight ahead.

I said, "Nothing you tell us will get back to him."

"We just want to know if looking at him is a dead end," said Bill.

She snorted. "And I thought the basement was going to be boring."

"You got assigned to this beat after McGraw—"

"—gave those other guys the axe?" Bill said.

I rolled my eyes. Juarez grinned and said, "Right, I got transferred down here after that." She paused, then went on, "I'm pretty sure Lucas, Sergeant Montero, he had no idea about any of that. Not just the nap room, but I can't see him just letting those guys not patrol that area if he knew they weren't. He's kind of loosey-goosey but I mean, that's ridiculous. McGraw . . ."

"Go on."

"Well, McGraw's not loose. Oh, man, the opposite—tight-assed, you know? Rules, time clocks, turn in those reports. He'll write you up any chance he gets. Tells everyone how to do their job. Won't leave the sergeants alone, guys like Lucas. Sticks his nose in everywhere. Especially when he might have a chance to rough someone up."

"Like when he responds to a call to the ER?"

"Exactly. Why should he do that? What are we for if he's gonna go running up there himself? Ask me, he misses the part of being a cop where you could harass people. Tell you this for free—when I have enough time on the job, ready for a step up, I'll move on."

"That doesn't sound like the kind of guy who wouldn't know six guys have a non-patrol agreement," Bill said.

"Well, they're his favorite guys. Were, I guess he fired them all? But if anyone was going to get away with anything, it was them."

I said, "He put his favorite guys on basement patrol?"

She glanced over at me. "It's easy work. Nothing ever happens down here."

At the bottom of the stairs another door opened into Corridor D. A few twists and turns and we were back at the nap room corridor, its crime scene tape now hanging in dispirited streamers from the walls on both sides.

"This is it?" Juarez said. "Where was she?"

"There." I pointed.

Juarez took two tentative steps forward to get a closer look at the concrete where Sophia Scott had died. "Not much to see, is there?"

"No."

"When I go," Juarez said, "I want to leave a crater." After another moment, "That the nap room?"

I nodded. She unlocked the door and stepped inside.

Bill began a slow walk through the room, his eyes searching in more detail than last time, probing the floor, the cots, the bookcase barriers. Juarez watched him. She craned her neck to peer through the room. "This is messed up."

"What do you mean?"

She bit her lower lip. "I have a GED, never even finished high school. Far as me, this is a good job. Took it when it opened up because I thought, a hospital, better than a department store, like where I was." She was echoing McGraw but I didn't tell her that. Her brow furrowed. "But nurses and techs and dieners, like that, they're professionals, they have degrees and shit. If they have to work doubles, there should be a real place for them to sleep. Or else they shouldn't be working doubles. This is just"—she waved an arm—"it's stupid."

"I can't argue. From what I hear, the nurses can't either. One of their contract demands is safe staffing."

Juarez nodded. "Yeah, I know. I—" She whipped around as a sound came from behind us. "Stay here!"

Benita Juarez took off through the nap room door.

Bill and I, naturally, did not stay there.

Juarez's long strides took her down the dim hall following a shadow that was running ahead. Ours took us racing after her. My strides were of course shorter than Bill's but I made up in speed what I lacked in stretch and I skidded around the corner up ahead before he did. That put me in time to see Juarez grab a man's arm, the man turn and throw a punch at her, and Juarez duck the punch. He twisted in her grip but all that did was throw him further off balance as she swept his foot, yanked him toward her when he staggered, and flipped him over her hip. He thudded to the ground as Bill and I pulled up.

"I told you to stay back," she snapped at us.

"You also told us all you had was a GED," I said. "You didn't mention your judo rank."

She grabbed the handcuffs off her belt and snapped them on the struggling runner. Hauling him to his feet, she said, "Useful in security. Employers look for martial arts skills."

"Black belt?"

"Brown. Working toward it. Test next week."

"I'd say you'll pass."

CHAPTER EIGHTEEN

So," Juarez said to the short, chunky man whose arm she held in a tight grip, "who the hell are you and what the hell are you doing down here?"

"Barry Sivek," he panted, his face still red from running. "Senior biomed technician. Come on, let go. My ID's in my shirt pocket."

Juarez didn't let him go, but she pushed his jacket aside to search his pocket. She read the ID card, checked his face against it, and put it in her own pocket. "And what are you doing here? This is a restricted area."

"I just wanted to see."

"See what?"

"You know. Where that nurse was killed."

"You're serious?" Juarez raised her eyebrows. "You don't think that's creepy?"

"Yeah, maybe." He gave her what Bill calls an aw-shucks look. "But I wasn't hurting anything. I just wanted to see. Take these things off, okay?"

Juarez knit her brows together. "Gotta admit, I didn't see that coming. Peepers down here. You work in a hospital! They got dead people up there all the time." She jerked her head upward.

"Yeah, but not someone I know, murdered."

"You knew her?" Bill asked.

"Well, okay, only maybe. I mean, I'm on the units a lot. Probably I've met her or whatever."

Juarez looked at me and Bill. "You believe this shit? Damn. Well, come on."

"Where?" said Sivek. "Like I say, I wasn't hurting anything."

"Like *I* say, this is a restricted area. You're not allowed here."

"Oh, come on. What I heard, people were sleeping and screwing all over the place down here. How come you didn't arrest any of them?"

"Uh-huh. I only just got assigned down here. And I'm not arresting you, either. I'm taking you to my boss. That's my job. Let's go."

"What about them?" He jutted his chin at Bill and me. "What are they doing here?"

"Plainclothes. I'm showing them the ropes. You two," she said, "stay here. I have to drop this guy off. I'll be back." Behind Sivek's back she flicked her head toward the nap room hallway. "Maybe fifteen minutes." She lifted an eyebrow at us. Then with a small smile she started down the corridor to the elevator, holding tight to the arm of her handcuffed prize.

After Juarez and her prisoner disappeared around the corner, I said to Bill, "Was that an invitation?"

"Engraved."

We spun and walked past the nap room. Around the next corner, as Jordy had said we would, we came to a door with a piece of paper taped to it. "The sign-up sheet," I said. "Except look. Drainboy. The Hulk. Calypso."

"Makes sense," Bill said. "The area's off-limits. You don't want to sign your name that you were here."

"And I guess Drainboy's lovebug would know. I wonder who'd call themselves Drainboy, though?"

"I don't think you really want that answered. Who's the last reserved time?"

I tilted the sheet toward the light. "That would be Calypso." I peered more closely. "Wait—they were here yesterday afternoon. Right around when Scott was killed."

"Crap. For real?"

"For real."

A possible witness. Right here on the list. Okay, we didn't know who Calypso was. Or whether they'd actually shown up. Or seen or heard anything. But Detective Church didn't even know they existed.

Bill tapped on the door.

"Why are you knocking?"

"Just in case."

No answer came, so I snapped on a nitrile glove—it had occurred to me Calypso's fingerprints might be on the lever—and I opened the door. The first thing that hit me was a floral, perfumey smell.

Bill flicked the light switch.

"Oh," I said.

A pair of mattresses scattered with pillows large and small lay on the floor, and a chair of the dentist's office reclining type took up one corner. Bolted into the concrete ceiling was a swing. The rest of the ceiling was taken up by swags of crimson fabric. We saw all this through the red gel pasted on the fluorescent fixtures.

"These people are medical professionals?" I asked.

"Hey, the heart wants what the heart wants."

"Sometimes it wants a transplant. Oh, God, now I'm making medical jokes."

"If that's a joke, you need to work on the funny part."

"This place is interfering with my conscious processes."

"It's supposed to."

We searched the room, but for all the lewd intimacy it advertised, we couldn't find anything that seemed remotely personal to anyone. I guessed the hookup room was like a kind of wilderness: carry it in, carry it out.

"I don't know what I expected," I said as Bill pulled the door shut behind us. "A note with a phone number, 'For a good time call Calypso and also I saw who killed Sophia Scott'?" I thought for a moment. "Calypso. That's music from the islands, right?"

"Trinidad and Tobago to start with, then it spread."

"How come you always know one more thing than I need? It would make sense, then, for Calypso to be a Caribbean nurse or tech or something."

"If you're right, that might narrow it down. Maybe we could ask people to sing 'Day-O.'" Bill stood looking along the corridor. "Nap room," he said. "Hookup room. I wonder what else?"

We made our way along the corridor and turned the corner into the next one, trying door handles as we went. Some doors opened into dim, disheveled rooms—only one with a working light—boxes and broken furniture throwing odd shadows as our phone flashlights slid and crossed. Other doors were locked, or maybe rusted shut. We'd gotten to the end of a corridor and were about to turn the corner into the next one when Juarez's voice boomed off the walls. "Yo, plainclothes! Where you at?"

"Here, boss," Bill called.

A few footfalls later, and there she was, grinning. "Make good use of your time, did you?"

"That was slick," I said. "Thanks. We saw the hookup room. Believe me, it's worth a peek. But so far, nothing else. A couple are locked—can you open them, just to see?"

She shrugged and went for the ring of keys on her belt. Only one lock responded, and the sagging boxes and musty smell we found didn't seem worth locking in, to me.

"Sorry," Juarez said. "Mostly it's key cards now."

"Okay," I said as we reached the end of a hallway, with no lights in either direction in the corridors branching off it. "Still, there was one thing that was worth the trip."

"What's that?" asked Juarez.

As we headed back the way we'd come I told her about Calypso.

Her eyes widened. "No shit. A damn witness?"

"Possible."

"And the cops don't know about this?"

"They already have a suspect."

"That's messed up. Well, come on, let me have a look and then I gotta report this."

"Can we just look around a little more?" I asked. "In the other direction? It's a fertile field down here."

She cocked an eyebrow at me. "Sure, why not? We already got a peeper and a possible witness. You two find anything else, I might get a raise."

CHAPTER NINETEEN

Juarez's raise was going to have to wait. We spent another half hour in the east basement, but though some of the doors were locked, most of them opened without protest into rooms that yielded up nothing but damp smells and abandoned boxes, broken furniture, and spiderwebs. A couple of times, opening a door prompted a considerable amount of scurrying within, and once, I saw red eyes gleaming in the light of our flashlights.

"Nasty," Juarez said. "I can see why those guys didn't want to come down here." Quickly she added, "Not that that's any excuse."

At a certain point, down a dingy hallway, it became clear we were treading in undisturbed dust. "I guess that's it," I said. "No more miracles."

"Who knows what Church will find, though?" Bill said. "When she follows up on Calypso."

"Who's Church?" Juarez asked.

"Detective Helena Church, NYPD," said Bill. "It's her case. She's the one who arrested Jordy. She's not going to be happy when she hears she missed something this big."

"Yeah," I said. "Can I be the one to tell her?"

We'd just about made our way back to the hookup room by then, and Juarez needed her peek. Her reaction was the same as mine, expressed in slightly different words. "Holy mother of God. These are, like, nurses and shit?"

We took the sign-up sheet off the door and went back to the Security office, where I didn't get to be the one to tell Church about our find. Sergeant Montero, Juarez's supervisor, called the detective, as protocol demanded. That was after he listened wordlessly to Juarez's report and, when she was finished, rubbed his hand over his face and said, "Good work, Juarez. Now if I were you, I'd start looking for another job, before the shit that's gonna hit the fan here splatters all over everyone."

"Nah," she said. "I've got your back, Sarge."

He gave her an appraising look.

Grinning, she went on, "Besides, if you and McGraw both get canned, and being those other six guys are already gone, you gotta know I'm gonna shoot right up that promotion ladder."

Montero stared, laughed, said, "Shit, Juarez," and made the call.

◆

By the time Bill and I left the hospital it was after eleven. Church hadn't been pleased at getting a late call telling her the noose she was trying to put around Jordy's neck had been loosened for a second time today—first with a new motive, now with a possible witness. Nor had she been happy that a hospital security assistant chief was wordlessly but very clearly telling her she'd done a sloppy job.

"She wanted to know why the hell you were down in the east basement tonight in the first place, Juarez," Montero had said when he hung up. "I told her obviously we'd decided it was time to start patrolling down there." He turned to Bill and me. "I didn't mention you guys. One thing if I make her look like a jerk. Another to admit you made me look like one."

"Wasn't our intention," I said. "Just doing our job."

"Yeah, and if we'd been doing ours, it wouldn't have happened. Okay, you guys, thanks, but you'd better blow. I have to deal with this asshole peeper now." He jabbed his thumb toward the window into the briefing room where Sivek sat scowling.

"What happens to him, Sarge?" asked Juarez.

"I'm going to read him the riot act in eight languages. Then I'll spring him."

"You going to write him up?"

"Probably not even. Hell, if we had sleepers and screwers coming and going down there like it was a train station, how am I going to write up a peeper?" He rubbed his forehead again. "Hey, Ms. Chin. Tell your brother I said hi."

"Lydia," I said, and then to Juarez's confused look, "My brother, Elliott Chin, head of Emergency Medicine. He and the sergeant here go skiing together."

"Oh," Juarez said. "You're related to Dr. Chin? Nice guy, when you can get him to stop moving. That's how you got this gig?"

"A little more complicated than that, but basically, yeah."

She nodded, taking that info in. "Come on, I'll walk you to the elevator." With the same small smile as when she'd escorted her prisoner out of Corridor D, she led us around corners, carded the elevator, pushed the Up button for us, and watched the doors close.

As we left the sharp cold hospital air for the slippery heat of the August streets, I said to Bill, "You think it's too late to call Cohen?"

"If all we had was bad news or no news, yes. But even if she's been sound asleep for hours this will make her day."

We went back to our bench on the driveway and Bill made the call, putting it on speaker so we could both be in on it.

"Cohen. This better be good." I heard what sounded like a basketball game go muted in the background.

"Oh, it is."

Bill went on to tell her about our full day of discoveries: that Scott was a mole and that there might be a witness. She swore like a happy sailor, then said, "God, that's fantastic! Did you tell Church?"

"We told her about the mole. The security guy at the hospital told her about Calypso," Bill said.

"Shit. I wanted to do it. Put it all in writing, yeah? And keep at it. Gotta go now, I'm calling Jordy."

She clicked off. I yawned, then said, "Hey. She sounded charmed."

"Yeah," Bill said. "Time to quit for the day."

The great thing about hospitals is that at all hours on all days, cabs pull up to them. We grabbed one and rolled down the FDR to Chinatown. We got out at Canal Street and Bill walked me home. "Let's keep walking," he said, nuzzling my neck. "Come back to my place."

"I told you I wasn't going to do that tonight."

"People so often change their minds."

"They're just not dependable, are they? People." I pulled back a little and looked at him. "They're really not. Like Sophia Scott. Never gave a damn about anything outside her own job and flirting with doctors."

"Except according to O'Brien's outlier opinion."

"Right. Then suddenly she joins the negotiating committee. A lot of extra work, the kind of thing she didn't do. Then, on the committee, keeps trying to get the nurses to take the offer, to take a for-sure losing strike vote. It's like she joined the committee specifically to make sure there wouldn't be a strike."

"Maybe she couldn't afford to be out." He kissed my ear.

"Stop that. I'm sure the nurses have a strike fund. We can ask Venturino in the morning."

"Think how much easier that'll be if we're together in the morning."

"We will be, after I come over at eight."

This time he pulled away to look at me. "You're not only refusing to come home with me, you're threatening to ring my doorbell at the crack of dawn and blast apart whatever pitiful shreds of sleep I'll have managed to get after tossing and turning without you all night?"

"Why would I ring your doorbell at the crack of dawn?" I asked. "I have a key." I wrapped my arms around him, stood on tiptoe, and kissed him.

Now there were two of us regretting I wasn't going home with him.

CHAPTER TWENTY

By the time I got to Bill's place the next morning he was up, showered and shaved, dressed, and sitting over a cup of coffee.

"Good God," I said. "Who are you?"

"I have no idea. Water's hot. Want a bagel?"

"No, thanks, Ma made congee. Because although she absolutely understands how important my work is, especially this case since it originated with Elliott, and I should go ahead and work whatever hours I need to because after all I'm a professional, she still worries because she never sees me because I'm never home and so she can't be sure how well I'm eating."

Bill drank coffee. "I'm going to refrain from commenting except to point out that I'm refraining from commenting."

I moved to the kitchen area—sink and appliances separated from the living/everything-else-but-bedroom area by a slate-countered island, all of it built by Bill—and reached into a cabinet for the Assam tea. As it was brewing, his bagel popped out of the toaster, so I put it on a plate.

"Jam?"

"Strawberry, please, ma'am."

My tea, with his bagel, butter, and jam, made their way on a tray carried by me to his easy chair. "Don't get used to the service."

"Apparently I can't even hope to get used to the server. 'Hello, I'm Lydia, I'll be ignoring you tonight.'"

I put the tray down and kissed his cheek. He turned his head and the kiss got more real.

"Okay," I finally said, "enough. We have work to do."

I took my tea and continued on to the sofa. I tucked my feet up under me as usual. The room had a comfortable breakfasty smell.

Bill's apartment, long and skinny, goes through the whole floor. If it had more rooms it would be called a railroad flat but he took some of the walls out when he moved here. The front wall is all steel windows from the days this floor was a button factory. No sun because it faces north but lots of light. His piano, which he tells me is a baby grand, gleamed in it. I nodded that way.

"I did you a favor. You had time to practice."

"All that did was make me even more frustrated by the time I went to bed."

Bill's a serious pianist. He's never let me hear him play. Or anyone else that I know of. "You lead a very tough life. Let's call Venturino."

He bit into his bagel, and I called, once again putting the phone on speaker. "Lucky for you I'm on the early shift," Venturino said when she answered.

"Not luck," I said. "Detective work. You were just getting off shift yesterday late afternoon. We have a question about the nurses' strike fund. Is there one?"

"Of course. Why?"

I told her what our thinking had been.

"Well, the fund's enough to keep everyone going for two weeks," she said, a note of doubt in her voice. "Sophia might have been in a hole, maybe not able to go for long after that, but honestly, nurses' strikes rarely last longer than that. Too much bad press for the hospital."

"Still, she might have been worried."

"Maybe. And it would be like her to want to stop the whole thing because it would be inconvenient for her personally. Though a better contract would—would've—benefitted her, too. And committee meetings and negotiating and all that—seems like a lot of work to stop something that might not happen."

"Yes, it does." I had a sudden thought. Maybe it was the Assam tea. "Your negotiating sessions—are they recorded? So nurses can watch them later?"

"The union has a YouTube channel, but you need a password."

"Can I get one?"

"A password? No, only union members—" She paused. "Oh, screw it, use mine. Management probably passes theirs around for shits and giggles. It'll help?"

"Honestly, I don't know. It might be just background but the more of that the better."

"Okay. It's Trillini92." She spelled it for me.

"What does it mean?"

I could almost hear her grin. "Look it up."

"I will. How will I recognize Scott?"

"Curly dark hair. Makeup. Sly smile. Batting eyes. Every man's nurse fantasy. Swear to God she was sorry we don't wear little white uniform skirts and perky caps anymore."

"All righty then. Thanks. Talk to you later."

"No, wait." Another pause, shorter this time, as though she'd come to a quick decision. "I was thinking of calling you anyway."

"About what?"

"I know it's not your lane, but it's about another member of the negotiating committee."

Bill and I exchanged a glance. "Okay, go on."

"Alon Bacay. He works in the ICU. Been here five years. Great guy, great nurse. Very pro-union, pro-strike. The exact opposite of Sophia. One of the strongest no-compromise voices we have. Out of nowhere he quit the committee this morning."

"I remember that name," Bill said. "He's one of the people I called yesterday."

"Oh, it's you," said Venturino. "Should've known you'd be lurking around. You called him about Sophia?"

"Like I called you. Why did he quit?"

"Said the whole thing was just too much stress, he needed to back off. Bullshit."

"Why?"

"Because 'stick it to the Man' is his middle name. And I say that with love. He's our most dependable table-pounder. He came here when the Philippines got too hot for him because he was a freaking revolutionary. And he's a bundle of energy. First guy to help out, on committees, on the unit, wherever. Too much stress, ha. He eats stress for breakfast. And when we're this close to a strike? I'm telling you, no way. What did he have to say about Sophia?"

While she took a breath Bill said, "He hasn't gotten back to me."

"No shit? I'd think he'd jump at the chance. He hates her, and he's not a guy who's stingy with his opinions. Something's going on."

"Like what?"

"I have no idea, but doesn't it seem weird to you? That negotiating committee members are dropping like flies?"

"Not exactly like flies," I said to Bill, pouring myself more tea after the call ended. "Only two. If Scott hadn't been killed, no one would think twice about—what's his name, Bacay? Alon Bacay, about him quitting."

"But she was killed. And he was a no-compromise bundle-of-energy guy."

"And she was a super-compromise that's-not-my-job woman. Hold on." I went to Google on my phone. "Ha. Giovanna Trillini. Most-medal-winning fencer in the history of the Olympics, either sex."

"Italian?"

"Of course."

He sipped his coffee. "Okay, Venturino's right and it's not our lane, but I think we should talk to Alon Bacay."

"I agree. But first I have an idea."

"Oh, good," Bill said. "That means I get more coffee before you make me go out."

By now it was nearly nine. If Bill thought eight was the crack of dawn, Wong Security considered nine the middle of the night. I called anyway; after all, I was a client.

"Hey, Lydia," said Trella. I heard, as usual, the speaker echo. "What's up?"

"Me and you, but I'm betting not Linus?"

"No, he's here, just a little groggy. We went to hear music last night. Mong Tong, Taiwanese electro-hypno-pop. Know them?"

"No. Should I?"

"Maybe not" came my cousin's voice, a little more hoarse and less exuberant than usual. "And Bill, for sure not. You calling about Eyegor and the DeBrengs? Hey, now that's a band name! Got 'em right here. Oh, God, thanks."

"Trella just give you coffee?"

"You know it." I heard a loud slurp. "You also know Eyegor's been in trouble? A drug arrest, charges dropped. DUI, charges dropped. Changed high schools twice. Hey, sounds like me!"

"You've been arrested?"

"Gimme a break. Too smart for that."

"Stop smirking."

"Don't pretend you can see me. We'd know."

"Don't pretend you're not smirking. When was the last time he was arrested?"

"Before yesterday? About five years. When he was still in med school."

"On?"

"That was the DUI."

As Elliott had said: Once out of medical school, Jordy's sea of troubles may not have totally evaporated, but they shrank to a puddle. Jordy had pretty much said that, too.

"Why were the charges dropped?"

"Officially? Not enough evidence. Really? Not enough evidence to outweigh someone with juice putting their thumb on the scale."

"Any idea who?"

"No. Want us to—"

"No. Besides, I have an idea of my own. What about the other guys?"

"DeBreng and Son of DeBreng? Well"—slurp—"Big Daddy, everything he touches turns to gold. Top of every list, head of every committee, chair of every department. Honoree at every function. Lives in Scarsdale, house in the Hamptons. Parties with the A-list. Hey! You think it's his thumb, right?"

"I do. Skeletons in his closet?"

"If they're there, they're probably gold, too. Didn't find any, but we could—"

"No."

"No, yeah." He sighed theatrically. "Now, Junior, he's another story. Oh, wow!"

"Wow what? Junior?"

"No. My mom just brought over a bunch of daan tāat from Legends. Hey, Ma, it's Lydia."

There followed a round of greetings in Cantonese to and from Auntie Nuanyi through which Bill contentedly sipped coffee. Finally I promised to give her love to my mother and sent mine to Uncle Ping. Since we were all on speaker, I heard her say "Baai baai," which is Cantonese for bye-bye.

Linus said, "Bye, Ma!" with considerably more verve than before. The coffee, along with the egg tarts from Flushing's best Chinese bakery, which he'd presumably downed two or three of while Auntie and I had caught the Wong and Chin families up on each other, had restored the vital sugar and caffeine levels in his blood.

"Now," he said, "Dr. DeBreng Junior. Bradley. Not exactly a loser, but not the guy his father is. Trying, though. Also an orthopedic surgeon. As was, by the way, Grandpa DeBreng. You get that one for free. Bradley gets three stars on Yelp. Fives for medicine, ones and twos for personality. 'Repaired my knee but arrogant and patronizing.' Like that."

"Met him, can confirm. How's Senior rated?"

"He hardly sees patients anymore, only the A-list and they don't do Yelp. They give him glowing recs on his website, though."

"He has his own website?"

"Duh."

"Yeah, okay, thanks. Put it all in the Dropbox. And there's something else. A nurse named Alon Bacay."

"Sounds familiar."

"He was on that list you sent of the negotiating committee. Check him out. Linus? Legally—"

"—only! Yeah, yeah. Sheesh."

"Trella? You still there? He needs more coffee."

CHAPTER TWENTY-ONE

Bill was, by that point, fully fueled and prepared to get up and go meet the day. We postponed that, though, and instead spent the next hour in front of his laptop. It's a little creaky, that machine, a few years old. He doesn't use it unless he has to. But he has Wi-Fi and Linus set him up, like he set me up, with security Fort Knox would envy.

We went back four weeks, to a negotiating session a while before the murder. The camera in the River Valley conference room, positioned high up near the ceiling, warped everything through its wide-angle lens. I settled in to watch fun-house-mirror nurses and lawyers scowl at each other across a bulbous Formica-topped table.

Venturino was easy to spot. Her lanky limbs, her relaxed posture, and, even with the camera's distortion, her sardonic smile, all the same as in the park.

"It's not even the fancy conference room," I said to Bill. "The one with the river views they take donors to."

"How do you know they have one of those?"

"Tell me you forgot the photos of my brother with Seymour Larson and Elizabeth Gordon-Platt."

"I only have eyes for you."

I rolled mine, then told him to glue his to the screen. "Let's watch these folks in action," I said.

You couldn't really call it action. A lot of talk, some of it indistinctly muttered; a lot of paper-flipping, some of it suspiciously ostentatious. I wasn't interested in the details of the contract offer anyway. I wanted to see people's faces, their expressions and their body language. Sophia Scott in particular: I wanted to get to know her, even a little, to try to understand why someone would want her dead.

She, like Venturino, was easy to spot. Talia Venturino's description had been on point, and as I watched Scott I saw more: a slight turn toward the person she was speaking to, as though he—it was always a he—now had her full attention and she was glad to give it, because he was really the one she'd been wanting to talk to all along. The briefest pause before she spoke so he would give her his focus, too. I could see her smile, the way I could Venturino's, but they were nothing alike. Scott's was sweet but knowing, a you-and-me-against-the-world look she bestowed on each man. She was pretty; she was poised; she was graceful.

"Manipulative bitch, huh?" said Bill beside me.

"Really?" I raised my eyebrows. "And here I was, thinking you were about ready to jump into the screen and run away with her."

"What would I want with an adorable nurse who looked at me as though I were wonderful and brilliant and the only man in the world, when I have a smartass black belt PI who won't even spend the night? Though if this thing had Smellavision and the pheromones came through—"

I whacked him.

"As I said." He rubbed his arm where my blow had landed. "Who needs her when I have you?"

I leaned closer to the screen. A bald and sour-faced management lawyer—one of the five White men Venturino had told us about—was expounding on the contract offer. I was just thinking that I didn't understand a word the guy was saying when a small brown-skinned man on the nurses' side of the table interrupted him.

"Bullshit."

"Hey," said the lawyer. "There's no need for that kind of—"

"Oh, yes, there is," the brown man said. "It's not a curse word, it's a description. Of what you're trying to hand us." In contrast to his sharp features and his stabbing eyes, his speech held the soft consonants and rolling rhythms of the native Filipino. "I wish I can say we're getting somewhere, but you just do tricks and think we're stupid. Move this money here, push that there, use fancy legal words and the nurses won't understand it."

"I bet that's Alon Bacay," I said to Bill. "Check him out?"

Bill scrolled through his phone as the chubby lawyer lifted a sheaf of papers and began, "This is just standard contractual language. If you haven't learned it yet I suggest you do."

"Coag panel," spat the man. "V-fib, A-fib, sed rate, retrocecal, PVST, ischemia, CPK. Just standard medical terms. Have you learned them yet? I suggest you do because maybe the next time you hear them it's from a nurse saving your life. Now tell us what that says in English." He jabbed his finger at the pile of papers. "O en Español. O sa Tagalog."

For a moment, silence. Then the older Black woman beside him said, "Ou en Français." A tiny Asian woman added, "Hoặc bằng tiếng Việt." I could see Venturino smirk as she put in, "O in Italiano." When a heavy White man at the end of the nurses' side of the table said, "Or yuh could just speak effin' English like a nawmal New Yawkah," Venturino cracked up.

Grins and high fives broke out among the nurses, tight lips and frowns among the management team. I watched Sophia Scott. She flicked a fast glance around at her fellow negotiators, smiled her smile at the bald lawyer, gave him an up-from-under-the-lashes look, and said, "Mr. Walsh? I do think if you could explain it to us, it would make things easier."

"I don't know why I should bother," the lawyer huffed, "since obviously you people don't really want to come to an agreement."

The Filipino started to say something but Scott smoothly overrode him while pretending not to notice him. "Please, Mr. Walsh?" Scott tilted her head. "I know it would help *me* understand it."

"Oh my God," I said. I was on the verge of adding that if I were on the committee I'd want to kill her, but that seemed monumentally tasteless, considering someone actually had.

"Okay, here." Bill showed me his phone. The River Valley Downstate website had photos of all the medical personnel, probably so you wouldn't worry that some random serial killer had just walked into your room. Bill had clicked through to the RN page. The negotiating firebrand was, in fact, Alon Bacay.

We watched as, on the screen, Mr. Walsh the attorney, referred to by Venturino as a dweeb, laid out in plain words and patronizing tones an explanation of the latest offer. The nurses took notes, conferred—I didn't see anyone conferring with Scott—and tightened their shoulders and jaws at his clear condescension. The other lawyers grew restive, like horses in their stalls when one's taken out for exercise and the others want to go, too. I was just wondering which side would erupt first when Venturino checked her watch. "Okay, that's it for today," she said. "Some people actually have to go to work. We'll see you Thursday."

The nurses collected their papers and filed out. The lawyers did the same, waiting until all the nurses had gone so they wouldn't get caught in the same doorway having to be polite to each other. Scott was the last nurse to leave, glancing over her shoulder with a smile I could see each man gathering in because he knew it was meant only for him. After a few more moments of fluorescent-lit stillness, the video ended.

"I thought negotiators were supposed to look for ways to actually come to an agreement," I said. "Walsh is just nasty, Scott's acting like she's on *The Bachelor*, and Bacay's lighting everything on fire."

"Unrehearsed versions of good cop/bad cop. They should take lessons from us."

We dipped in and out of a few more sessions. No progress was made that I could see. One session ended with the management team, led by the sour Mr. Walsh, abruptly gathering their papers up and walking out, as Venturino had said they did from time to time. From our ceiling perspective, however, it was obvious—quick glances, tiny nods—that the walkout was coordinated and planned in advance.

We did see a couple of notable things, though.

It became clear as we watched that the best prepared, most hard-line, slyest negotiator on the management team was the woman. "What's her name again?" I asked Bill.

"Margaret Weldon, I think Venturino said. You know they can't hear you?"

"Of course they can't. Why did you say that?"

"Because you're whispering."

I shot him a dirty look and went on watching. Weldon was a take-no-prisoners bulldog in a blue business suit. The soft blonde waves falling to her shoulders and the understated pink of her lip gloss and nails were camouflage, like the pretty colors on an insect-eating plant. She interrupted. She listened, then twisted people's words. She slapped down facts and figures when other people were speaking in abstractions, and blew up abstractions from other people's facts and figures, and it didn't seem to matter which team those other people were on. She was icy, razor-edged, and constantly ready to pounce.

"It's a game to her, isn't it?" I said. "I don't think she even cares what the fight's about. She just wants to win."

"To be fair, that's how lawyers are taught."

"Why are we being fair to lawyers?"

As we watched a while longer something else became clear. Margaret Weldon was irritating the men on her own side as much as she was the nurses. "Dancing for the master," Venturino had said, but the masters didn't seem impressed. Why should they be? They were completely outclassed.

"I'm torn," I told Bill. "I almost want to root for her because those patronizing clowns don't like her. But she's the opposition."

"Only if you think we're on the side of the nurses."

I turned to him. "Aren't we?"

"It's probably better for the investigation if we don't take sides." He looked at my face and laughed. "I guess it's also probably too late. Jordy, Elliott, Venturino—"

"On one side, and these condescending jerks on the other." I waved my hand at the screen. "If I wasn't pro-union before, I am now."

We switched to the next session. The more we watched, the more I could see why Venturino thought Alon Bacay wasn't likely to quit the committee out of stress.

"If Weldon's a bulldog," I said to Bill, "this guy's a terrier. He's the only one who's really a match for her and he is *so* not letting go. I might have to agree with Venturino that something's up. Also," I added after another few minutes, "I'm totally ready to agree with Venturino that this contract negotiating business is excruciating. Let's—"

I stopped my hand on its way to the keyboard. The conference room door had opened and Elizabeth Gordon-Platt had walked in.

"Well," Bill said. "She sure classes up the joint, huh?"

She did. Mahogany hair in a low chignon, patrician posture, red power jacket over black power slacks—Prada, I thought—and the

Ferragamos Jordy had said management was quaking in. Gordon-Platt was not quaking. Or smiling. All faces had swung toward the door but she greeted no one, just took a seat along the wall behind her negotiators.

"Is that normal?" I asked. "For the chief administrator to descend to the earthly realm? To sully her ears with talk of shift staffing levels, healthcare coverage, and full-time-equivalent employment days?"

"She's there to intimidate," Bill said. "I guess things aren't moving fast enough for her."

"Boy, that's below the belt."

People shifted in their seats and picked up from where they'd stopped. The management team, without the benefit of seeing her, could only feel her stare on their backs. The nurses kept flashing glances at her, watching for her reactions. If a face were ever made of stone, though, it was Gordon-Platt's. She might have been livid, she might have been bored, she might have thought the whole thing was hilarious. There was no way to tell. She sat straight-backed, her black-clad legs crossed and her manicured hands in her lap.

After a couple of minutes I said, "I don't think it's working. Bacay's on a roll and Venturino's smirking again."

"It's not the nurses," Bill said, "that she's there to intimidate."

CHAPTER TWENTY-TWO

Ten minutes after Elizabeth Gordon-Platt made a splashless but resounding entry into the negotiating room, she stood and left. I caught Venturino's smile, saw her gaze follow the chief administrator as she closed the door. Across the table, lawyers shifted in their seats again, a weight lifted from their backs.

"Let's go," I said. "I've had it."

"I'm with you on that. Where are we going?"

I shut his laptop. "I almost don't care. Just not a closed room where everyone hates everyone."

"You're exaggerating."

"Yeah, okay. But don't you agree that was pretty unpleasant?"

"Excruciating."

We locked up his place and trotted down the stairs into the swampy day. Our plan was to head back up to the hospital. We wanted to talk to Alon Bacay and, if possible, a couple of other people on that committee who hadn't gotten back to us. We also had another goal, and before we reached the subway the goal called us.

"Smith," Bill answered when his phone rang. "Oh, good. I was hoping you'd call back. Uh-huh. That would be great. You sure you're okay with that? Wherever you say. About half an hour. Thanks." He slipped the phone back in his jacket and said, "Benita Juarez will meet us in the lobby. She can take us to Supplies."

Biomed techs worked in Medical Supplies and Equipment. We wanted a conversation with Barry Sivek, assuming he hadn't been fired after last night. If the guy was a peeper, who knew what he might have peeped besides the crime scene?

Juarez was waiting in a rectangle of sunlight near the visitors' desk. She wore gray jeans and a blue denim jacket.

"You work nights," I said. "When do you sleep?"

She grinned. "Should be doing it right now. But working with you guys is much more fun."

"Umm . . . Working with us?"

"Considering this my private investigator practicum."

"Oh," I said,

Bill said, "Why not?"

We got our photo ID badges from the desk and followed Juarez to the red-stripe elevator. "We're going to the basement?" I asked. "Quick Draw won't be happy."

"He's already not happy." Her eyes sparkled as she swiped her card on the keypad and the elevator started down. Fingers making air quotes, she said, "He's at an 'information meeting' with the disciplinary committee. They want to know how six guys could not patrol the east basement and McGraw didn't know about it."

Like the morgue, the Supplies and Equipment department was reached through a double door off a corridor. These doors, though, had pebbled glass in their upper halves and were locked.

"I could badge us in, but there's people in there, so it would be kind of impolite," Juarez said. She pressed the buzzer. After a few moments the door buzzed back; evidently the camera above had decided we weren't a threat.

Not so the spectacled Black man who met us as we walked into what seemed like a very large room. He wore a white coat, held an e-tablet, and gave us a stony look. “Yes?”

“Juarez,” said Juarez, showing him her Security ID. “Plainclothes today. Chin and Smith.” She nodded at us.

“Bob Forrest.” He didn’t smile; it occurred to me that what we were a threat to was his schedule. Behind him steel shelves stretched away to infinity and people in white coats moved back and forth, some also with e-tablets, some with carts they were filling with items they selected from here and there. The lights overhead glared brightly and the flooring was scuffed vinyl tile. It looked like a Costco for medical supplies.

“What can I do for you?” Forrest said.

Juarez told him, “We’re looking for Barry Sivek.”

“Join the club.”

“He’s not here?”

“Not here, didn’t call in, doesn’t answer his phone, his email, his text. We tried his emergency contact. They haven’t seen him. I had to call three people before I found someone who could cover his shift.” Bob Forrest eyed us. “Why does Security care?”

“Just need to ask him something,” I said. “Does he do this often?”

“Are you kidding me? I don’t know how Quick Draw runs his department, but in mine, people don’t pull this crap twice. If I ever do see Sivek again, I’ll fire him.”

“Aren’t you worried?” I said. “Something may have happened to him.”

“Yeah, maybe.” Forrest gave a cynical shrug. “But before it did, he emptied out his locker.”

CHAPTER TWENTY-THREE

We went with Juarez back up to the lobby. "That's weird," she said.

"I agree," I answered. "I'd say he just wanted to leave before he got fired, except Montero said he wasn't even going to write him up."

"I don't know what he was doing down there in the basement," Bill said, "but I'm beginning to think it wasn't peeping."

"You think he was cleaning up his tracks?" Juarez said, eyes shining. "Making sure he hadn't left any evidence behind when he killed her?"

"That's a reach," I said. "But it's at least one more thing that muddies the waters of the case against Jordy."

"I feel another call to Church coming on," Bill said.

"You bet."

I made the call, but didn't get Church. I left a message, as instructed, though I was pretty sure I'd have to be the one to call her back. In case I was wrong I wanted a warning, so I gave her her own ringtone: the Fordham University church bells said to have made Edgar Allan Poe a little nuts.

Then I called Linus.

"Hey," said Trella. "What can Wong Security do for our favorite client now?"

"Barry Sivek," I said.

"Same to you. What's that?"

"A medical tech here at River Valley. I want his contact info."

"Gotcha. Want to hold on?"

"No, just send it when you have it."

"Your will, my lord." She clicked off.

"Who was that?" asked Juarez, who'd been leaning in close.

"Trella Bartoli. She works with my cousin Linus Wong at Wong Security. The tech arm of Chin and Smith Investigations."

"You guys are even cooler than I thought."

"We generally hide how cool we are. It's better for business."

Juarez left us, heading home to get some sleep. "Call me if you need me, boss," she said to me.

"You know," Bill said, after she was gone, "my ego is taking a beating here. I really have charmed people in my life."

"I believe you. I bet I've even seen you do it. Let me try to think back—"

"Nuts," he said. "I'm going to go out and have a cigarette."

"No, you're not. We're going to go up to the ICU and see if Alon Bacay is on duty."

Bill tilted his head as if weighing the two options. He slipped the pack back in his pocket and we walked to the elevators. By the time we got upstairs my phone had buzzed with Barry Sivek's information.

"Downtown from here," I told Bill. "Not real far."

"Which Detective Church will be delighted to hear."

"If she deigns to call back," I said.

Alon Bacay, as it turned out, was on duty but, his supervisor told us, he wouldn't be able to speak to us until his break. "This is the ICU," she said coldly and needlessly, standing in front of a nurses' station with a stainless steel sign reading ICU, which we'd reached by going through double doors marked ICU. "The nurses can't just leave their patients to take care of personal business. And frankly Mr. Bacay is too good a nurse to even want to. What do you want with him, if I may ask?"

"We'll wait." I smiled. "Please let him know we're here." I gave her my card.

She frowned as she read it. "If I may—"

"You may ask him," I said.

Bill and I left through the double doors and went to the visitors' lounge just outside the ICU. It was furnished with comfy couches and chairs, its walls decorated with colorful gardeny watercolors, the floors a calm blue-gray vinyl. Beyond the wide windows clouds drifted above the East River. The sun sparkled on the water, cast long shadows from the new towers in Queens, and made a barge's wake look like cotton fluff. Cars, trucks, and subway trains flowed across the bridges. So much distracting beauty for worried visitors.

No other visitors this morning, though. We were alone in the lounge, and that was a good thing because just after we settled in, my phone started to sing "Bad Boys."

I answered it and was rewarded with "Yo, cuz."

"Hi, Linus. Was that a yawn?" I put the phone on speaker but kept the volume low. Bill leaned over to hear.

"Late night. Plus I got Alon Bacay here for you and the guy's a snore."

I glanced at Bill. "Is he really?"

"From Quezon City. That's in the Philippines. Did his nurse training there. Troublemaker over there, good trouble I mean—revolution yes!—but since he came here, zippo. Came here with an RN, got the job at River Valley five years ago. Active in the nurses' union. I don't know, maybe that's interesting. Sends money home on the regular. Lives small, in Queens, commutes. Driver's license but no car. Two bank accounts, one checking, one savings. Three credit cards, rent, pays everything on time, not early, not late. Has a green card, working on citizenship. Maybe another six months for that. Goes home twice a year, a week each time. Married two years ago."

"Did he meet his wife here or there?"

"Husband, and there. The guy—Carlos Fernandez—lives there and comes over here twice a year, too. The wedding was here. Had to be because gay marriage isn't a thing in the Philippines. Pretty much being gay isn't a thing in the Philippines, actually. He was here about six weeks ago, Fernandez. He's a writer, a poet, edits a Tagalog-Spanish literary magazine. He can't get a green card."

"Why not?"

Bill answered that one. "An employer has to state they made a good faith effort to find a citizen to hire for the job before they can hire an immigrant. There's a nurse shortage but there's no poet shortage."

Linus said, "Tru dat. For a living the poet-husband teaches Spanish and Tagalog to people new to the Philippines. Not a lot of call for that here, either. When Bacay's a citizen he'll be able to bring Fernandez over. Maybe if he does it'll be party time. Meanwhile I can find zero interesting about Bacay."

"No reason you can see that he quit the negotiating committee suddenly?"

"Actually that's about the most interesting thing he's done in years, from what I see. But there is one thing."

"You just said there was nothing."

"Not about him. About looking stuff up about him."

"Meaning?"

"Just like with that nurse, Scott. We're not the first. The footprints of a gigantic hound! That's from Sherlock Holmes. Someone else has been pawing around in here."

Bill got there before I did. "Linus—"

"Yo, big man!"

"Yo. Do a random check on some of the other negotiating committee members. Talia Venturino, two or three others. See if it's the same, that we're not the first."

"Will do."

"And Linus?" I said. "If there's any way of finding out whose footprints they are—"

"Legally only?"

"Yes!"

"Ah, but you hesitated. She hesitated, didn't she, Trella? Woof? She did, didn't she? Never mind, I'll be careful."

"I'm not interested in careful!" I said. "I'm interested in legal."

"Uh-huh. Talk to you later."

Linus clicked off. I looked at Bill. "Did I hesitate?" I demanded.

"Afraid so."

"Damn." I deflated. "I'm going to call him back." As I lifted my phone to do that, though, it rang. The number wasn't familiar, so I said, "Lydia Chin," in English and "Chin Ling Wan-ju," in Cantonese.

"Lydia Chin?" came a vaguely familiar male voice. "You're some kind of detective?"

He'd chosen English, so I did, too. "Private investigator. Who's this?"

"Alon Bacay. You were asking for me. Leave me alone."

"We're working for Jordy Kazarian's lawyer," I said fast. "It's about Sophia Scott."

"I don't know anything about it and I don't want to talk to you. Leave me alone."

"We're right nearby. In the ICU visitors' lounge. We just—"

But he hung up.

"Alon Bacay," I said to Bill, lowering my phone. "He's not charmed and he doesn't even know us. He said to leave him alone."

"Word about us is getting out. Well, we know he's at work and he hasn't walked by. We could wait and trap him when his shift's over."

"He'll want to talk to us even less if we do that. And we'll waste a lot of time sitting here until then. Time we could be spending doing what, I don't know, but—"

My phone chimed out "Bad Boys." "Linus!" I barked into it. "Whatever illegal thing you're doing, knock it off immediately."

"Me? All I did was what Bill asked for. Talia Venturino and two other random people on that committee. If you actually want stuff about them it'll take longer, but we were just checking for footprints. They're everywhere."

I thought. "Could they be background checks? You know, due diligence when they were hired?"

"They're recent. Last month."

"Hmm. And you don't—"

"No, but I could—"

"No, you could not. And I mean *not*. Thanks, Linus. And Trella and Woof. We now return you to your regularly scheduled legal-only programming."

I slid the phone back in my pocket and said to Bill, "You were right. Footprints everywhere."

"So." His eyes followed the flight of a helicopter past the window. "Someone's been looking for skeletons in the committee members' closets."

"And whatever they found forced Alon Bacay to quit the committee."

"Except there's nothing interesting about Alon Bacay."

I was about to suggest we leave the ICU floor and discuss this outside when Bill's hand went to his cigarette pocket. Obviously there was no smoking in the ICU lounge, so he dropped it again.

"Okay," I said, as if I hadn't noticed that. "We need to know who."

"You have a lousy poker face," Bill said. "I can go for about another half hour before I get really crabby."

"Pretend we're on a long airplane flight."

"In that case, a bourbon, please. And you look really cute in that little flight attendant hat. Also there's something else."

"One word about my legs—"

"Your legs?" He made a show of looking my corduroy-clad legs up and down. "I guess they're cute, too. When Sophia Scott volunteered for that committee, everyone was surprised."

I took a beat. "You're saying if you can blackmail someone off a committee you can blackmail someone onto it." I pulled out my phone again.

"Who're you calling?"

"Our employee."

The phone, again on speaker, rang three times before Benita Juarez picked it up. Her sleepy voice offered a hoarse "Hello?"

"It's Lydia," I said. "Sorry to wake you."

"Boss? What do you need?" I could hear her trying to snap to. "Muscle? I'm your girl."

"No, thanks. Just a question. Who does investigations at the hospital?"

"Who does—what do you mean by investigations?"

I was impressed that her instinct was to stop and let me define it, not jump in with what she thought I might mean. "Say something goes missing from people's lockers, like that."

"Oh. Quick Draw contracts with an outside firm that sends people in to work undercover as janitors, cleaners, plumbers, whatever. You know, unfamiliar faces. It's pretty standard."

"And what about background checks, say for new hires? Does Security do those?"

"No, that stuff is always contracted out, too. The Security Management Handbook warns you about that. Too great a risk to do in-house. People sue, stuff like that."

"You know who the contractor is?"

"Security handles the investigation contract but not the background check one. Legal does. I don't know but I could find out."

I looked up as a pale, teary-eyed woman walked uncertainly into the lounge. I gave her a quick smile and said to Juarez, "No, thanks. It's the other one I need. Go back to sleep."

"No, wait, you gotta tell me why—"

"I will, but not now. Good night." I put the phone away, nodded to Bill, and we stood and left.

CHAPTER TWENTY-FOUR

Thank God this flight's landing," Bill said as we waited for the elevator on the ICU floor. "It was interminable. Movie was good, though."

"We need to find out who's authorizing those background checks."

"We need to go out and have a cigarette, and then I might have an idea about that."

"You can't have the idea first?"

"Where do you think I get my ideas?"

We had to cross the street for Bill to smoke. I waited silently beside him, trying to enjoy the sunshine bringing my body temperature back up to normal and to not radiate impatience.

"You know," Bill said, "I can see it coming off you in waves like in a cartoon."

"What?"

"Impatience." He ground the cigarette out. "All right, let's go."

"Where?"

"We're going to do this the old-fashioned way."

Back into the ice-cold building. I actually shivered. A security guard checked us out as we did the same to the directory.

"Help you folks?"

"Legal?" Bill said amiably. "We have an appointment with Margaret Weldon."

He glanced at our jackets, saw that our badges were in place, and pointed us to the Admin tower, where the lawyers dwelt.

"What's the plan?" I asked as we followed the green line. "Are we really going to see Weldon?"

"No. First name that came to mind, is all."

We got to the elevator just as it was opening. Other people got on with us, so I didn't have a chance to ask anything else. We got out on ten, facing double glass doors with the River Valley logo etched into them and a bronze plaque reading LEGAL DEPARTMENT beside them.

I said, "Are you going to tell me—"

"Nah. More fun this way."

A discreet black button waited for a gentle thumb push, which Bill applied. The response was a single click so hushed I almost missed it. He pulled the door, held it for me, and walked in after I did. Well, I walked, he ambled. We were in a carpeted anteroom across from a sleek dark wood wall with the River Valley logo again, this time in bronze. In front of that stretched a sleek dark wood desk. On the desk sat a sleek black monitor and keyboard and behind it sat a sleek dark-skinned woman. Her name plate read VIOLA LEWIS, her nail polish matched her lipstick perfectly, she wore a delicate microphone headset, and her eyebrows were raised.

"Yes?"

"Morning, ma'am." Bill slipped a card out of his wallet. One of the "Smith and Chin" cards, I saw, not the "Chin and Smith" ones. Well, at least my name was on it. As the receptionist read it, Bill smiled. "Not to chase around Robin Hood's barn, Miz Lewis, me and my partner here, we're looking for work." His Kentucky accent, which all these years in New York had just about obliterated, was on full display.

Viola Lewis glanced up. "Looking for work?"

"Yes, ma'am." He slipped a hand into his pocket and shifted his weight to one hip. If I hadn't known better I'd have sworn he was wearing cowboy boots. "You see, it's been my experience that every large organization comes to a time when some reprobate can't resist taking something that isn't his, or selling some information he knows to someone as oughtn't to know it, or trying to take liberties with the wrong individual. Now, when those things happen, the organization is going to want to look into the situation. Right then a private investigator who isn't familiar to anyone in the organization can be of great assistance. My partner and I have been in the investigative business quite some time and can provide excellent references. I'd be appreciative if we could talk to one of your attorneys. Just to introduce ourselves, you know." His smile was so ingratiating I had to struggle to keep a straight, though hopeful, face.

"I admire your enterprise." Viola Lewis returned his smile. I got the distinct feeling she was amused at this country bumpkin but didn't want to be unkind. "But when the hospital needs investigators, the attorneys contract with a large firm. One we've been using for years. I don't think a two-person office . . ." She glanced at the card and shook her head.

"Oh," said Bill. "Why, that's a shame." He took a beat, as though he were wondering whether to go all in, and said, "In that case, ma'am, would you be good enough to tell us who that firm might be? I ask because we've also had the opportunity to work with firms larger than ourselves, and it's been a fruitful collaboration each time. Except that one time—darlin'"—he turned to me—"what was the name of those fellows, the ones we didn't get on with?"

"Spencer and Guster," I said. I'd lost the thread of what he was doing but I was willing to ride with it.

"Right, that was them. That won't be the firm you all hire, would it?" Bill gave Ms. Lewis an expectant smile.

"That sounds familiar but I don't think we've worked with them. Generally the attorneys go to The Michael Group."

"Is that a fact?" Bill's face lit in a grin. "Chris A. Chambers, would that be? Partner there. Army buddy of mine."

Viola Lewis seemed on the verge of a reply, but a door in the dark wood wall opened silently and Margaret Weldon stepped through. I guessed we were seeing her after all. "Viola, could you—" She stopped and glanced at Bill, and then at me. "Is there a problem?"

We'd only ever seen Margaret Weldon from above on a wide-angle video. Standing here in front of us, stopped in the middle of a gesture, eyes blade sharp, she gave me the eerie sense I was seeing a predator spotting what might be prey. After a moment she closed the door behind herself and stood, each movement small and balanced, a hunter hiding in tall grass.

"No, Ms. Weldon," said Viola Lewis evenly. "These folks just had a question." She handed Bill back his card, saying, "I'm sorry I couldn't help you."

"Ma'am, we appreciate your time." He smiled at her, and, not having a hat to tip, he nodded. Another nod, this one to Weldon. "Ma'am." He turned, so I also nodded at both women and walked through the door he held open for me. From behind I felt the disappointment of the carnivore when the small unsuspecting animal she thought she saw turned out to be just a shadow in the canes.

Neither of us spoke until the elevator doors closed behind us.

"Spencer and Guster?" Bill said.

"Hey. You keep me in the dark, you get what you get. Though except for a sighting of Margaret Weldon, which was pretty scary but which you said wasn't why we were there, I don't see that we got much of anything."

"How wrong you are. Can't blame you, though. You were forced to make that judgment while lacking critical data." He handed me the card Viola Lewis had returned to him. I looked at it, at Bill's smug face, and turned the card over.

"Darius Georges" was written on the back.

CHAPTER TWENTY-FIVE

Outside on our bench, I found the website for The Michael Group. Security consultants, like Linus and Trella, but with a more boring slogan: "Risk Management and Cyber Safety." Yawn. Darius Georges was a managing director and expert witness. Witness to what, I wondered, as I made the call. The receptionist passed me to a secretary, who told me she'd be happy to make an appointment for me to see Mr. Georges. I thanked her and suggested half an hour from now would be an excellent time.

"Oh, no, I'm sorry, that's not possible. The soonest I can get you in would be . . . Hmm. Not this week, but let's see . . ."

"I'm thinking the soonest would be half an hour from now. Tell Mr. Georges I'm also an investigator, Smith and Chin Investigations. My partner and I are at River Valley Downstate Medical Center, so we're right nearby. We're on our way."

"I can't—"

"Oh, I think you can, and probably, you should."

"I—"

"You know," I said, "I can tie up your phone lines all day. Automated calls from random numbers. Or you could tell Mr. Georges all we want is a few minutes of his time. Actually, since we're at River Valley—don't forget to tell him that part—we can be there in twenty minutes. Does that help?"

Silence, then the coldest "Please hold" I'd ever heard. I held, through some interminable easy-listening pop. After what seemed like an hour of that stuff, but by my watch was seventy-two seconds, the non-music went away and the icy voice came back. "Mr. Georges will see you in twenty minutes, and he said to tell you he doesn't appreciate being threatened."

"No one does," I said. "It's an undervalued art."

The Michael Group had the twenty-fifth through twenty-seventh floors of a glass tower on Lexington, as boring as their slogan and their hold music. In the boring gray-veined marble lobby, we had to show ID to get through the turnstiles and into the boring wood-grained elevators. At twenty-seven we emerged into a wide, high, gray-carpeted lobby. The gray wall in front of us held six-inch-tall bronze letters claiming this floor for The Michael Group. Each letter was bolted at the corners by the kind of hardware you see on old bank vaults.

"Not just boring, but cheesy," I whispered to Bill. Through a gray smoked-glass door in the wall to our right vague outlines could be seen. Once we opened the door, they resolved into a brown-skinned woman with feathered blonde hair. She sat at a desk presiding over groupings of gray chairs in a waiting area. I presented my card to her—a Smith and Chin card, in deference to the way Bill had started this—and we sat. She murmured into the earpiece she wore.

"He's gonna keep us waiting," I said to Bill.

"You bet. Giving me the chance to ask—you really know how to do that random number dialing thing?"

"Are you kidding? All I know is it can be done. Linus told me."

We waited in companionable silence, companionably ignored by the receptionist. Bill leafed through a copy of *Security Today* while I went back to The Michael Group's website and studied up. Twelve minutes after we'd come in—under ten minutes shows dominance but a certain amount of respect, over ten is a power play, but you have to calibrate it; fifteen and we might have kicked up a fuss—we were summoned to follow a thin young man through a door into a gray-carpeted corridor that ran between a glass-enclosed bullpen and smoked-glass-walled, windowed offices. The young man stopped at one, gave a knock on the door, and opened it for us. He left, closing the door behind us.

A Black man with a receding hairline and a close-cropped beard remained seated when we came in. Another dominant move, like the wait time. Talk about boring. I walked forward, gave him a warm smile, and stuck out my hand. "Lydia Chin. It's a pleasure, Mr. Georges."

He half rose—how could he not, to shake hands?—but said nothing. Bill and I sat in boring gray chairs opposite his desk. He wore a gray pinstripe suit, a white shirt, and a yellow tie. Behind him the window offered a sliver of sky—gray—but mostly it was filled with the upper floors of the boring next-door skyscraper. How anyone kept their eyes open at The Michael Group I had no idea. Maybe they played power games to stay awake.

"I checked you out," Georges began abruptly, dropping into his chair again. His clipped voice carried a nasal Midwest accent. "You're both licensed but only you"—me—"have an office. You've both had brushes with the law. Neither of you has ever been on the Job, either civilian or military, which is a big neon tip-off that someone's a low-rent back-alley PI."

"Admirably thorough," I said. "We checked you out, too. You *were* a cop, so I guess you're from a better class of back alley. Quit to go into security, joined this firm's Chicago branch, then to San Francisco, came here ten years ago to run the New York office."

"Right. I paid my dues. You didn't, so who the hell are you to threaten me and what the hell do you want?"

"I appreciate a man who doesn't chase around Robin Hood's barn," I said. "Although I wouldn't have had to threaten you if you'd extended a little professional courtesy to begin with." His lip curled slightly on that one. A Canal Street back office versus three floors of a Lexington Avenue skyscraper; denim jacket, jeans, and cords versus a Brooks Brothers suit; brushes with the law versus upstanding boringness. Seems like he thought maybe Bill and I weren't really in the same profession as he was after all. "We want to know why you did backgrounds on over a dozen people who work at River Valley Downstate Medical Center a month ago."

"What makes you think we did?"

"Your footprints are all over them."

"Footprints?"

"E ones."

"I have no idea what you mean."

I peered over his shoulder. "I see Robin Hood's barn coming up fast."

Georges worked his clamped jaw. Someone on a floor below was in for a dressing-down.

"A client requested them," he said.

"River Valley Downstate." I nodded. "The Legal department. Why did they want them?"

"Who our client is is obviously confidential. Everything we did for them was within their right to ask for and was done within the law and according to industry best practices." I wanted to shout *Legally only!* but he went on. "Why do you want to know?"

"Fair enough. We have a client, too. He's a person, not a department. His name is Jordy Kazarian and he's accused of killing one of the people you did backgrounds on. Sophia Scott. You know she was found dead at the hospital?"

A pause. “I’d heard.”

“That doesn’t concern you?”

“I went back through that file.” At least he spared us some pious variation of “anyone’s death concerns me.” “I found nothing that could have been related to the incident.”

Incident. Sophia Scott hadn’t been well-liked—including, posthumously, by me—but I didn’t think she deserved to have her death downgraded to an incident. “How were you able to determine that?”

“Ms. Chin. We were hired to do a job and we did it. You asked why, I’ve told you why. I think we’re done here.”

“I also asked why your client—and we know that was River Valley, so you don’t have to bother to stonewall that anymore—wanted that job done.”

He rubbed his forehead as though I was giving him a headache. “You can’t really think I asked. Do you ask? If the request is legal and the work is legal it can only increase your exposure to know the reason.”

For the first time, Bill broke in. “So, to limit your exposure, you just took a list of sixteen people and started going down it. The fact that that’s the same number of people as on the nurses’ union negotiating committee was purely coincidental.”

“First, I have no reason to know the number of people on the nurses’ union negotiating committee. Second, yes, that’s what we did. If you’d pressed me, I’d have said I thought the people on the list were being considered for promotion and someone was doing due diligence. But I really didn’t care. I’m paid to do a thorough job for the client, not to care why.”

CHAPTER TWENTY-SIX

"Oh my God," I said, slumping against the wall in the wood-grained elevator as we escaped from the twenty-seventh floor. "If I ever get the urge to go corporate, you'll stop me, right?"

"Don't worry," Bill said. "You've been working with me long enough to guarantee that no corporate firm would hire you."

"I suppose I should be grateful."

"I live to serve. Bet Juarez would like it, though."

"Only if she could shoot right up that promotion ladder and grab a corner office. I wish I could get my hands on those background checks."

"I know someone who can."

"No you don't! You don't know anybody who can."

The elevator door opened and people got on. From the marble lobby, we revolved out of the building. Bill lit up a cigarette as soon as we hit the sidewalk. "Could it be," he said, "that all this is a distraction?"

"You mean"—I waved a hand in front of my face—"a smokescreen?"

"Very funny," he said, but he blew out his next puff way above my head. "No, because that implies deliberate misdirection. I'm just wondering how much of this stuff has anything to do with Jordy."

I considered that. "Maybe none. But aren't we thinking Scott's killing didn't have anything to do with Jordy, either? The more complicated this gets, the better it is for him."

Bill nodded. He took another draw and ground the cigarette out. "Do I get points for only smoking half?"

"No."

"Seriously? You know how much these things cost?" He shook his head sadly. "Well, despite your disregard, I'm going to continue working with you—"

"Lucky me."

"—and what I want to do now is fill in some blanks. Who in the River Valley legal department ordered the background checks? What made Bacay quit the committee? What made Scott join it? Why was Scott so against a strike? Where's the peeper?"

"Sivek," I said.

"Yeah, him. And who's Calypso? And did either of them really see anything?"

We crossed the street and came to one of those pocket mid-block parks New York gets every now and then for letting a developer add a dozen shade-casting stories to his building. The whole park was in that shade, and would probably be a windswept tundra in the winter; but right now, with the cool mist added to the air by a waterfall that poured over the rear wall, it was perfect. Three young women in blazers and slacks sat at a table eating salads out of plastic clamshell boxes; at another table a middle-aged couple and two tweens, all tall and blond, were chowing down hot dogs and pretzels and consulting a guidebook.

"Okay," I said to Bill when we'd chosen a bench. "Maybe you do know someone who can get their hands on those background checks. Watch this." I tapped Detective Church's number.

"Yeah, what now?" Church snarled in my ear. Because of the waterfall I kept the phone off speaker.

"I have some more tit but this time I want some tat," I said. Beside me, Bill laughed.

"What the hell are you talking about?"

"I want to know if you've found Calypso yet."

"Good luck with that."

"Not where they are, not what they said, because I know you won't share that. Just if you've found them. I'll trade."

"What've you got?"

"Uh-uh. We've done that already. This time you go first."

"If you have information pertinent to an active investigation and you withhold it—"

"Who are you and what have you done with Detective Church? Last I heard from her she was telling me not to call again."

"God, you people like to skate on thin ice, don't you?"

I didn't answer, just waited.

"Where the hell are you? Sounds like a bathroom."

"It's a park with a waterfall."

"Oh. How lovely, to be able to sit in parks all day. Meanwhile I've got my captain riding my ass to clear this case, and that's because he's got fifteen layers of assholes at One PP riding his. And every time you call, things just get more complicated and the finish line gets farther away."

I glanced at Bill. "Why does anyone at headquarters care?"

"Because the fucking mayor cares, which makes the commissioner care, and it's assholes all the way down."

"Do you know why?"

"Why what?"

"Why the mayor cares?"

"Something about one of his rich pals. How the hell should I know? Get lost."

"You don't want my tit for tat?"

"Oh, shit." A breath. "Yeah, fine, okay, no."

"Fine, okay, no, what?"

"Did I find Calypso yet, you wanted to know. No. Now you."

"Did you figure out who it is?"

"Are you fucking kidding me?"

"Just asking."

She hissed out a breath. "No. You have any idea how many people from the islands work at that place?"

"Damn."

"Why?" she asked quickly. "Something you're not saying?"

"No, I was just hoping you knew, and even if you didn't find them, you'd be willing to trade for the name. I guess we'll just have to keep looking. Bye."

"Don't even. You offered, you'd better come across."

"Okay, but it was a good try, you've got to admit. Every member of the nurses' union contract negotiating team was the subject of an outside private investigation firm's background check in the month leading up to the contract talks."

A pause. "Not surprising. A little dirty, maybe, but union negotiations, anything for an edge."

You were the one who said no one gets killed over union negotiations, I wanted to say. But I settled for "What if something in—"

"—Scott's past was turned up by the check, yeah, yeah. You really think we're that stupid? We ran a background on her, of course we did. One arrest, age seventeen, six months probation. You know about that, Miss Wiseass?"

"Actually," I said, "we did."

"Of course you did. And the hospital would've run a background check as part of her job application. If there was something else why didn't it—"

"—turn up then, yeah, yeah. The company that did the checks was The Michael Group. The guy we talked to, Darius Georges, just about but not quite admitted it was the hospital Legal department that ordered them. Well, if you don't like that one, I have something else for you."

"How did I get so lucky?"

"A medical technician named Barry Sivek was caught sneaking around the basement near the crime scene last night."

"From what I hear everyone and his monkey was sneaking around that goddamn basement."

"Maybe, but this guy's disappeared."

"What the hell does that mean?"

I told her about his boss's unsuccessful attempts to reach Sivek, and about his cleaned-out locker.

"So the guy decided he doesn't want to work in a place where people get killed."

"Yeah, especially if he killed them."

"Oh, for Christ's sake."

"Uh-huh," I said. "See you around." I hung up.

"How is it possible," I said to Bill's raised eyebrows, "for someone that obnoxious to get more obnoxious?"

"I hope you're not asking me because you think I have some unique insight into obnoxiousness. What was she saying about the mayor?"

"Apparently Hizzoner wants this case cleared soonest, so he's riding the commissioner who et cetera and it's pissing Church off."

Bill raised his eyebrows. "That's pretty strong language coming from you."

"I think Church may be catchy."

"Why does Hizzoner care?"

"Church says, and I quote, because of one of his rich pals." I met Bill's eyes.

"You think Larson?"

"I do. I think he wants to make his damn donation but he can't until this blows over."

"I'm going to have to get used to you swearing."

"Maybe I'll go back to normal after this case is over. Listen, that list of things you wanted to know. Let's go down it. I—"

My phone interrupted me, the screen usefully informing me my caller was Benita Juarez.

"Hey," I said. "I thought you were supposed to be sleeping."

"How'd you know it was me, boss? You give me a ringtone of my own?"

"Not yet."

"I want 'Bad Boys.'"

"Someone has that already."

"Oh. How about 'Hard to Kill'?"

"Don't know it. Send me the link. What's up?"

"Where are you? Sounds like a bathroom."

"It's a park with a waterfall."

"Nice. I couldn't sleep. So I had an idea. I called Leo Brown."

"Who's that? And why?"

"Bad, bad Leo Brown, baddest man in the whole damn Security department," she sang. "One of the six guys Quick Draw fired. Him and me had a thing, once."

"Um, Juarez," I said, "I'm not sure you should—"

"Yeah," she said. "Because I don't really work for you, so there's no presumption of confidentiality. And besides, I don't know what you're doing, so I could screw something up. I know. But this was just me calling an old boyfriend. Just checking in, ask how he's doing. Sympathize, all that." She paused. "Was going to see if he really did know something about the east basement, that was all."

"Someone got killed down there!" I said. "You can't just go around asking questions like that."

"Why not? Everyone in the hospital's talking about it. It's not like I would've stood out."

She had a point there.

"Anyway, no harm done because he couldn't talk to me. He was at work." She finished with a note of triumph in her voice I didn't quite get.

"Well, good, but then why are you calling?"

"He was at work," she repeated.

"Yes, and I—" The light dawned. "Where?"

"A freight company on the west side. Tolen Forwarding."

I scribbled that down. "Can you give me the names of the other guys who were fired?"

"I'll text them."

"Thanks, Juarez. This is good. But you've got to stop going out on your own, okay?"

"Then you better give me an assignment, boss."

"Yeah, okay. Your assignment is, go back to sleep."

I clicked off and lowered the phone.

"Juarez," said Bill, just so he could sound smart. "And she had something."

"One of the guys Quick Draw fired. She used to date him. So she called him for the tea on the east basement. But he couldn't talk to her because he was at work."

"At work? That was fast for a guy who just got fired a few days ago. For dereliction of duty."

The three young women packed up the lunch debris from their table, smashed it into an overflowing trash can, and headed out.

"No kidding," I said. "We need to make another phone call, but not from here."

"Why not?"

"Because," I said, "it sounds like a bathroom."

CHAPTER TWENTY-SEVEN

To find a quiet spot in east Midtown, somewhere that could believably be an office, was not simple. Most places that were public, and therefore accessible to us, were either building lobbies, made of echoing stone and glass; libraries, where phone calls were frowned upon; or stores where peppy Muzak played in the background to energize shoppers. We left the waterfall park and looked up and down the street. "Got it," said Bill, starting to walk east.

"Where are we going?" I caught up with him.

"Yale."

All the Ivy League schools have private clubs in New York. They're open to any alum willing to pay dues. Neither Bill nor I was an Ivy League alum and we hadn't paid anything. Nevertheless I quick-walked with him to the Yale Club, a few blocks from the tiny park and near Grand Central Station. Handy for those Yalies who hankered after a quick squash game or a quiet drink before boarding their trains to the suburbs.

We entered through a bronze-and-glass revolving door. Just inside, Bill scanned the quiet lobby, surveying the upholstered chairs and loveseats arranged into conversation areas around dark wood coffee tables on a patterned carpet. "He's not down yet," he said to me in conversational tones.

I checked my watch. "Well, we're early."

"We're meeting a friend," Bill told the concierge, who offered a professional smile and a seat.

We chose a small sofa in an unoccupied grouping in the corner, at a distance from a pair of young women in business suits scrolling through their phones and, at the other side of the room, two older men leaning forward, forearms on knees, in intent discussion.

"How do you know about this place?" I asked Bill.

"My clients are a more classy breed than you might think. Why are you giving me that look?"

"You forget I've met a lot of your clients."

This phone call had to be mine, because Bill had called our quarry before and his number might be in their system. I was glad; I was looking forward to it.

"Which one, do you think?" I asked Bill, showing him the list Juarez had texted me.

"Delgado, no? He was on duty." Bill read me the number I needed off his phone and I tapped it in on mine.

"River Valley Medical Center Security Services. How may I direct your call?" I heard. I pictured the Black woman with the fingernails in the many-windowed outer office.

I pitched my tone low and sharpened my consonants. "James McGraw, please."

"May I say who's calling?"

"Rhonda Phillips, Human Resources, the Yale Club."

"Just a moment," I heard, and then another familiar voice.

"You've got McGraw." He sounded tired.

"Good afternoon, Mr. McGraw. Rhonda Phillips, HR, the Yale Club. We've had an application for a security guard position from a Jaime Delgado and he gave your name as a reference."

"Delgado, yes, great guy. Wish I could've kept him."

"May I ask why he's no longer in your employ?"

"He wanted more money. Deserved it, too. But my budget's fixed and I couldn't get it for him. I gave him overtime, best I could do, but he wanted forty steady hours at a better hourly."

"I see. Would you say he's dependable? On time, presentable, quick thinker? Does he do his paperwork? Will he be willing to work nights and swing shifts?"

"Yes, all that."

"Anything I should know about him?"

"Nothing. You'll be lucky to get him."

I thanked Quick Draw and cut the call. "Wow," I said. "Hell of a reference for a guy whose ass he fired. Should we go see Juarez's ex?"

"You bet. And for the record, I like this new you."

◆

Tolen Forwarding Co. had a yard and warehouse spread over a couple of mid-block lots in the west fifties between Eleventh Avenue and the highway. It was one of a few surviving remnants of the numberless businesses that had bustled on the waterfront for three centuries before the freight trade all moved to the container ports in New Jersey. I suspected Tolen Forwarding Co. was only holding on to this piece of property while they waited for an offer from a condo developer, someone who'd pay them a bundle and squeeze as many stories as possible onto the site. Then Tolen Forwarding Co. could move to New Jersey, too.

A guard in a booth by the gate checked the credentials of a trucker and handed him back his paperwork. The gate swung open. Once the truck was inside, it creaked shut again. Juarez had texted me a photo of her ex; even with the distraction of the photo's sunlight, sand, and Speedo, I could tell the guy in the booth wasn't him. The truck pulled up to the warehouse loading dock and Bill and I crossed the street.

"Hey," Bill said when the guard slid his window back. "Can we talk to the site super?"

The guard, sallow-skinned and wispy-bearded, said, "Depends why."

Bill gave the guy his card but didn't say why. The guard looked at the card, at Bill, at me, and shrugged. He picked up a handset, spoke into it, and pressed the button that opened the creaky gate.

As we crossed the yard, a door in the warehouse wall opened and a big-shouldered man stepped out. He had the kind of ruddy complexion that makes people look permanently sunburned. "Help you?"

"Bill Smith. This is Lydia Chin. We're private investigators." Bill handed over another card. "You in charge?"

The guy glanced at the card and nodded. "Dan DiMenna."

"We'd like a word with one of your guards. Won't take long."

"Who, and why?"

"Leo Brown. It's about something that happened on his last job. We're hoping he might be able to point us in the right direction."

DiMenna narrowed his eyes. "Should I be worried about him? He just started."

"No. Not his problem. He's just a possible witness. We're looking at someone else there. Brown's good."

DiMenna nodded. He searched the yard, spotted a man in uniform walking the fence, looking for potential breaches. Diligent security guard behavior as befitted someone new on the job. DiMenna shouted, was drowned out by traffic noise, sighed, and shouted louder. "Brown!" He waved the guard over.

Leo Brown was tanned and ponytailed, and had pale blue eyes in an angular face. He gave us a lopsided, quizzical smile. I thought I knew what Juarez had seen in him.

"Private investigators," DiMenna said. "Need to talk to you." Brown's smile vanished, as so often happens when people hear that. So sad. "I'll be inside," DiMenna told us all, and walked back to the warehouse. From that I understood that, one, he didn't want to intimidate Brown into not talking because his new boss was there, and two, that whatever this was about, DiMenna didn't want to hear it.

Brown eyed us warily. "If this is about that girl that got killed at the hospital, I don't know anything about it. In fact I got canned because I was skipping that part of the basement."

"Yeah, that's what McGraw said," I told him. "He said he canned all six of you. Looks like you landed on your feet, though." I gestured around, at the trucks, the warehouse, the shipping containers.

Brown shrugged. "I was lucky. Answered an ad."

"And got a glowing recommendation from the guy who fired you." I was guessing, but after my conversation with Quick Draw about Delgado it wasn't much of a stretch.

"Like I said. Lucky."

"No," said Bill. "No, I don't think so. I think it was part of the deal."

"What deal?"

"The deal you had with McGraw," I said. "All six of you. You'd keep out of the east basement, and if it ever caught up with you, he'd have to fire you but then he'd give you great recommendations for new jobs. That plus the cash he was slipping you was enough. We know all you guys he put on the basement were his favorites. The rest of the guards think it was because it's easy work, the basement. But that's not it."

“The question we’re asking,” Bill said, “is why?”

Brown attempted a confused scowl. “I have no idea what you’re talking about.”

“Look,” I said, “it’s hot out here, it’s stinky and loud by the highway, and we’re not here to bust you but we will anyway if you keep up this crap.” I saw Bill grin at that. “Let me remind you a woman was murdered.”

“On Delgado’s watch, not mine!”

“Yeah, fine. You were bribed by your boss not to do your job. Why?”

No answer.

“Ah, Jesus.” Bill took out his phone.

“What are you doing?” Brown demanded.

“We’re private. Obviously this needs to go to the cops.”

“No. No, wait.”

Bill lowered the phone.

“I need this job.”

I said, “Sophia Scott needed to stay alive.”

“I had nothing to do with that.”

“Which we’re more likely to believe if you tell us what was really going on.”

“You’ll keep me out of it?”

“You’re already in it. You don’t want to dig yourself deeper, tell us about it.”

Brown rubbed a hand over his mouth. “I don’t know.” He glanced at Bill’s phone, which was beginning to rise. “I don’t know but you’re right. McGraw gave us bonuses. Bigger than the other guys, and twice a year.”

“For what?”

“Like you said. Staying out of the east basement.”

“Why?”

He shook his head. “Honest to God, I have no idea. He didn’t say and none of us ever went in there to see.”

"Just because he told you not to? You're a troop of goddamn slacker Boy Scouts?"

Brown's jaw flexed, but Bill's phone wiggled.

"Well, it was more like because we thought if we did we might get caught."

"And lose your golden eggs."

"Sure. It was a good deal. Why blow it?"

"When did it start?"

"Three years ago."

"Before that you patrolled that area?"

"Stuck our heads in. Most nights. It's been off-limits since the flood."

"I'm sorry, I'm not buying it," I said, though I pretty much was.

"We did hear rumors there was some kind of sex room in there," he said quickly. "We thought maybe people were paying Quick Draw—I mean, McGraw—not to see that. Or even, I don't know, maybe McGraw was running hookers out of there."

"Out of that disgusting basement?" I said.

"Hey. Some people, you know, it might be a turn-on." He winked. I thought I knew why Juarez had broken up with him. "Like I say, I didn't know what was going on and I didn't want to know."

I looked at Bill. That might be all we were going to get. At the entrance the gate creaked open and another truck lumbered through. DiMenna eyed us from across the lot.

"All right," I said to Brown. "Like *I* say, we're not after you. But if McGraw hears we talked to you, we'll nail your ass to the wall. If he doesn't, we won't say anything to your new boss about why you were available for this job. Do we understand each other?"

Brown nodded, and Bill and I headed out.

CHAPTER TWENTY-EIGHT

Running hookers out of that disgusting basement?"

"Hey, for some people it might be—"

"Don't." I gave Bill a dirty look.

"Okay, I won't. Besides, I agree with you. Not out of the hookup room, anyway. One, McGraw seemed genuinely surprised to hear about it. Two, there's the sign-up sheet. Amateurs were using that room, so if McGraw had professionals in that basement they'd have had to be somewhere else. I wouldn't put it past him, but I don't think that's it."

"What is it, then?"

"You got me."

I was going to tell him I already knew that but luckily for him his phone rang. "Smith." He didn't put the call on speaker, so all I could do was listen to his half of what seemed like a bad-news conversation. "Damn." An exasperated breath. "When? How's he doing? No, of course not. Based on what?" A longer silence, Bill leaning over his phone to cut out the traffic noise. "Do we know who? All right, but do we know why it took this long?" Surprisingly, one side of Bill's mouth lifted into a half smile. "Yes, I think we are. Okay, we'll call you later."

He lowered his phone. "Cohen. Jordy's been re-arrested."

"Oh, no! When? Why?"

"Just now, and because they—Church, I assume—has a couple of witnesses who saw him with Sophia Scott."

"He said he didn't know her."

"I know."

"Who are these witnesses?"

"Cohen doesn't know yet. One seems to be, and I quote, 'very credible.' The other corroborated the first one's story."

"Why didn't they come forward before?"

"What she said when I asked her that is something the new you could take lessons from. Cleaned up, it was about people—not the word she used—always being reluctant to get involved."

"I talked to Church an hour ago. She didn't say a word about this."

"Would you really expect her to?"

"No. But it makes me feel like an idiot, sitting there in the park giving her information. Dammit. That's the last time. She's cut off."

"You know we can't do that? Withhold things."

"All of a sudden you need to do things legally? Just when I'm ready to go over to the dark side, too. Is there something Cohen wants us to do now?"

"Yes, find something to help Jordy. She asked if we were getting anywhere and I said I thought we were. She told me to keep going and call her later."

"All right. I think I need to sit and absorb everything we just found out. If we—" This time the phone that interrupted was mine. Another day, another unknown number, this one so secret the screen just said "Private." Either we were coming up in the world or someone was about to try to sell me crypto.

"Lydia Chin," I told it, and then, "Chin Ling Wan-ju."

"Lydia Chin." The voice was a woman's, controlled and patrician, making a definite choice between the two. "The private investigator?" She sounded like she'd never said those words before and didn't like them.

"Yes," I said. "With whom am I speaking?" That one was a definite whom, I knew.

"This is Elizabeth Gordon-Platt. I'd like to see you as soon as possible."

I could feel my eyebrows jump up practically into my hair. From the tone of her voice I was sure I was expected to squeak *Yes, ma'am!* Instead I said coolly, "Of course. Can you give me an idea what this is about?"

"I will when you get here. As soon as possible, please."

I guessed there was no question of her coming down to Canal Street, then. "My partner and I can be there in thirty minutes."

"That's the best you can do?"

"Yes."

A second, probably for grinding of teeth. "Passes will be ready at the visitors' desk. They'll tell you how to reach my office." She cut the call.

I slipped my phone away as Bill said, "Where have you just committed me to being in thirty minutes?"

"Oh, you'll love it. Let's go."

From way west Midtown to the way Upper East Side at this time of day, there was no possibility anything—a cab, a bus, a Citi Bike—would be faster than the subway, especially as close as we were to the big fancy 7 train station at Hudson Yards. We hotfooted it on over, ran three steps at a time down the escalator—a sensation not unlike jumping out of a plane, I realized—and swung onto the train just as the doors were closing. The car's a/c felt great for a couple of seconds. Then my damp shirt iced over and the sweat dripping down the back of my neck turned into arctic rivulets.

"Did we really have to do that?" Bill panted, wiping his face with a handkerchief.

"Probably not. I just wanted to see if we still had it."

We made the connection at Grand Central, zipped uptown, and were at the hospital twenty-seven minutes from when Gordon-Platt had hung up.

However, it still took us five minutes to get our passes, find the right elevator, and emerge into the calm pale blues of the main Administration floor. They had five, of which this was the highest. We approached the gatekeeper, a super-efficient-looking parchment-faced woman with seriously short gray hair. I was opening my mouth to speak when she lasered us with a look of disapproval, which might have been for our rumpled sweaty states, or for the fact that we were two minutes late. She said in a steely voice, "Ms. Chin and Mr. Smith? Please wait." She pressed a keypad, announced us through her headset, nodded at what she heard, looked at us, and repeated, "Please wait." She went back to her monitor and keyboard as though she were already rid of us and glad of it.

Bill and I exchanged a look, chose two square upholstered blue chairs, and waited. I scrolled through my phone. Bill flipped through a copy of *The Journal of Healthcare Management*. Not for long; although I had to think Elizabeth Gordon-Platt was entirely familiar with the rules of executive suite power games, we were fetched within five minutes by a precisely put-together young woman in a navy business suit. Since I didn't for a second imagine this promptness was an expression of Elizabeth Gordon-Platt's high regard for us, I had to think it was because you don't bother to play power games with the hired help.

The young woman escorted us to the fancy conference room I'd seen in newspaper photos, where Gordon-Platt and Seymour Larson wore happy smiles and my brother Elliott looked like a kid ordered to stop playing and stand still for a family portrait. She pushed open the heavy glass door on its squeakless square hinges. "Dr. Gordon-Platt will be with you shortly," she told us, and left.

"She's a doctor?" Bill asked me as the door closed without a sound. "They put a doctor in charge of a hospital? Will wonders never cease."

"Don't get excited," I, who had Googled Gordon-Platt, said. "What she's got is a PhD in healthcare management."

Bill sauntered past the polished wood conference table and its ergonomic chairs to the window. I followed him.

"Does it seem darker outside?" I asked. "I mean, it's not cloudy, the sun's out, but still."

"Polarized glass," he said. "Like in sunglasses. So the people facing the window aren't looking into the glare behind the people on this side."

"Expensive?"

"Very."

I stood beside him and looked through the very expensive glass. The view over the East River to Queens and beyond was similar to the one from the ICU waiting room where we'd failed to talk to Alon Bacay, except this was a higher floor and thus the executives up here could be more far-seeing. As they should be, having in their hands the welfare of River Valley Downstate Medical Center.

Which, it turned out, was what Elizabeth Gordon-Platt wanted to talk about.

The glass door behind us opened as silently as it had closed, but in the window, we'd already seen Gordon-Platt's ghost reaching to push the bronze plate. We turned to face her.

She gave us one sharp nod. "Elizabeth Gordon-Platt," she said, wearing the same stone face we'd seen in the negotiation video. "Please sit down." Making no move to shake hands, she crossed the room and sat at the head of the table, clearly her accustomed spot. I considered taking a chair on the window side to see if the polarized glass really worked or if she had to squint but decided that would be childish of me. I walked the long way around the table to a seat on the other side. Bill took the chair beside me.

Elizabeth Gordon-Platt wore a cobalt suit with an ivory silk shell, a gold chain, and a delicate gold watch. She'd brought no purse and sat with her hands folded on the table, regarding us wordlessly. She might have been taking our measure, or just wondering how two such, er, imperfectly put-together people ended up in her conference room. Or since, as before, her face and body language gave no sense of her thoughts, maybe she was about to tell us a really funny joke.

"Ms. Chin," she finally said. "What are you doing in my hospital?"

My hospital. "A member of your staff was murdered in your hospital," I said. "Another member of your staff has been accused of the crime. I think that warrants investigating. That's what we're doing."

"The police are professionals at that."

"So are we."

"So are many people in this city, I imagine. Can I expect to see them all in here tripping over one another?"

"I'm afraid I don't know what you can expect."

Bill added, "We haven't tripped over anyone yet. But we'll be sure to be extra careful."

Though Gordon-Platt's face didn't change, I had a sudden vision of a pair of broad-shouldered thugs grabbing Bill from behind and dragging him out of the room. It was all I could do not to turn around to see if they were there.

"You're working for Jordan Kazarian? The morgue assistant who was arrested?" Gordon-Platt asked.

I said, "His lawyer hired us."

"What makes you think he's not guilty?"

"What makes you think we think that?"

Now her eyes flashed, though nothing else, not her features, not her posture, betrayed any emotion.

"That's not our job," I went on. "To make judgments like that. We look for facts. We tell our client what we find. That's it."

"You know Jordan Kazarian is the son of my chief of medicine."

My chief of medicine. Boy, she was grabby. I said, "Dr. DeBreng, yes. And the brother of one of your orthopedists. I know that makes his arrest embarrassing but I'd think it would also make you all the more anxious to be sure he gets a fair shake."

"I'm not interested in what you think. And both Doctors DeBreng have told me they feel that the sooner this is concluded, the better."

"I'll bet. We've met them. They're convinced Jordy did it. Some family."

"I thought you didn't make judgments." Okay, touché. "The police think it's likely he's guilty. So likely that I understand he's been re-arrested. I get frequent updates on their investigation."

I almost said, *Wonderful for you, so do we*, but it could get very playground in here very fast.

Gordon-Platt went on: "And talking of family, I understand you're Elliott Chin's sister."

I nodded. "That's right. And it's another reason I'm concerned with finding out what really happened at this hospital."

"You might want to show some concern for your brother's career."

"My—I'm sorry, what?"

"Your presence is disrupting the functioning of this hospital. I'd expect Dr. Chin to be aware of that."

"To the extent you're right, which I don't think is very far, I'm sure he is."

"If so, he's doing nothing about it."

"He hasn't locked me in my room since I was five."

Now as well as her eyes flashing, her nostrils flared. If we worked at it, we might get her whole face going.

"Dr. Gordon-Platt," Bill said, "Dr. Chin didn't hire us. I'm not sure what 'doing something about it' would look like."

"Don't play stupid," she snapped. "If Dr. Chin were to ask you to resign from this case I'm sure you would."

"Are you?" I said. "I have four brothers. Ask them how often I do what they ask."

"It probably depends on how much it matters to them. If their livelihoods are affected, for example."

I stared. "You can't possibly be threatening my brother's job as a way to get me to drop this case."

"I won't have the workings of this hospital disrupted."

"My brother," I said slowly, "has nothing to do with the investigative work we're doing here." I warmed up. "However, he does have a great deal to do with why this hospital, at least its emergency department, functions as well as it does. His staff loves him. He gets awards. He wrote *the* manual on gunshot wounds. He founded and donates time to a free clinic—"

"I'm familiar with Dr. Chin's many sterling qualities. All of which have another side. He indulges his staff. I've had to speak to him about that. He earned the experience he drew on for that manual here at River Valley. And if that clinic didn't exist, its patients would come to our emergency room."

At least this time it was "our," not "my." "No, they wouldn't. They're afraid to. They're—"

"They're illegal immigrants. But we, like you, don't judge"—her perfect lips curled into a little gotcha smile—"and we'd treat them no matter what."

"They don't know that. If you reached out into the community—"

"Oh, stop it. You're parroting your brother, which I suppose is to be expected. However—"

I didn't want to hear her "however." "My brother saved the life of the daughter of one of the richest men in New York, who now wants to donate millions to 'your hospital.'" Yes, I made air quotes. "And you're telling me—"

She slapped the table. "He turned that money down!"

Whoa. A frown, and movement. When we left I'd pat myself on the back. "He did not turn down the money," I said. "How could he? Grab Seymour Larson's hand before he wrote the check? What Elliott said was he didn't want his name on an unnecessary new building when the hospital has other more urgent needs."

Resuming her iron control, Gordon-Platt said, "Mr. Larson has put the donation on pause."

"That has nothing to do with Elliott! He did that because Sophia Scott was murdered here!"

A brief silence, while Gordon-Platt drilled into me with her eyes. She said, "What happened to Nurse Scott was tragic. The police are investigating, with the full cooperation of the hospital, and they will arrive at the truth."

I wasn't crazy about the idea of throwing Detective Church under the bus, but then, she was no prize, either. "A couple of times so far our investigation has uncovered facts the police had missed."

"Probably because they're of no consequence!" Gordon-Platt barked. "All this is, is you stirring up anxiety among my already tense and distracted staff, and I won't have it."

"No," I said. "What it is, is you wanting to be the one to create the distraction. You want Larson's millions under your belt before the nurses' strike. Huge donation, fine new pavilion, the nurses look petty and the public forgets all about this pesky murder, which has so gotten in the way of your plans. Very inconsiderate of both the killer and the victim, not to think about the good of your hospital before proceeding."

Gordon-Platt drew a long, slow breath. "What I want," she said deliberately, "is for you to stop interfering with my staff. You have no business meddling in this hospital, just as Dr. Chin had no business refusing Mr. Larson's donation. These actions lower both of you in my estimation."

"I don't think I was ever very high there, so I don't care," I said. "And if being more concerned about nurses' salaries and water bills than having a monument to himself lowers your estimation of Elliott, I don't think he'll care either."

"He will if a prospective new employer asks about him."

"Oh. My. God. You're not only threatening to fire him, you'd blackball him?"

"A cooperative attitude is an important factor in hiring decisions. I've been overlooking Dr. Chin's failure to display that attitude for quite some time. Maybe long enough." She sat up, if possible, straighter. "Going forward, this investigation will be handled by the police, and the police alone." She took a pause, looking from me to Bill. "In medicine, an important skill is to be able to separate the relevant from the extraneous. It takes a lot of training and practice to learn to do so. The police, in investigative work, are analogous to doctors. People like you more closely resemble faith healers."

Bill glanced at me. Using his unparalleled ability to know when I was about to detonate, he stood. "Thanks for your time, Dr. Gordon-Platt," he said. If there was a slight sarcastic stress on the "doctor" it was fine with me. I stood, too. Bill said, "We understand your position, though I think you're misguided in taking it. I hope you understand ours. Until our client tells us to stop, we're going to continue doing what we were hired to do." He turned and walked to the door and held it open for me. Just before he followed me through it, he turned back to Gordon-Platt. "And your faith healer analogy is faulty. What we're offering is a second opinion."

CHAPTER TWENTY-NINE

"Why that—!"

"Yes."

"How could—!"

"You're right."

"I'll—"

"You'd better not. It's against the law."

This conversation, me spluttering and Bill filling in the blanks, went on as we waited for the elevator in the pale blue executive suite lobby, which was much calmer than I was.

"And the DeBrengs! Some family. But we knew that. I can't believe this. Cannot believe this."

The elevator came, which was a lucky thing. I decided I didn't want the guys in the basement security room, or wherever these elevator cameras were watched from, to see me explode. I breathed three-counts, in and out, until we reached the ground floor. As soon as we were back in the lobby I took out my phone.

"Who're you calling?" Bill asked.

"I know what we said to that witch. But I have to talk to Elliott."

Two rings, then, "Hey, Lyd. What's up?"

"I need to talk to you."

Immediately into doctor mode, which was the same as big brother mode: "You sound serious. Everyone okay?"

"Everyone but maybe you. Are you home? Can we come up?"

"Sure. I was just about to stop for lunch anyway. I'm putting up bookshelves in Craig's room."

"Lunch!" I checked my watch. It was almost two. "We'll bring the bagels."

"And the lox? And the cream cheese?"

ER doctors worked varying kinds of schedules, depending on the hospital. At River Valley, Elliott had set it up so that his doctors, including himself, regularly worked four ten-hour shifts a week, allowing them, as much as possible, to schedule themselves to accommodate their families, religious holidays, and whatever sidelines they had. Like skydiving. It was one of the reasons his staff loved him. His own schedule sometimes fluctuated, because of the admin work and because he often covered for the other doctors. When he could, he took Sunday, Tuesday, and Wednesday off. Today was Wednesday, and he was home.

Bill and I headed to the Chin-Ling family homestead, a condo in a high-rise a few blocks south and east of the hospital. We stopped on the way and bought bagels, lox, and cream cheese. "Tomatoes," said Bill. "Red onions, and it's no good without capers." So we bought those, too. "And a chocolate babka."

Carrying our bounty, we stepped through the automatic glass doors and past the desk where the doorman knew me. I waved, he waved, and as he called my brother to say we were coming up, the elevator whisked us to the twenty-fourth floor.

"Hey." Elliott was waiting at the open door. He took the bag I was carrying. "What's up?"

"You guys go on," Bill said. "I'll put lunch together. Lydia shouldn't be around the knives anyway."

Elliott raised his eyebrows, then took me out onto the big slate terrace. The view was the same as the hospital's: river, buildings, boats, bridges, sun. The glass-topped table was already set for three.

"Janie's at work?" I asked.

"And the kids are at school. After school Craig has tap and Elaine has basketball. They'll be unhappy they missed you. Unless this is such a long story you'll still be here."

"I don't know." I flopped into one of the cushioned wicker armchairs beyond the table. Elliott took another. The sun glinted off his glasses.

"Bill and I were summoned to see the Wizard of Oz," I said. "It turned out it was really the Wicked Witch of the West."

"Umm . . . could you be more—"

"Elizabeth Gordon-Platt! She called and demanded we come up. She wanted us to drop Jordy's case."

"Oh."

"Don't just give me 'oh.' For one thing, Jordy's just been re-arrested."

"Shit, really? Why?"

"A couple of witnesses say they saw him with Sophia Scott."

"I thought he said he didn't know her."

"He did. And I believe him. I don't know what that's about but I feel like this really isn't the time to drop the case. But."

"But?"

I met his eyes. "She threatened to fire you if we didn't."

My brother put his hand on his chest. "Me? I'm just a little old emergency room doctor. Who'd want to fire me?"

"Don't make jokes. This isn't funny. She meant it. Fire you, and blackball you."

I described our encounter with the stony chief administrator, possibly using more hand-waving and verbal exclamation points than were strictly necessary. As I was winding down, Bill came onto the terrace carrying a tray mounded with the makings of a classic New York Sunday brunch. That it was Wednesday bothered none of us, that's the kind of mavericks we were. Elliott and I helped unload the contents onto the table.

"Wow," Elliott said. "Brings the food, prepares everything, and makes the coffee, too?"

Bill lifted the kettle and a tea canister off the tray. "Plus hot water for tea. Assam, is that right?"

"There may be a place for you on my staff," Elliott said. "They make terrible coffee. May I ask under whom you trained?"

"Lydia Chin. All I want is for good reports about me to get back-channeled to your mother."

Elliott grinned. "I speak well of you at every opportunity."

"How often does she give you one?"

"Never."

We took chairs at the table and were briefly silent while our plates got piled.

"I don't know if you know this," Bill said to Elliott, "but Lydia is always really hungry after a fight."

They both eyed my everything bagel, heaped with cream cheese, lox, tomatoes, onions, capers, and more cream cheese.

Elliott raised his eyebrows. "Uh-oh. Did you forget to tell me you punched her?"

"I don't know why you aren't taking this seriously."

"Actually"—Elliott poured himself a cup of coffee—"I am." He looked out across the river, the view he'd had since Janie had gotten pregnant with Craig and they'd decided to stay in the city and not move to Scarsdale or Port Washington. The downside: no backyard, no bike rides on quiet suburban streets. The upside: New York City. And family, both the Chins and the Lings in Chinatown and elsewhere in the boroughs.

"Could she do it, Ell?" I asked. "Fire you and blackball you?"

He nodded. "If her chief of medicine wanted to keep me, there'd be pushback, but I'm not on his Christmas list, either." He put the coffee down and bit into his bagel.

"Why does she care so much? It's almost like she has something to hide."

"About the murder? I doubt it. I think what you said was right—she wants Larson's donation and she wants it now, before the nurses go out. The longer this investigation is open, the worse the hospital looks. And we're losing money. I told you, canceled surgeries, diverted ambulances. Things like that. The worse River Valley looks, the worse she looks."

"To who?" That probably should have been a *whom*, but Bill knew better than to correct me right now.

"The board. She can always be replaced."

"Is that a real possibility?"

Elliott nodded. "Even without the murder she must have been worried, with the strike looking likely. Anytime a hospital can't come to an agreement with one of the unions and there's a walkout, the board will look seriously at the administration."

"True in any organization," Bill said. "Someone has to get elected to hold the bag."

"Then add a murder because the hospital's security chief was asleep at the switch and you have a ready-made fall woman right there," Elliott said.

"I can't believe this," I said. "I'm really stuck defending her? The murder's not her fault, and neither will the strike be if it happens. We watched the negotiations. A couple of those lawyers aren't negotiating in good faith and that's the nicest thing you can say about them."

"Those lawyers all report to her. As does Quick Draw."

"So the board would fire her because they need a scapegoat so they don't look bad, and she'd fire you to keep that from happening? I thought this was a hospital. I thought everyone was in the business of saving lives, not their own butts."

"'In the business,'" Elliott said. "Start from there."

I took another bite of bagel. Bill was right; I was as hungry as if I'd been sparring at the dojo—or in a real fistfight.

"What would happen?" Bill asked. "If she fired you?"

"I'd find another job."

I swallowed and said, "She'll give you bad references."

"It doesn't matter. Obviously if she fires me, any prospective employer will assume we weren't getting along. They'd take that into account but they'd also look at my resume, my publications, talk to my staff, look at my budgets, my outcomes—no, I'm not worried about getting another job."

"I'm glad someone's not."

"The problem," he said, "is where."

"What do you mean?"

He looked back across the river before he answered. "New York has a finite number of emergency medicine departments and right now they're all run by people happy in their work."

"What are you saying? You'd have to leave?"

He shrugged. "I hear Montana's beautiful. The kids could learn to ride horses."

"Are you insane? You can't. Ma would have a fit. She practically took to her bed when Ted moved to Queens."

"Yeah." He smiled. "I remember when Andrew was living in Hoboken. The first time she went she took her passport. Just in case, she said."

"Elliott, come on. You can't leave New York."

"I'd have to go where the work is."

"What about Janie? Her parents are in Chinatown too. And the kids?"

He met my eyes. "We'd work something out. It would be a big adventure for all of us."

"No. No. Absolutely not. I am not going to let that woman fire you."

"You can't stop her."

"I can quit the case."

"No. No, you can't."

"That's what she wants."

"She won't care about that if I accept Larson's donation."

"What? You can't."

"Of course I can."

"It's too important to you. It's a matter of principle."

"And not being blackmailed off a case is too important to you."

"It isn't blackmail. It's extortion."

Elliott and I stared at each other.

Bill laughed. "My God, you two. Does anyone in the Chin family ever let anyone else win?"

"No!" my brother and I snapped at the same time. We kept the staring going for another few seconds.

Then he cracked up.

I blew on my nails and polished them against my shirt.

Bill poured Elliott and himself more coffee.

"Elliott—" I began.

"Lyd? The guy who's getting left out of the equation here is Jordy. He'll be in prison for decades if they can pin this on him."

"Maybe he did it."

"You think so?"

I bit my lip. "Okay, no. But there are other investigators he could hire."

"Not as good as you guys. And you have contacts now, facts you've gathered. Gut feelings, right? By the time someone else can get up to speed the police will have a long running start."

"They already do."

"All the more important for you to stay on the case."

I slid my gaze from his glinting glasses and looked across the river. "I don't want to make this a problem for you, Ell."

"I appreciate that. Think about it this way, though. If a guy I like—a guy who came to *me* for help—ends up in prison for a crime he didn't commit because you were trying to protect me, that will make a much bigger problem for me than moving to Montana."

"You don't know he'll end up in prison."

"You don't know I'll end up in Montana."

I looked at him, this man who'd taught me to ride a bike but had let me fall so I'd figure out how not to, and then had dried my tears and put a Band-Aid on my knee. This man who'd pushed me out of a plane yesterday morning.

"I hear it's beautiful," I said. "Montana."

Elliott grinned at me and I beamed right back at him. Bill poured more coffee.

"That's what I like to see," Bill said. "Family harmony. Is it okay if I smoke out here?"

"On the ER doctor's terrace? You trying to get me thrown out of the building? Yeah, go ahead."

"You're not going to tell him to stop?" I said as Bill struck a match.

"He's a grown-up. He already knows he has to stop. Besides"—Elliott turned the grin to Bill—"think how happy it would make Ma if it killed you."

Bill took the cigarette from his mouth and looked at it. "That right there is the best argument for quitting I ever heard."

"Whatever works," I said. "Though she'd also have one fewer objection to you if you didn't smoke."

"Increasing the chances of that family harmony thing," said Elliott.

Bill took a long pull and put the cigarette out.

"Well, at least some people around here are interested in family harmony." I sat back with my tea.

"What do you mean?" Elliott asked.

"The DeBrengs. Doctor Senior said yesterday if Jordy didn't do it his way—DeBreng's way—he was on his own. Can you imagine Ma saying that?"

"The part about doing it her way, yes. But leaving you on your own? Not on your life."

"And now according to Gordon-Platt both Senior and Junior personally told her they want this wrapped up fast."

Elliott crossed one ankle over his knee. "Jordy's been a thorn in DeBreng Senior's side for years. Part of the problem is he's twice the guy Bradley is. Twice as smart, twice as . . . human. DeBreng knows it and had Jordy's life all mapped out, from what I hear, except Jordy didn't want that life. Now all DeBreng has left is Bradley. Mediocre in all ways."

"I hate the idea of a mediocre doctor."

"People graduate from medical school with C averages all the time, Lyd. It just doesn't say that on their licenses."

"Thanks, bro. You're cheering me up enormously."

"DeBreng consults on all of Bradley's difficult cases, and 'assists' in surgery sometimes. He was the guiding hand that got Bradley through his boards. Bradley's what DeBreng has left and I'd be surprised if he didn't fight to protect him."

Bill said, "I get the feeling that for both of them, Senior and Junior, it's not beyond the realm of possibility that Jordy did do it."

“I agree,” said Elliott, “and if they think that, it’ll be much better for them if Jordy’s charged, takes a plea, and it’s all over.”

“I don’t get it,” I said. “How’s he protecting Bradley by throwing Jordy to the wolves? What’s he protecting him from besides being embarrassed by his brother yet again?”

“If the investigation’s not stopped here it’ll eventually get to him.”

“To Bradley? Why?”

Elliott looked from me to Bill. “Because he knew her.”

CHAPTER THIRTY

Doctor Bradley DeBreng wasn't happy to see us. But he saw us.

Not that we'd wanted to see him, either, at first. What Elliott had told us was that a few weeks ago, stopping in the place with the cheery yellow walls for a quick cortadito, he'd seen Bradley DeBreng and Sophia Scott leaning toward each other across a Formica table. "Up in the balcony, toward the back. The kind of vibe you don't interrupt." So I'd called Church.

"Jesus Christ," she muttered when she picked up. "What now?"

"Did you know that Jordy Kazarian's brother, Bradley, knew Sophia Scott?"

"Of course I did. Is this news to you? You mean I finally win one?"

I was taken aback, which luckily she couldn't see. "He seems to have known her pretty well."

"Good for him. It's a hospital. Are you surprised the doctors know the nurses?"

"Bradley and Jordan look a lot alike. Your witnesses could be mistaken about which brother they saw."

"How do you know about my witnesses?"

"We work for the lawyer, for Pete's sake. It seems to me—"

"Do you know how tired I am of what seems to you? This witness isn't mistaken."

"How do you know?"

"Next question."

"Did you interview Bradley DeBreng?"

"Of course we did! We really are cops, you know. We interviewed the father, too."

"Separately?" Because if Bradley had anything to hide he'd likely have been more desperate to hide it from his father than from the NYPD.

"Jesus."

"Still—"

"For God's sake. I'd like to play this game with you, Chin, but I have things to do, which I'm guessing you don't. Bradley DeBreng was in surgery all afternoon the day Sophia Scott was killed. And his father was in a committee meeting about some damn thing or other. Happy? Good. Goodbye."

I put the phone back in my pocket. "Alibis," I said to Bill and Elliot. "She knew they knew each other and they both have alibis." To Bill I added, "And she cut me off before I could really get up in her grille about re-arresting Jordy without mentioning it."

"To you?" Elliott said. "Why would she have mentioned it to you?"

"I thought we were secret buddies. I gave her a bunch of useful info. She acted like she was pissed but I thought that was just kind of because she had to. Wrong."

"Senior and Junior both have alibis?" Bill asked. "Did Senior know her too?"

"Church didn't say." I surveyed the lunch debris on Elliott's terrace. "You know what? I want to talk to him anyway."

"Senior?"

"Junior. And then maybe Senior."

So I called Bradley DeBreng's office to make sure the doctor was in. I left no message.

"He's there." I stood.

"You guys go ahead. The least I can do is clean up," Elliott said. "And thanks for lunch. If you need me I'll be here, searching properties in Montana."

◆

"This is a busy practice," Bradley DeBreng said when Bill and I were shown into his office. "I'm seeing you as a courtesy to my brother but I don't have time for nonsense."

The office was part of a ground-floor suite in a medical building on the next block down from River Valley. The suite's waiting room looked out onto the plantings near the sidewalk but the offices were windowless. At least, Bradley's was. Big brown desk, fancy mesh chair, computer monitor, keyboard, mouse on a miniature Persian carpet pad. Mandatory row of thick medical texts standing on the cabinet behind him. I checked out the framed certificates and degrees on the walls. MD from Albany Medical College—Jordy had been at Columbia before he'd changed career tracks—Board Certification, FACS Certificate. That was it. Elliott had a dozen more, from post-docs, fellowships, and a volunteer stint with Doctors Without Borders. Okay, not everyone could be like Elliott. But DeBreng Junior seemed to be hanging on in the medical world by his fingernails.

"We're trying to keep your brother out of prison," I told him as I sat. "I'd think that's worth a few minutes of your time."

"If Jordan's innocent the police investigation will clear him. If he's guilty there's nothing I can do."

"And what if you're guilty?"

He yanked his head back as if he'd smelled something awful. "What?"

"You knew her."

"Sophia Scott? Is that who you mean? So what? She was a nurse at River Valley. Hundreds of people knew her."

"Not all of them were seen in deep discussion with her in that Puerto Rican café a few blocks over a couple of weeks before she was killed. The café not a lot of doctors go to. If you have no time to waste, then maybe don't bother to deny it," I said as he opened his mouth. "We have a witness and I'm sure there are more."

DeBreng Junior flushed. "What's there to deny? We were discussing a patient."

"OB/GYN and Orthopedics share a lot of patients?"

"Sophia was temporarily reassigned."

"I doubt it," Bill said. "She hated being reassigned. And that's a really easy thing to check. You can't do better?"

Before he could try to do better, I said, "And she wasn't the kind of nurse to spend time discussing patients over coffee outside of work. And hey, Dr. B., your face is flushed. Embarrassed much?"

Bradley's jaw muscles clenched. He spoke slowly, as though he were lecturing medical students. "Flushing—dilation of the blood vessels in the skin of the face—can be caused by many strong emotions. Like anger at stupid and insulting questions."

"Listen," I said, "you met with a murder victim not long before she died in a place where you must have thought you wouldn't be seen by anyone who knew you. You had what a witness described as an intense conversation with her there. I'm betting that wasn't the only time or place and if we look we'll find others. We know you have an alibi for the time of the murder and I admit I was only trying to shake you up by saying maybe you did it, but I want to know what you and Sophia

Scott were wrapped up in together and so help me if you don't tell me I'm going to ask your father."

Over many years in this, my chosen profession, I've made some enemies. I've seen people give me looks that clearly said if they could explode me right then, they would. The molten glare coming my way from Dr. Bradley DeBreng's eyes, though, was such next-level hate that it took me a little aback.

"My father has nothing to do with this."

"If we're right," I said, "whatever it is, he doesn't even know about it. But if you don't tell us, he's our next stop."

"Hey," said Bill, "look, if you two were having a thing, nooners, whatever, it's easy to understand. She was hot, no question. Maybe you want Lydia to leave and you can tell me about it?"

"What are you—I'm a married man!"

"And married men never have affairs," I said. "Especially married doctors, and especially not with hot nurses who come on to doctors, so I guess that's that." I stood. "Okay, Bill. Let's try the other Dr. DeBreng."

"Goddamn it. You don't give a damn, do you? Leave me alone!"

"That's not going to work."

"Goddamn you." Bradley's desk phone buzzed. He picked it up and barked, "What?" After a moment, "Well, she'll just have to wait a while longer, won't she?" He slammed the receiver down.

"It's very obnoxious when a doctor keeps his patients waiting," I said. "But yours will be waiting as long as it takes for you to come clean, because"—I dropped back into my chair—"we'll be sitting here until then. Come on, Doctor. We know you didn't kill her and we have clients all the time who're having affairs. We don't judge but we do need to know."

"Having affairs. You people have some goddamn nerve." This time it was I who started to speak and he who cut me off. "There was no affair!

But that won't stop you from ruining my reputation and my marriage if you think that would help Jordan."

"If you—"

"Oh, shut up. I'll tell you. But it has nothing to do with Sophia's murder and if anything I say gets back to my father I just want you to remember he has powerful friends."

The logic of that threat seemed jumbled but Bill and I sat and waited.

"Sophia was on the nurses' negotiating committee. For the new contract."

I nodded. "We knew that."

"Aren't you smart? She was . . ." He trailed off, took a breath.

"She was a management mole," Bill said. "And you were her contact."

DeBreng Junior snapped Bill the same lava-of-loathing look he'd given me before. Bill's impervious to that sort of thing, though, and besides, the look *I* gave Bill was admiring.

"Wow," I said. "I wasn't quite there yet. But it's true, isn't it? She told you what the nurses were thinking. You relayed that to *your* management contact. A game of negotiation telephone. Then management would pull the rug out from under the nurses by offering a mangled version of whatever it was she told you they wanted." I glanced at Bill, then back to Bradley. "Oddly enough, I believe you. You do seem like that kind of guy. So, no affair, okay, fine. Why?"

"Why weren't we having an affair?" He scowled.

"No, I don't care why that. Why were you willing to be the go-between in this sleazy business?"

Bill threw me a look. Okay, I probably should have phrased that more neutrally. Witnesses take it better when you don't sneer at them.

Bradley shook his head. "You asked why Sophia and I were having an 'intense conversation' in a place we weren't likely to be seen. I've told you. I'd like to know who saw us, by the way."

"I'm sure you would. I'd like to know who killed Sophia. Go on."

"I have nothing more to say. That's what we were doing. It's not against the law and as I said—"

"Your dad will sic his powerful friends on us if we open our mouths. You're a piece of work, Doctor. Who was your management contact?"

"Are you serious? I'm not about to betray—"

"God almighty, Scott was betraying the nurses and you were helping her do it," Bill said. "I don't think honor is really on the program here. If the reason wasn't sex it probably has to do with money."

"Dr. DeBreng," I said, "we don't actually give a damn about you. Our concern is keeping your brother out of prison. We don't think he killed Sophia but someone did, over something, and being—and running—a double agent is a dangerous business. Oh, and you have patients waiting." I recrossed my legs.

"Rest assured, if I ever find a way to get back at you for this, I will," Bradley growled. "I passed Sophia's information on to Albert Walsh."

The round bald dweeb? Now, that was a surprise. I'd been expecting to hear "Margaret Weldon."

"And you may not believe me, but what I did was for the good of the hospital. To avoid a strike."

"I don't know about Bill," I said, "but personally, I don't believe you." I looked over at Bill; he was shaking his head. "If that's true, why would your father be upset to hear it? I'd think he'd be proud as punch that you took the initiative."

He flushed again. "My relationship with my father is none of your business. Nothing you asked about is any of your business. I want you out of my office."

"All right, we're going. Although if any of this isn't true, we'll be back."

"If you come here and occupy my office again, I'll have you arrested for restraint of trade."

I stared. Bill laughed.

"Call your waiting patient in," Bill said. "And I hope she's really annoyed."

We stood and left.

CHAPTER THIRTY-ONE

Back on the sidewalk in front of the medical building, Bill grinned and said, "Hey, he really got your goat, huh?"

"The whole herd! Every goat! You remember that giant goat statue we saw on that Route 66 trip? A whole herd of *those* goats! I mean, come on. What he was doing might not be illegal but it was unethical by any standard. Aren't doctors supposed to be ethical?" I stopped. "Though I guess they're supposed to be smart, too. This case is very disillusioning."

"What was it Jordy said? 'Reality's a bummer'? So, what's our next move, boss?"

"How about you be the boss for a while and make the decisions?"

He slid out a cigarette. "Well, if I were doing that, I'd really want to know who these witnesses are, and where they think they saw Jordy with Scott. I'd also want to know—"

He stopped as my phone rang. I lifted it from my pocket. "After this case I'm throwing this thing away. Hey, Juarez, what's up? You on duty already?"

"Came in early, boss. To reconnoiter. I'm not on the clock yet and before I am I have something you want to see."

"I do?"

"Guarantee it. Can you get here soon?"

I glanced at Bill. "We're on the next block. Where do we find you?"

"Meet you in the lobby, like usual."

So five minutes later there we were in the lobby, getting what were now our usual passes from the usual sweet young man.

Juarez, in uniform and with a bulging canvas crossbody bag, badged us into the elevator and down to B3. She led us past the nap room, down the hall past the hookup room, and beyond into one of the branching hallways.

"We were here," I said.

"Right you are, boss. And some of these doors wouldn't open, remember?"

"I do."

"Well, I thought, maybe my basement master key just wasn't high enough on the key ladder. You know? So I borrowed the grandmaster."

"Borrowed?"

She grinned. "Quick Draw really needs to upgrade Security's internal security."

"Are you nuts? You could get canned for something like that."

"Yeah, but then I'd come work for you, so it's all good."

"I—"

"And the grandmaster opened the other three doors. But not this one." She took a small flashlight from her uniform pocket and pointed its powerful beam at the lock on the door we'd stopped at. "I could've gone back for the ggm—the great-grandmaster—but the grandmaster doesn't even fit in here. This one's keyed to a totally different system. So I brought this." With a triumphant smile she reached into her bag and produced a drill.

"You want to drill it out?" Bill asked.

"Hey, I'm Security. Who knows what's going on in there? I'm taking initiative."

"Where did you get that?" I asked. "Does Maintenance also have a problem with internal security?"

"Nah. I borrowed it from the dieners."

"Seriously? Ugh."

"What? They rinsed it off for me." That knowledge didn't make me any less queasy but Juarez positioned the drill just above the keyhole and powered it on. A few seconds of screechy whine and then it abruptly stopped. She tried again. The same thing happened. Juarez gave a sheepish grin. "Sorry, boss. I'm not real handy."

"Me either. Bill is."

"Cool." She handed him the drill.

"Okay, but you have to call me boss, too."

She grinned. "No problem, Boss Two."

He rolled his eyes but took the drill from her, positioned it where she had, just above the keyhole, and clicked it on.

The screechy whine continued but more steadily. Bill leaned into the drill. Juarez hovered nearby, watching. I vaguely wondered what would happen if anyone heard us, but as Juarez said, she was Security, and I was much more interested in the question of why this door down here, deep in the east basement netherworld, wasn't keyed to the hospital system.

Twice Bill stopped and changed drill bits. To Juarez he said, "When you drill out a lock you need to make sure you're straight on, not at an angle. That's pretty much true whenever you drill. In a lock plate, when the drill stops, don't force it, move to a larger bit." Like he was talking to an apprentice. Oh God. She nodded. He clicked the drill on again and leaned in. More whining, and then, with a sudden clonk, the chuck hit the lock plate. "We're through. Got a screwdriver?"

Juarez brought one out of her bag and slapped the handle into his palm as though they were a doctor and nurse in surgery. He gave her back the drill and worked the screwdriver between the door and the jamb. Patiently, he pried.

The door moved. Bill pried some more, then pushed. It opened.

Juarez started into the room but Bill put his hand out to stop her. "Look first," he said. That was the way he always did it: standing in the doorway running his gaze over everything before he stepped inside.

Though "everything" was pretty much nothing. Juarez's flashlight played over a couple of folding chairs and a card table in the center of the room. Steel shelving wrapped around three walls. All the shelves were empty.

Without stepping in, Bill took out his handkerchief and with it felt around the wall beside the door where the switch should be. He found it, flicked it, and the light blasting out from the fluorescent ceiling fixtures almost knocked me down.

"Wow," I said. "What is this, a rogue operating room?"

My question wasn't serious; nothing about the room except the light level said "OR." We stepped in one by one and started to walk around, peering at this and examining that. Whoever had created this room put a lot of effort into installing the new lock, these shelves, and these lights, and an equal amount of work into cleaning it out. It seemed like nothing was left except the odd rubber band or paper clip. Bill ran his hand along the highest shelves; Juarez poked her light into shadowy corners. As the shortest among us I took it upon myself to search under the shelving units.

Virtue is occasionally rewarded.

At first all I saw as I crouched on my elbows and knees was dust. But then my phone flashlight illuminated something else. Squeezing my arm into the darkness under the bottom shelf I grabbed at the something else and pulled it out.

"Hey, you guys," I said, scrambling to my feet. "Look at this."

I was holding a torn, uneven scrap of carboard roughly the size of an index card. Letters, numbers, and part of a picture covered one side. The other was blank.

"Looks like maybe a piece of a box," I said.

Bill took it from me and examined the picture. "I think that's an otoscope head."

"What's an otoscope head?"

"An otoscope is the thing the doctor sticks in your ear. The head is the replaceable part."

I considered. "Couldn't that just mean this room was used as a storeroom? Before the flood?"

"Maybe. But that doesn't explain the lock."

We finished our sweep of the room with no additional finds. Juarez checked her watch. "Forty-five minutes before my shift," she said. "I have to return the tools to the morgue. Want to come?"

Bill grinned. "Dying to."

CHAPTER THIRTY-TWO

Save your life, did it?" Paul asked when, after he and Valerie welcomed us back to the morgue, Juarez handed him his drill.

"I owe you one," she said.

"Trying to be a nice guy. You reap-er what you sow-er."

I said, "We have a couple of questions, if it's okay."

Paul shrugged. "Sure, go ahead. Nothing going on in here. Silent as the tomb."

"But you'd better ask now before things get grim," Valerie said.

Sighing, I took the cardboard scrap from my pocket. "First, do you know what that is? Bill thinks it's an otoscope head."

Valerie looked. "We don't have much use for them down here, but he's dead on."

"Is there a way to tell how old it is, this model?"

Paul leaned over, peering at the scrap. He took it and pushed off from the autopsy table, gliding silently—almost ghostlike, but I'd never tell him that—across the floor on his rolling stool until he stopped at a counter by the wall. He clicked away at a computer keyboard. The screen changed, and changed again, as the rest of us walked over—except Valerie, who slid her stool along the polished vinyl as Paul had.

Paul looked over his shoulder, pointed to the screen, and said, "New. Introduced six months ago. This is the manufacturer's website."

So much for the once-a-storeroom theory.

"What do they cost?" Bill asked.

"Eighty bucks retail."

"Killer price," Valerie stuck in.

"The hospital buys them for a third of that," Paul went on.

"No kidding?" I said.

"Most things your doc uses in the office the hospital buys in the kinds of numbers that get us huge discounts. It's a plot."

"Oh, thank God. I was worried. You hadn't made a joke for the last half dozen sentences."

"Hey, I'm a serious guy. If this is about helping Jordy, I understand it's a grave responsibility."

◆

I called Venturino as soon as we left the morgue, putting her on speaker so Bill and Juarez could hear her too.

"Hey," she said.

"Hey. How do you order supplies?"

"You know, you might have to start paying me as a consultant. Did you enjoy the negotiation videos?"

We crowded the phone in the hallway. "Every bit as good as *Game of Thrones*," I said.

Venturino laughed. "Better, because our negotiations are even bloodier. What do you mean by supplies? How does who order them?"

"Thermometers, scissors, otoscope heads, things you need on your unit. Small stuff. When you need more."

"The nurse supervisor's responsible for keeping track. Something's running low, they send a requisition down to Supplies and Equipment."

"Electronically?" said Bill.

"What do you think, pneumatic tubes? Carrier pigeons?"

Juarez looked at me with raised eyebrows.

"And then?" I asked.

"What you ordered comes up on carts, usually the next day, sometimes the day after, unless it's an emergency. That kind of stuff rarely is, though."

"So it's all routine? And it's the same process for all departments?"

"Why wouldn't it be?"

"I can't imagine. Listen, as long as we're here there's one more thing. An OB/GYN nurse quit the day after Scott was killed. I want to know who he was."

"Ask the supervisor."

"I don't want the supervisor to know I'm asking."

"Oh, shit. Is this going to be trouble?"

"I got the feeling you liked trouble."

"Not the kind other people get me in. What about your secret databases, like where you found me?" Luckily she didn't actually want an answer to that, because I'd have had to admit I'd rather get her in trouble than Linus. She said, "All right, give me some time," and clicked off.

"Wow," said Juarez. "Snarky much?"

"Up until now, mostly with Bill," I said.

He shrugged. Juarez grinned.

"What do the supplies have to do with the nurse who quit?" she asked.

"Nothing."

Juarez knit her brow seriously. "Ask irrelevant questions to throw suspects off. Cool. That woman on the phone, then, she's a suspect? Who was she?"

I laughed. "Calm down. She's not a suspect and the question's not irrelevant. It's just a loose end we need to follow up. Let's focus on the supplies. Because I'm starting to think Sivek wasn't peeping."

She grinned. Then, "Wait, let me! Not peeping. He was—storing stolen supplies in that room and selling them! How'm I doing?"

"You're a natural. And after the murder the east basement suddenly got hot, so he cleaned it out," I said. "But if that's what was going on, how come no one missed the stuff he skimmed?"

Bill squinted up at the ceiling. "The orders come in electronically. I'm thinking out loud here, but I bet it wouldn't be hard to alter them by, say, ten percent. In the Supplies and Equipment department records, not the originals."

"Two sets of books."

"Exactly. The orders logged in from the suppliers would be right. The orders that went to the units would be right."

"And no one compares the two. Sivek skims the ten percent, stores his take in that room, and sells it on eBay!" Juarez said triumphantly.

I said, "Wait. Seriously, eBay?"

Juarez crossed her arms and leaned back against the corridor wall. "When I was first working retail, my manager told us to keep an eye out for smalls. Two kinds of shoplifters, he used to say. One steals things they want. The other steals things they can sell. The first ones, they try to sneak out with a blouse or a pair of shoes, usually they're not hard to spot. The second kind are in it for the money. They go for socks, wallets, makeup, cheap jewelry—not gold or diamonds, just junk, but a lot of it. Some of those kind, they come in like customers. Some of them work at the store—on the floor, in the stockrooms, on the delivery trucks."

"And they sell what they steal on eBay?"

"Showed us a case study. A different, bigger store, but the same idea. Read it from cover to cover. The next week I caught a girl working the Clinique counter with two dozen lipsticks in her purse. She had an eBay store. Makeup, hair clips, combs, gloves, socks."

Bill laughed. "Damn. Fences in the backrooms of bars all over the world must be crying in their beer right now."

"And you think this could work with medical supplies?" I asked.

"You're a small practice," said Juarez, straightening up off the wall. "Maybe you go through two dozen pairs of scissors, four dozen suture kits a year. You look to see where you can get your best price. Google sends you to eBay. MedSupply, some store with a name like that. Looks legit, merch arrives, it's good, what's the problem?"

I looked at both of them. "How much do we think this scheme would be worth?"

"Hundreds of thousands," Bill said. "Whatever percentage of the budget Sivek felt safe skimming. Not things anyone keeps a close eye on, but like Juarez says, scissors and suture kits, and I bet stuff like gauze, boxes of Band-Aids, Q-tips, mouthwash. A quiet, steady stream diverted off a huge river of a budget."

Juarez rolled her eyes. "I like the dead jokes better."

"Metaphors-R-Bill," I said to her. I looked at Bill, and then back to her. "And something else," I said carefully.

"Something else, other products in the stream?" It took a moment. Then her mouth dropped open. "No! Not products. Day-um. Oh, day-um. Quick Draw. That's what you're saying, right? My boss was in the protection racket."

"Do not," I said, "do *not* do anything rash."

"Rash? No, for real—Quick Draw was shaking Sivek down for hush money. Right? Leo and Delgado and Quick Draw's other favorite guys were shaking *him* down to look the other way. Right? That's why he gave them such great references that they could get new jobs right away, guys he supposedly canned. Right? And that SOB Quick Draw docks me if I get a report in late! That mother! I should—"

"But you won't."

"Why won't I?"

"Because," Bill said, looking at me, "we're going to give this to Church."

I rolled my eyes the way Juarez had. "You know what, between calling Church and listening to dead jokes, I like the dead jokes better, too." I took out my phone.

"What?" Church said when she answered.

"You arrested my client an hour after we talked without giving me any clue you had that in mind."

"You've got to be kidding."

"He still says he didn't know her."

"To me too. Except I have witnesses."

"They're mistaking him for his brother. Who did know her."

"Not these witnesses. Is that it?"

"No. There's a room in the basement, in the no-go zone. It had a lock not keyed to the hospital system. We think it was a stolen-supplies storage room and we think it was that biomed tech, Barry Sivek, who stole the supplies."

"What the hell are you talking about?"

I detailed for her our basement expedition, leaving Juarez and the dieners out of it. "We think that's what Sivek was doing down there when Security found him. Not peeping, clearing out his stuff. We think the east basement got too hot with you guys crawling all over it after the murder, and obviously Security is now patrolling there. He may have been visiting his storeroom to make sure there was nothing left."

A long silence.

"What you guys did, that's a B&E if I ever heard one."

"You want to arrest me?"

"Actually, I do. But I'm busy."

"Fine. If it really was Sivek down there moving those goods—"

"And Scott ever saw him there, it's another fucking motive, yes."

"And at the least, another possible witness. Plus . . ."

"What the fuck is that, a dramatic pause? Plus what?"

"Plus, we think the security chief, McGraw, we think he was providing protection."

"The hell does that mean?"

"He knew what Sivek was doing. He let it go on for a percentage of the take."

"That—He's an ex-cop. Are you sure about that? How do you know?"

"Ask him," I said shortly.

"Oh, I will. I will, goddamn you. Does he know he's in your sights?"

"No. You can pretend you thought this up all by yourself."

"Making enemies, is that your hobby? And where do I find Sivek, can you tell me that? Do you have him wrapped in a pretty package with a bow on it?"

"No. I mean, I can give you his address, but aren't you already looking for him?"

"Yeah, and a fat lot of good it's doing. The guy's nowhere."

"He has to be somewhere."

"You got any bright ideas?"

"You know," I said, "it's almost like what you want is to close this case, not to solve it."

She didn't even say goodbye.

CHAPTER THIRTY-THREE

I know, I know," I said to Bill and Juarez as we headed to the elevator to lift us off the Pathology floor. "There's a difference between failing to charm someone and pissing them off. I can't help it with her. What are you grinning about?"

"I'm thinking what a good thing it is you're not a cop," Bill said. "All the politics. You'd have been canned and you'd have to go to work as a sleazy private eye."

I considered. "Well, at least Darius Georges would like me better."

"Who's Darius Georges?" Juarez asked.

"A private eye we just met."

"Sleazy?"

"God no. Sharkskin-suit-straight-arrow-boring corporate."

"Does he need an apprentice?"

I raised my eyebrows. "Does he sound like your type?"

"I dunno. Might be interesting, working corporate. And speaking of work, I have to go do that, so see you later, Boss and Boss Two." She got off at the Security floor, waving goodbye.

"See?" I said to Bill. "Just give her that corner office. So, what now?" We stepped out into the lobby.

"I'm the boss again?"

"You got the most votes."

"I'm pretty sure Juarez didn't vote for me."

"But I did."

"And I voted for you. So you win."

"Lose, you mean. All right, as boss, it seems to me we're at a crossroads. We can say 'okay, it's time to step back' and let Church take up Sivek and McGraw. Once she figures out which one is guilty, or both of them, Jordy's free, we send Cohen our bill, and we all go home."

"You really think that'll happen?"

"Not on your life. First, I'm not sure how committed Church is to this Sivek-McGraw angle. Second, they may actually not be guilty. In that case the waters are nicely muddied but Jordy's still in jail."

"And third," Bill said, "Cohen hired us to 'find out what happened.' Isn't that what she said? All this muddying the waters is great, but I don't have much faith in Church, either."

"So you think we should just keep going?"

"I do."

"Me too."

"Good. In that case"—he took out his phone—"let's try this." Tapping buttons, he gestured me over to a secluded corner of the seating area. We sat, he put the phone on speaker, and one receptionist and two minutes later we heard "Ronald Scott."

"Bill Smith, Dr. Scott. Thanks for taking my call."

"You're a private investigator? This is about Sophia? I already told the police, we haven't spoken in years. Not since the divorce."

"I'm just looking for a little background. Different from what the police wanted, maybe. My partner is also on this call, by the way. Lydia Chin."

"Hi, Dr. Scott," I said, leaning toward the phone. "We won't take much of your time." Plus, the police didn't share your conversation, I didn't say.

"Who are you working for?"

"The lawyer for the man the police are looking at," Bill said. "Just making sure all the bases are covered."

"Did he kill her?"

"We don't think so."

A brief pause. Then, "All right, well, go ahead."

Bill said, "You say you and your ex-wife hadn't spoken in years. Any particular reason?"

"Nothing to talk about. No kids, no common property. When we split, I still had med school debt and she was free and clear. Med school debt is a bear but the silver lining was it meant no issues about alimony. I moved back out to Seattle, she stayed in New York, and there was nothing more to say."

"If you hadn't been in debt, you think she'd have asked for alimony?"

"No question. She talked to a lawyer before we split—before I even knew we were splitting—to see if there was any way at all she could claim to have supported me while I was in school. But she hadn't and there was no way to fudge it."

"She'd decided to break up the marriage before you did?"

"She was having an affair."

"Who with?" I asked. Oops, that would be a "whom."

"Another doctor. I forget his name and it didn't last." He sighed. "Listen, Sophia is—was, I guess—a user. She'd just left home when we met and she latched onto me because I was older, knew the ropes, knew how to show her a good time. I thought we had something real. But I was a stepping-stone. After a couple of years she didn't need me anymore."

"Meaning?" Bill asked. Actually what he meant was pretty clear but the longer a witness talks the more you can learn.

"I'm a pediatrician," said Scott. "We're not at the top of the income pyramid and she knew I wanted to come back here eventually and work at Indian Health. She was from the Midwest, Chicago suburbs. We met in Florida, came to New York together, and as soon as she got her New York legs under her she went looking for someone higher on the food chain. I'm pretty sure the reason that first affair didn't last was because she found someone else even higher up. By then I was out of it and wishing I'd paid attention at the beginning."

"To what?"

"Lots of things. You ever in a relationship you knew almost from the start was a bad idea?"

"Yes."

I looked at Bill when he said that but he just shrugged.

"There are always signs," Scott said. "But you don't pay attention except looking back."

"Can you give us an example?"

He was silent for a moment. "In high school Sophia had been arrested. You know about that?"

We did, but Bill said, "Tell us."

"She and two other girls, and a guy. A drug arrest, just weed, but the girls were minors. The boy was nineteen. He and Sophia were an item. The girls got off with warnings and the boy spent a year behind bars for supplying the drugs." We knew all that, but then came the part we hadn't known. "But he wasn't the only one selling. He was Sophia's wholesaler. She was dealing to the kids in her school."

"Damn," Bill said.

I glanced at Bill, and said to Dr. Scott, "Is that what you wish you'd paid attention to? That she dealt drugs?"

"No, no, it's not that. Sophia was always good at learning from other people's mistakes. By the time she came to New York she'd given that up."

"Selling, or using?"

"Both."

Bill said, "You know she OD'd on fentanyl and heroin? That she died with a needle in her arm?"

"The police told me. But that's not Sophia. If she used anything harder than weed it would be coke, MDMA, meth. Stimulants, not narcotics. It's much more likely, if that's how she died, that someone killed her."

"What did you mean, then?" I asked. "When you said you wished you'd paid attention? To what?"

"Not that she'd been arrested or even that she'd used drugs or sold them. It was the way she told me. The fact that she told me at all. She'd been seventeen, the charges were dropped. There was no way I'd ever have found out and no reason to tell me. But she was so pleased with herself for getting the boyfriend to take the rap." A heavy sigh. "Listen, it might have worked out that way anyway, an older Black boy, three blonde high school girls, Chicago suburbs. They might not have believed the boy if he said it wasn't him. That's the world we live in. But for Sophia to use that . . . She told him if *she* confessed, they'd think she was just trying to protect him and they'd throw the book at him for trying to let his underage White girlfriend take the fall. But if *he* confessed, they'd cut him a deal. Plus, his father was a cop. That would help, she said."

"Doesn't look like it did," Bill said.

"The DA was looking at his reelection prospects. Plus the father was a cop in Chicago. The police department in the White-flight suburb where they were arrested couldn't have cared less. But understand, it's not that any of this surprised me. The kid would've gone to jail whether or not Sophia went too. But it's how Sophia told me. She was—gloating, that's the word. Not a moment of regret, no guilt. She even promised she'd wait for him."

"But she didn't."

"Are you kidding? She split for nursing school in Florida two days after graduation."

"That's where you met?"

He gave a rueful laugh. "Gainesville. I was doing my residency. I'd never known anyone like her. She just did whatever she wanted and never looked back. I was—well, now I'd tell you I was infatuated, but then, hell, I was head over heels. We were married within six months." A brief silence. "She told me the arrest story soon after we got to New York. That was the first of those signs, anyway the first I noticed. I said I thought what she'd done was wrong but she asked me if I'd rather *she'd* spent the year in prison and not been able to be a nurse and we'd never have met. Things . . . went on from there. With Sophia, they usually did."

This time what he meant was so clear neither of us asked him to elaborate.

"She never married again, did she?" he suddenly asked.

"No."

"Sure. Why would she? Easier to get what you want and move on if you're not attached. I'm a little sorry she kept my name, but I guess that's one more thing she was able to use. Easier than Kanellopolous. Look, I need to get back to work. Anything else I can help you with?"

Bill looked at me. He said, "Just, is there anyone you can think of who might have wanted to do something like this?"

"Kill Sophia? I've been out of her life for a long time but I'd suggest you look at whatever string of ex-boyfriends she'd been trailing behind her lately. Or anyone else, a colleague, another nurse, who she might have taken advantage of. Not everyone takes being used quite as charitably as the high school boyfriend did."

◆

"I hope you got something out of that that I missed," I said when Bill cut the call. "It seems to me he just underlined what everyone's been saying about her."

Bill said, "No, I agree. Let's get out of here."

"You want a cigarette, right?"

"And a little action."

I was freezing again so I didn't argue, but once we were through the revolving doors and into the blessed smelly soggy New York August heat, I asked, "What action, exactly? It being much too early to call it quits for the evening and go home."

He turned to stare at me. "Seriously? That's what you thought of when I said 'action'? This case is doing wonders for you. No, we can save that for later. I want to take a look at Barry Sivek's place."

"Where he isn't, along with all the other places he isn't?"

"Not knowing where a man is, to the place where he once was, one turns in hope."

"Yoda?"

"PI Handbook, 1895 edition, written by Sherlock Holmes."

"You're lying."

"Yes." He struck a match.

The address Trella had given us for Sivek was walking distance from the hospital. River Valley Downstate was in an interesting neighborhood; generally speaking, the farther south you went, the more expensive real estate got. North was East Harlem, tenaciously resisting gentrification with more muscle than its western counterpart. Central Park was a few blocks from River Valley's west flank, and those blocks between the hospital and the park were mostly townhouses and condos, golden real estate for finance bros, old money, and doctors and administrators who wanted, and could afford, both park and hospital proximity. Directly east of the hospital was the Upper East Side, but not the super-rich, high-class part, just the part normal people can barely afford like most of Manhattan these days. I thought we'd be heading that way, because there were still apartment bargains to be found, but I was surprised to find Sivek's building just a block east and nine blocks south.

The address turned out to be an elegant side-street brownstone, built as a townhouse a hundred years ago. It had probably been divided into apartments, and if we got to the door we'd know, but right now we couldn't get any closer, because there was another surprise. The street was blocked by NYPD emergency vehicles including an EMS ambulance, into which a gurney with a body bag was being loaded.

"Stay or go?" I asked Bill as we stood across the street watching a couple of Tyvek-suited crime scene techs issue out the front door. "Could be coincidence."

"Uh-huh," Bill said. "Except look out, here comes Church."

CHAPTER THIRTY-FOUR

It was indeed Detective Helena Church, bearing down on us like a hawk on squirrels. There were no trees close enough to run up, so we stood our ground.

"Jesus," she said when she reached our side of the street. "The bad two cents."

"That's a joke," I said. "Be careful or I'll start to think you're human."

"No such luck. What the hell are you two doing here?"

"We came to talk to that tech. Barry Sivek."

"You just happened to turn up at this very moment? You want to tell me you didn't know?"

"We still don't know. What happened?"

She narrowed her eyes at me, then tilted her head toward the building. "The tech. Barry Sivek. He's dead."

I said nothing while Bill said, "Crap. When and how?"

Church pushed her unkempt hair back off her forehead. I thought she might not answer, but she said, "Sometime last night, single bullet to the gut."

"Signs of a struggle?"

"Billboards. His place was a wreck."

"So the killer might have been a wreck when he left."

"Oh my God, a genius."

"Security here?" I asked.

This time she actually didn't answer. A long stare, and then she said, "I need to talk to you two."

I spread my hands. "We're here."

"Yeah, well, let's not be. I don't get into some air conditioning soon, I'm going to bite someone's head off."

I was pretty sure she'd do that anyway, but I didn't say so, in case she decided to do it right then.

"Wait here," Church commanded. She waved her arm in a couple of broad arcs as she went back across the street, calling, "Ahn!" A broad-shouldered Asian man in a sharp gray suit spoke briefly to the two uniforms he was standing with and started across, meeting her halfway. They conferred, she gestured to us, he raised his eyebrows, they conferred some more, and they parted again.

Church came back to our side of the street, jerked her thumb east and kept going without speaking or stopping. We could've turned tail and run the other way, as any sensible person might have done, but no one's ever accused me of good sense. Bill and I fell in behind her. She stalked on until she hit Third Avenue. Stopping, she wiped her forehead, looked around and said, "Thank God," pointing to a mid-block pizzeria. She marched down there and yanked the door open. A blast of cold air escaped like it knew who she was. We were right behind her as she stomped inside.

Dropping heavily onto the vinyl seat of a tubular-frame café chair, Church said to Bill, "Get me an iced coffee. Black. Large." Without a word—but with a tiny smile only I saw—he went to do that.

"They call this air conditioning?" she said. "I ought to take them up for fraud." She slipped her phone from her blazer pocket and scrolled through it. I bit my tongue and waited. It seemed plenty cool in the pizzeria to me, though I myself was beginning to get hot.

Bill came back with two black iced coffees, a hot tea, and a plate of cannoli. One side of Church's mouth screwed up. "Won't work." She picked up a chocolate cannoli.

"What won't?" Bill asked as he sat.

She gestured with the pastry she'd just taken a bite of. "This shit. I haven't been nice to anyone since 1998." She put the cannoli down and pulled a napkin from the dispenser on the table. "But I clear cases." Wiping her fingers, she muttered, "Fucking Ahn."

"I'm sorry, fucking what?" Bill said.

"Hyo-sung Ahn. That was him." She nodded vaguely in the direction of Sivek's building. "Detective from the one-nine. He caught the case because this is his lah-di-dah precinct. Silk stockings and all that shit. I'm from the two-three, up there where the hospital is, where we have real crime."

Without pointing out that a bullet in the gut in a wrecked apartment fit the definition of real crime, I said, "Your border's Ninety-Sixth Street?"

"God, the knowledge on display here." She slugged some coffee. "So the Sivek homicide is Ahn's. I'm only here because my lieutenant mentioned it at the briefing. That's SOP with homicides in adjacent precincts. But it made me sit up. Because unless this is the world's biggest coincidence, kind of like you two showing up here, any asshole can see it's connected to my case." She took another gulp of her coffee. "Jesus, that's foul." Bill shrugged as Church gave him a glare that said since he was the one who'd brought the coffee its quality was his responsibility. "Now, I hate this shit." I thought she meant the coffee, but she went on. "Because for my case, the dead nurse, I have a guy behind bars with witnesses"—Bill opened his mouth but she held up her hand—"and all the shit I need. The DA's about to charge him and bingo, Church clears another one. This time, one the brass cares about, for whatever stupid reason brass have for caring about shit. Once the lawyers start crapping around in court, maybe they convict, maybe not, but it's not my problem. Once he gets charged, I'm done." With claps she dusted Jordy off her hands. "But now there's all this other crap floating around. Another related homicide. Stolen supplies. A security chief who was maybe in on the game. And you two. Every time you call me everything that's neat and squared away blows up. I know you think Kazarian didn't fucking do it but I don't even want to talk about him. I want to know what else is going on up there. In the hospital, in *my* precinct. Everything you masterminds think connects to my case."

Scowling from one of us to the other, she bit into her cannoli.

"Can we do the tit for tat part first?" I asked, trying not to be impressed that anyone could eat a cannoli through a scowl.

"What the hell?"

"Before we talk about all the other things, can you give us the details on what happened to Sivek?"

She swallowed the cannoli bite. "Oh, why not?" She shrugged. "Ahn tells me he'll liaise but he's not turning the case over *until* the forensic evidence is all in and *unless* it points to Kazarian. That's a pain in the ass but if it means you'll start calling him and pissing him off instead of me it's all good. What do you want to know?"

I looked at Bill.

"Security at the building?" He repeated my question from before.

Church shook her head. "Four-unit co-op, no doorman, not even a damn camera."

"Only four units?" I said. "Sivek owned a floor-through co-op on the Upper East Side?"

Church shook her head. "Rental."

"Oh."

"Don't 'oh.' Five grand a month. Two bedrooms, fireplace, roof terrace, the whole nine yards."

"Oh."

"Impressive for a biomed tech making around ninety a year, wouldn't you say?" Church sipped her bad coffee.

"That's what Sivek was making?"

"What he was actually making is Ahn's department. Ninety is the average senior biomed tech salary in New York City. I looked it up."

"So he was living larger than you might expect," Bill said.

"Damn right he was. And you geniuses think it's because he was black-marketing hospital supplies, am I right?"

"He clearly had money coming from somewhere," I said.

"Maybe he had a rich uncle. Or a sugar daddy." She looked at my face. "Yeah, me either. Let's say you're right. Ahn's stuck with following that up. What I want to know is how does it tie in to my dead nurse?"

I started to tell her we weren't sure yet but it turned out to be a rhetorical question.

"Here's what I think," Church said. "Being as Sivek was down there in the basement all the time, he clocked Kazarian killing her. Or maybe just Kazarian thought he did. So Kazarian came over here and killed him."

"Jordy Kazarian's back in jail," I pointed out.

"Nice try, but that's today and Sivek's been dead since last night."

"Haven't you had Jordy under surveillance, though?"

Church laughed out loud. "Damn, that's cute. You serious? My lieutenant would lock me in a rubber room if I asked for that. I wouldn't do it even if we could afford it because Kazarian would sue the department and my ass personally for harassment. You can't just sic surveillance on a guy out on a misdemeanor. Nice if you could, maybe, especially when that misdemeanor was just a lawyer's bullshit trick, but no."

So much for Juanita Cohen's warning to Jordy. I hoped he'd believed it, anyway. And had had friends over and had ordered from DoorDash last night.

"So," Church said, taking another long pull on her coffee. "Change my mind."

Okay, why not try? "McGraw would've had as strong a motive for killing Scott as Sivek had," I started, "if she'd found out about him being in on the stolen supplies. He'd have a pretty strong one for killing Sivek, too."

"McGraw was on duty when Scott was killed. I don't know where he was last night but if he has no alibi, that puts him on equal footing with Kazarian, but no worse."

I guessed Jordy hadn't gotten quesadillas delivered last night.

"And," she added snidely, "I don't have a witness who says they ever saw them together. Scott and McGraw," she added, in case we'd missed her point.

"Yeah, okay," said Bill, probably in response to the steam coming out of my ears. "Leaving that aside, Sophia Scott was a management mole."

"So who does that mean killed her?" Church asked.

"A nurse who found out?"

Even as he said it, I heard Venturino: *We bust our humps to save lives every goddamn minute of every goddamn day. We don't kill people.*

"Ah, you see, but all the BS Kazarian's lawyer was talking about, the knot that was wrong, the needle that was wrong—a nurse would know the right way to do those things just like a diener would."

"A nurse deliberately trying to make it look like it wasn't a nurse?"

"A diener deliberately trying to make it look like it wasn't a diener? Anyway, you have a name for me? A nurse suspect? Yeah, yeah, I'll interview the committee members, but you know it's a goddamn waste of time that's going nowhere. Next."

I met Bill's eyes. His look said he knew what I was thinking and it was up to me. I considered briefly. I wasn't scared of DeBreng Senior but DeBreng Junior obviously was and though I didn't like him even a little, I had no real reason to screw him over.

Except, I decided, to keep his brother out of prison.

"Scott's management contact was Bradley DeBreng."

After a moment a smile broke out on Church's face. Probably it had gotten lost on its way to someone else's. "No shit? Kazarian's brother?" Then the smile realized where it was and vanished. Church said, "Wait, you're saying DeBreng was a contract negotiator for management? The doctors do that shit?"

"No. He was the handler. *His* contact on the management negotiating team was a lawyer called Albert Walsh." Silently I added, *The Dweeb.*

Church looked into space while she drank more coffee. She said, "Well, this is interesting, but I don't think I care who DeBreng's contact was. I'm not surprised management was pulling dirty tricks—you should see any NYPD negotiations with the city. Running a mole might be against some labor law or other but that's not my lane. I still don't see any motive in it for someone else killing Scott. DeBreng being Scott's contact might give Kazarian a motive, though."

"How?"

"I don't know. Protecting his brother?"

"From what?"

"Looking sleazy?"

"To whom? Besides, they hate each other."

"People say that. But blood's thicker and all that shit."

I shook my head and reached for a cannoli of my own.

"Well," Bill said as I bit into it, "how about an old boyfriend, then? Maybe someone she dumped? We talked to the ex. He says she was a user. Not drugs, people."

"I talked to him, too. Sounded pretty bitter. If he hadn't been able to prove he was in Seattle at the time, I might suspect him. Did he give you any names, guys she was seeing?"

"No."

"I couldn't find any either."

"That doesn't mean there weren't any."

"No, it doesn't." Church finished up her coffee. She looked from me to Bill. "What she said"—she pointed the empty cup at me—"that I'd rather close this case than solve it, that's not really true. But see, we're looking at it from different angles. From mine, I have a viable suspect with a shit-ton of evidence pointing to him. From yours, your job is to muddy the waters around that suspect." Once again she held up her hand to ward off objections, and since we'd used the same phrase ourselves we probably didn't have any right to object anyway. "Perfectly understandable. But until I have a quarter of the evidence against anyone else that I have against Kazarian, I'm not running around on any wild goose chases. Capeesh?"

"The evidence," I said. "Your witnesses who claim to have seen Jordy with Scott—how can they be sure? Jordy and Bradley DeBreng look so much alike. And Bradley admits he knew Scott. They can be hard to tell apart."

"Not in this case."

"Who are these witnesses?"

"Who's your mama?" This was delivered with a raised-eyebrow stare.

My mama could take you, I thought.

"All right," said Bill, employing that sixth sense. "What about Calypso?"

Church turned to Bill. "What about him?"

"Oh, come on."

"Yeah, fine. I haven't found him."

"Whoever he is, he might not be a witness—he could be the killer. Scott could've been in the basement to meet him."

"And coming up on the rail, a dark horse! Calypso, running at six hundred to one! Damn, you people will try anything, won't you?"

"It's not unreasonable," I protested.

"I suppose not. We'll keep looking, and when we find him, we'll ask. Though tell me this—if it was him, why did he stage the killing in the hallway right outside the nap room when he had the hookup room reserved? I think it's much more likely he met his squeeze, had his afternooner, and tiptoed away before anything went down."

"You also think it's likely Jordy did it."

"Yeah, I do."

Church popped the last of her cannoli in her mouth, and when it was finished she wiped her hands on a napkin and said, "So what else?"

"What else what?"

"This is your last chance. What else is going on at the hospital that you want me to think has something to do with this case?"

"Well, did you talk to Darius Georges at The Michael Group? About the background checks?"

"He had no problem admitting the hospital's law department asked for them."

"He had a problem admitting it to us."

"Cops one, PIs zero." Another smile, this one tight and smug.

"We think the hospital used something they found in those backgrounds to blackmail one of the nurses off the negotiating team."

A brief, considering silence as Church stared at the ceiling again. "If they did, it sucks but it might not even be illegal, and if it is, it's labor law again. How is it related to my homicide?"

An answer, outlandish but not impossible, popped into my head. I looked at Church's face, which managed to be both pugnacious and exhausted. I imagined her scornful response if I told her what I was thinking, and I imagined myself at a loss to respond to that response because the outlandish idea was based on nothing solid, and I imagined her snootiness at my non-response, and I said, "I don't know."

She narrowed her eyes, as though she knew I was thinking something I wasn't saying. "Yeah, well, you figure it out and give me a buzz. Until then, go bother Ahn and leave me the fuck alone." Helena Church stood and ended the conversation exactly as she had the last time. "Thanks for the coffee," she said while she yanked the door open and stalked out into the late afternoon heat.

CHAPTER THIRTY-FIVE

"Hey," I said to Bill as I stared at the door Detective Helena Church had just let close behind her. "You almost charmed her. In fact that may be as close as anyone's come since—what did she say? 1998?"

"Something's seriously wrong with a person who can be charmed by me and not by you."

"You're the one who said it." I finished my tea, now long cold.

"And you're the one who didn't say anything about whatever brilliant idea you just had while we were talking to her."

I stared at him. "Oh my God. It was that obvious?"

"Sorry."

I shook my head. "I'm slipping. It's about Bacay. We don't know what they had on him, but what if whatever it was was enough to get him to kill Scott for them?"

"That would have to be something pretty goddamn big. And who's 'them'? And why Scott?"

"All good questions. And I can only think of one person who might be able to answer them."

So we headed back to the hospital.

As we walked I called the ICU and asked for Alon Bacay. A woman told me to hold on and she'd get him. I hung up; all I'd needed to know was whether he was there. He must be working the same hours as Venturino, which meant his shift was nearly done.

When we got to the hospital Bill went up to Intensive Care while I waited in the lobby in case Bill somehow missed Bacay. We were gambling he wouldn't linger on the unit or in the locker room, or slip out the back, but as backup we had his home address, too, and Linus's assurance that he lived a quiet life. We'd both seen him on video but he'd only spoken to us on the phone, so when one of the elevators opened and a stream of people flowed out, I wasn't surprised to see both Bacay, looking oblivious, and Bill, looking preoccupied, among them.

We trailed him at a discreet distance until we were two blocks from the hospital. He was headed for the subway but before he could go down the steps we pincered him. "Mr. Bacay?" I said. "Can we talk for just a minute?"

His head snapped around. "What? Who are you?"

"We're private investigators, working for—"

"That guy they arrested for killing Sophia. You called before. I told you I don't want to talk to you."

He tried to brush past me but Bill blocked him.

"Right here," I said, pointing to the park across the street. "In public. Just a few minutes. Nothing to worry about."

He sneered. "You think I'm afraid of you?"

I said, "I think you're afraid of something. I'm sorry but we really need to know what it is."

"It's none of your business."

"Jordy Kazarian is in jail."

"I don't know him."

"Do you know I'm Elliott Chin's sister?"

He took a longer look at me. "Dr. Chin from Emergency?"

"The hospital thinks our investigation is disruptive. They threatened to fire my brother if we don't drop it. I told him. He said to keep going. Because both Jordy and Sophia Scott deserve justice." I paused, glanced toward the park, and said, "Just a few minutes."

Bacay muttered, "Pakshet." He nodded and we followed him across the street to the park.

We found an empty bench close to the gate; I had a feeling he'd be more comfortable if he felt like he could bolt at any time. I sat next to him and Bill next to me, so Bacay wouldn't feel boxed in. Bacay leaned forward, forearms on knees. He was a handsome man, short and sharp like a penknife. Right now he was practically vibrating. With anger? Worry? Unspent energy? After a moment he straightened up and snapped, "All right, what?"

"You were blackmailed into leaving the nurses' negotiating committee," I said.

He shook his head. "I just need a break."

"You don't even sound like you want me to believe that."

He didn't answer, but his dark look told me he was seething.

"Try this," said Bill, leaning back and looking into space. "Say a gay man on an H-1B visa is working on getting US citizenship."

Bacay cut his eyes to Bill.

"He marries another man from his home country," Bill went on, seeming unperturbed by Bacay's radiating anger. "They keep it quiet because it's not safe for the one who's still back home, not safe to be married to a man, not really even safe to be out. The one who's here will apply to bring the husband over as soon as he's a citizen, maybe six months from now. But to stay here and see the citizenship process through, he has to stay employed. If he loses his job and can't get another, he not only can't become a citizen, he might have to go back. That would put both him and his husband in a dangerous position."

Still nothing from Bacay.

"The person at the hospital who threatened to fire my brother also threatened to blackball him," I said. "To keep him from getting another job."

Bacay looked down at the asphalt again. He clamped his jaw shut and I had to wonder if he'd actually be able to keep himself from exploding. Between clenched teeth he said, "Putang ina mo."

Bill answered, "Tayo o sila?"

Bacay looked up, startled. He said, "Sila. Them. Do you speak Tagalog?" He included me in the wave of his hand.

"I do, some," Bill said. "We lived in Manila when I was a kid."

"I don't," I said. "So whatever we're talking about here, can we do it in English?"

Three young boys came charging into the park laughing and raced each other to the basketball court. Bacay watched them shooting, dribbling, taking their measure against each other. Quietly, he said, "How do you know?"

"About your marriage?" I said. "We're investigators. It's what we do. It's what the company the hospital hired does, too. The Michael Group. Heard of them?"

"No."

"They've heard of you. They ran background checks on all the committee members."

"I'll bet they were really happy to find something they could use against you," Bill said. "We watched some of those negotiating session videos. You were a pain in their puwit."

Bacay smiled slightly. He lost the smile and waited some more. Finally, looking at neither of us, he spoke. "It's right, what you said. If I don't quit the committee they're going to fire me and give me bad references. If I can't get a job, I'll have to go back home. It will be the end of a dream for Carlos and me." After another pause he said, "They also say I can't tell anyone."

"Of course they did. What else did they say?" Bill asked.

Now Bacay turned to Bill. "About what?"

"Maybe about Sophia Scott?"

When Bill said that, I held my breath.

Bacay's expression didn't change. "Nothing. Do you mean, did they tell me what they found out about her? No, why will they?"

As Bacay looked at Bill I looked at him. If this was an acting job it was a good one. I didn't think it was, though. So much for my inspiration.

"Who's 'they'?" I asked.

"They?"

"The person who talked to you. Who told you to quit the committee." He hesitated, so I added, "We'll keep it to ourselves."

While we waited for Bacay to decide whether to tell us, I reflected. I'd love to hear it had been Darius Georges, with his holier-than-thou sneering, but I doubted he'd go so far as to personally strong-arm for a client. It might be one of his underlings from a lower floor, though. My other favorite was Elizabeth Gordon-Platt. It was unlikely that she'd deign to talk to a mere nurse, but on the other hand the blackmail-and-blackball tactic was hers, and she'd attended at least one negotiating session, so she knew that as a negotiator there was nothing mere about Alon Bacay. I was prepared to offer her name but before I spoke Bacay said, "Margaret Weldon. Puta."

That was a word I didn't need translated. "Weldon? Did she speak to you herself, or did she use a go-between?"

"Herself. After a negotiating session. She stops me and says she will buy me a drink, we can talk, it will be informal, just the two of us. I tell her I don't drink. She says, meet her anyway, we'll have coffee. She tells me where and when. I understand she's not saying 'please' even when she's saying 'please.' I go and she tells me she knows the status of my citizenship application and she knows about Carlos. She says congratulations on my marriage." He paused, and spat, "Demonya yang Weldon na yan!"

I didn't know those words but nothing could have been clearer than their meaning.

"It was secret, my marriage. We don't tell anyone, to keep Carlos safe. How does she find out? And then she says bringing my husband here where we'll both be safe is the most important thing. More important than hospital staffing ratios, which, let's admit it between us, since we're talking informally, won't be followed anyway. She tells me she knows it's important that I keep my job and don't get a reputation as a troublemaker. Troublemakers, they can get fired and it can be very hard for them to get another job. She says she hopes that doesn't happen to me."

I said, "Puta."

Bacay smiled and Bill laughed out loud.

"May I ask, did anyone else know?" I said. "About your 'informal' talk with Margaret Weldon?"

He shook his head. "I didn't tell anyone. I understood what I was being told. I quit the committee. I said it was stress."

"Did she tell anyone?"

"Margaret Weldon? I don't think so. Why will she? Probably later, after they win and we get a bad contract. Then she'll tell everyone what dirty things she did and be a big hero. But not yet. In case something backfires." Bacay narrowed his eyes. "Those people, they're paid to take care of the hospital. If the hospital tells them it wants the buildings painted red, they'll try to put that in our contract, to paint the buildings red. They don't care what it is. It's just a job for them, to make the hospital win and the nurses lose. Next year, maybe they get a new job at Uber. It will be the same thing, to make Uber win and the drivers lose. Maybe they get a bonus if our contract is bad enough, I don't know."

We all sat in silence for a few moments, watching the kids on the basketball court. I asked Bacay, "Could you just tell me, what did you think of Sophia Scott?"

He looked at me. "I think she's stupid. Also a coward."

"Why?"

"Every offer management makes, she wants to take it. Every time, it gets a little better, and every time she says to take it because it won't get better again. Why won't it? It just did, and if we push them, it will again. She says she doesn't want a strike. Nobody wants a strike. But we have to be ready to put our money where our mouth is or we get nothing. Sophia just says no, take the offer, no strike. Talking to her—sayang ang oras." This one he translated for me. "A waste of time."

Bill asked, "Do you have a theory on why someone would kill her?"

Bacay opened his hands. "A lot of people don't like her. But kill her? No, I don't know why someone will do that."

"Was she dating anyone, do you know?"

He shook his head. "I don't know, but that doesn't mean she's not."

Time now for the big question. I said, "Did you know she was a management mole?"

He frowned at me. "Mole?"

"Double agent. She was working for management. Reporting on your internal discussions."

His eyes widened. "Susmariosep! It's true?"

"Yes. She would meet with someone who'd report back to one of the management committee members."

"Margaret Weldon?"

"No." I watched him closely. "Albert Walsh."

Bacay frowned. "Walsh? You're saying Sophia was reporting our discussions to Walsh?"

"What's wrong?" Bill asked.

Bacay's thick eyebrows knit together. "He's the opposite of Sophia. She always says take the offer, she always says no strike. But that man Walsh, he's so sure we'll strike he just tries to make us mad so it happens sooner."

"Why would he do that?"

Bacay shrugged. "Maybe he has a bet on it. I don't know. But you can see him doing it. The other lawyers, they actually negotiate. 'We can give you this if we don't give you that.' If we agree to something, they're happy. But Walsh, he's never happy when we agree. If we finally settle and don't go on strike at all I think he'll be disappointed."

I thought back to the session we'd seen where Walsh and Bacay got into it over contract jargon and medical terms.

"Good cop, bad cop?" I suggested.

"Walsh is the bad cop and the others are all good cops?" Bacay sounded dubious and I didn't find it convincing either. "Sometimes," he said, "they make an offer about one of our demands that's close to what we want. Some of us, we have no poker faces. But that's not a problem, we think. Probably it will be fine, if the lawyers see the nurses are happy. It will make everyone feel like we're getting somewhere. Most of them, yes, it's true. But if Walsh sees someone on our side likes something, he loses his temper about something else. Even Sophia looks confused."

Why wouldn't she, I reflected. He pays her—or blackmails her?—for information and then doesn't use it.

I fed her bullshit, I heard Venturino in my head.

"Did management ever make an offer that seemed to come out of nowhere?" I asked.

Bacay cocked his head. "Yes, two times. Things we'd never discussed. No one understood why they thought to offer them."

"Because someone made them think you wanted them."

He waited but I didn't fill him in.

"I have to go," Bacay finally said. "Carlos will be calling me. You won't . . ." He trailed off. A young man pushed a stroller through the park to the gate.

"We won't tell anyone about this conversation," I said. "Good luck to you and your husband. Thank you for talking to us."

He stood. "If that diener is not guilty, I hope you can help him. I hope you can find who did kill Sophia." He broke into a smile, his teeth dazzling in his brown face. "And I hope, I very much hope, it will be Margaret Weldon."

CHAPTER THIRTY-SIX

What do we think?" I asked Bill, watching Alon Bacay cross the street and disappear down the subway steps.

"It wasn't Margaret Weldon."

"Who killed Scott?" I said. "Or who blackmailed him?"

"Who killed Scott. It's very easy to believe the blackmail was her. She seems like that kind of a shark."

"But not the kind that kills people?"

"Nothing's impossible, but no, I don't think that kind."

"Me either. And I can't see a motive. I'm kind of sorry to disappoint him, though. Now myself, I'm stuck on Walsh."

"And all this time I thought you were stuck on me."

"With. You, I'm stuck with. Walsh, I'm stuck on."

"I'll take what I can get. Walsh, in what way?"

I leaned back and let my eyes track an escaped balloon wiggling into the hazy sky. "From what we saw, it seems true that Walsh isn't interested in negotiating. In settling. When we watched those videos I thought he was just being a jerk. But if Scott was reporting to him through Bradley that makes it even weirder. Why would Walsh get involved in something like that unless he was looking for leverage on the nurses? To make them settle. But if he doesn't want them to settle, what's going on? *Is* he just being a jerk? That's a lot of trouble to go to, just to be a jerk. Or is he looking for something else?"

"Door number two. And that something else?"

I bit my lower lip. "Bacay says he's trying to make the nurses mad so they strike. He said maybe he's got a bet on it."

"No one would bet on something like that. Not big enough to make it worthwhile endangering his own bonus."

"What if someone he knew had a bet on it and he was fixing the game?"

"Again, what nut would bet big on that? And who'd take the other side?"

"Boy, you're argumentative."

"You're completely wrong, I'm not. Though if we got out of this park and I could have a cigarette I might revert to my more agreeable self."

"I never met that guy."

I lifted off the bench, Bill joined me, and we left the park. Standing on the street corner, where it was legal to smoke—the city council must figure the smoke will know how to keep itself out of the park—Bill lit a cigarette and inhaled deeply. "Okay," he said. "People's motivations, though often appearing convoluted and anomalous, rooted in the particularities of their distinctively singular lived experiences—"

"Oh my God, what's in that cigarette?"

"—mostly come down to sex or money. Is it sex?"

"Well, not Walsh and Scott." I watched the three boys jump and shoot on the basketball court, showing no signs of slowing down despite the thick heat. "He wants, or at least expects, a strike. She was trying hard to prevent one. It's an odd way to show affection, on either of their parts. To push for the thing your lover doesn't want."

"I agree. So, Walsh and someone else?"

"Who else wants a strike? The hospital is desperate to avoid one. Maybe not desperate enough to meet the nurses' demands, but it wouldn't be any of the other lawyers. Or Elizabeth Gordon-Platt. Anyway she'd eat Walsh for breakfast."

"So, money?"

"But it's the same problem. No one makes money during a strike."

"Well, here's the thing about money," Bill said. "You can either be motivated by the opportunity to make a lot, or to avoid losing a lot. Or, if you've already lost a lot, and you can't pay what you owe—"

"Then someone has leverage and you might act against your own interests, like your bonus, if they tell you to. Though still, why would the someone want you to?"

The smoke Bill streamed out climbed up to join the balloon in the sky. "We might want to go ask Walsh. I mean, if you want to talk about leverage, blackmail seems to be something of a lifestyle at River Valley. Maybe Walsh has a skeleton in his closet."

"So maybe we should look for it before we ask him." I regarded Bill for a moment, then took out my phone. "I hope it's not really true that you get your best ideas from cigarettes."

"It is. Once I stop smoking you'll see how stupid I really am. Who're you calling?"

"The skeleton in the closet crew."

Two rings, then, "Cuz!"

"Hey, Linus. You sound like you're out on the street."

"I'm walking Woof. How's the case going? Did Eyegor do it?"

"The case is complicated and we still don't think so."

"Complicated how?"

"I'll tell you later."

"Compartmentalizing! Need-to-know basis!"

More like *it's a long story*, but I said, "Is it legal for you to look into someone's finances?"

"Umm . . . What do you mean by 'into'?"

"That's not the word I was thinking you'd pick to ask about."

"No, seriously. Legally, we can find anything that's public record. Purchase or sale of real estate or stock, bankruptcies, alimony, anything FOIA, like that."

"Foya?"

"F-O-I-A. Freedom of Information Act. And just so you know, we can also find lots of other things but—"

"But not legally. Okay, start with what you just listed. A lawyer at River Valley named Albert Walsh."

"Start with! Woof, she said start with! That means if we don't find what you need—"

"It certainly does not mean that." Although I had to admit—to myself, not to Linus or even to Bill—it sort of did. "I want to know if there are any recent changes in his financial situation. In either direction."

"On it. Come on, Woof, gotta get back to work."

"Call me as soon as you have something."

"Sooner."

I hung up and Bill and I started heading back toward the hospital, for no particular reason, like homing pigeons.

"What now?" said Bill.

"You're the one who just raised his IQ. Think of something."

"Can I have another cigarette?"

"No way."

"Then there's only one thing on my mind. Dinner."

I considered. "Will food work as well as tobacco?"

"To make me smart, no. But it'll keep me Mr. Nice Guy."

"'Keep' may be stretching it. Now that I think of it, so may 'nice.' Okay—" I was saved by the ringing of my phone. I checked the screen, put the phone to my ear, and said, "Hey, Venturino."

"Got a pencil? Marshall Holcombe."

"Marshall—oh, the OB/GYN nurse who quit? You have an address?"

"Jesus, you're a private eye. How come you can't find things yourself?"

"How do you think we find things?"

She snorted. "Five ninety-three East Ninety-Third."

"Apartment number?"

Venturino laughed and hung up.

CHAPTER THIRTY-SEVEN

Five ninety-three East Ninety-Third was a well-kept six-story brick building of the type that, if you'd been living there long enough, your rent was probably just about manageable; and if you were a two-income family, you'd be doing okay. We buzzed apartment 5G, whose button, labeled HOLCOMBE, made it unnecessary for us to have to detour to the super and ask. I identified myself to the man who answered my buzz as a detective: technically, not true. Bill and I were investigators. People employed by the NYPD were detectives. But the "detective" label was perennially voted by private investigators "most likely to get us through the door without actually impersonating a cop." And it did.

Up on five, a freckled Black man stood in an open doorway waiting for us. He smiled almost eagerly, as though he had no idea what was going on but since he had nothing to hide he'd be happy to help.

"Mr. Holcombe? I'm Lydia Chin. This is Bill Smith. We just have a couple of questions about someone you used to work with. Sophia Scott?"

Private investigators don't carry licenses in our wallets in New York State, but people are always asking for them, so most of us have state-issued ID cards with our photos. Bill and I showed ours to Marshall

Holcombe, and while it's clear they're not NYPD badges, they do say "New York State" so unless people have extremely suspicious natures they usually work.

"Um, sure, come on in," he said, standing aside so we could enter the living room. An aroma of tomato sauce drifted out of the kitchen on the left. As we entered, two girls, maybe seven and five, looked up from jumping off the sofa onto a pile of pillows.

"Hi!" said the younger one. "We're superheroes."

Bill said, "I can see that."

"Girls, I just need to talk to these people for a few minutes," Holcombe said. "Go on into your room, okay?"

"Aww—"

"You can fly off the couch some more when we're done."

"Yay!" The girls ran off.

"Kid duty," Holcombe said, watching them disappear down the hall. "My wife's at work and I'm a stay-at-home dad until I get a new job."

"You quit at River Valley the day after Sophia Scott was killed?" I asked.

He shuddered. "I couldn't stay. Sophia and I worked together for years. Murdered in the basement. I mean, how creepy is that?"

"Creepy," I agreed. "What did you think of her?"

"Sophia? She was a good nurse."

"Cooperative? Willing to step up?"

"Sure."

"Were you friends?"

"Outside of work? Not really. Sophia didn't hang out."

"We're trying to get a picture of her," I said. "To understand why someone would want to kill her."

Holcombe gave me a quizzical look. "They caught him, didn't they? That diener."

"Jordy Kazarian. We think he didn't do it."

A pause. "Shit, really? You mean the killer's still out there?"

"Out there somewhere," Bill said. "Let me ask you this. Scott was seeing someone. Was it you?"

Holcombe's eyes flew wide. "Me? My God, no." He gestured around the apartment, as though to show us his domestic bliss. "I told you we weren't even really friends."

"That's what you told us, yes," I said. "We also talked to your supervisor. Liam O'Brien?" I paused and waited.

"Liam said I was seeing Sophia?" Holcombe's surprise and confusion were what Linus would have called epic.

"No," I admitted. "But he was hiding something. We figured he was either protecting you or himself." Actually we'd figured nothing of the kind, but it wasn't a bad theory. "If you weren't seeing her—were you?"

Emphatically, he shook his head.

"Then maybe it was him." I looked at Bill. "Maybe we should be looking more closely at O'Brien. His records, his past, that sort of thing."

"No. No, you don't have to do that," Holcombe said. "Liam wasn't seeing Sophia, either." He looked past us, then back. "Sophia was dating a pharma rep."

Bill and I glanced at each other. "A pharma rep?" I said. "That's who her new boyfriend was? Seems a little low on the food chain for her."

"Are you kidding? You know what those guys make?" Holcombe seemed to relax. "But it's not really cool. Not that Sophia ordered the meds or pharma products or anything. I mean, that's the doctors. But still. It looks bad if anything happens."

"If anything happens."

He shrugged. "With the products."

"Like, it turns out the hospital's ordering too many, or paying too much, that kind of thing?"

He nodded. "The reps work on salary plus commission. So cozying up to them's a no-no."

"But Sophia was. Cozying up to one."

"Well, yeah, but . . ."

"And something did happen. Someone killed her."

Holcombe didn't meet my gaze.

I said, "Boyfriends sometimes do that kind of thing, you know."

He said nothing. The happy shrieks of little girls came from down the hallway.

"Didn't you think to tell the police who the boyfriend was?" I said. "Because no one else seems to know."

"No one asked me. The police didn't come before this. You're the first people I've spoken to."

Of course. Of course we were.

He frowned. "You mean really, no one knew this but me? About Manan?"

"That's his name? This pharma rep?"

"Manan Namboothiri. He's with Unilab. No one told you about him?"

"A couple of people said they thought she had a new boyfriend. No one seems to know who."

"Well, it was a secret. Like I said, it's not cool."

"Does O'Brien know?"

"No. That would have been bad. For Sophia's supervisor to know. He'd probably feel like he had to report it."

"What would be the result?"

"Manan would've lost the route. Maybe gotten fired. But you don't think he had anything to do with it?"

Anything to do with it. A tip-toeing-up-to-it phrase if I ever heard one, and I heard that one every time someone was talking about something bad. Like murder.

"We don't know. But it's interesting he hasn't come forward. Yes, I know, seeing her was not cool. But someone murdered his girlfriend."

Holcombe nodded. "You can see the spot that put him in, though, right? If he doesn't know anything about it, what good would it do to come forward? He'd just lose his job. But if he doesn't say anything and then people like you find out about him, he looks guilty and could lose his job anyway. Poor guy."

"That's very empathetic of you, Mr. Holcombe."

Holcombe shrugged.

I got up to go. Bill stood also. Holcombe, with evident relief, walked us to the door. As he opened it I said, "One more question, though. If neither you or O'Brien was seeing Sophia Scott, and O'Brien didn't know about Namboothiri, what was he hiding?"

"What was who hiding?"

"O'Brien was obviously hiding something. If it wasn't his relationship with Sophia, what was it?"

"I . . ." He opened his hands. "I have no idea."

"Okay, well, thanks. If you think of anything, call us." I gave him my card.

◆

"Jesus Christ, what?" Church demanded when she picked up my call. Bill and I stood outside Holcombe's building in what should have been the cool of the early evening but was just the early evening. "What part of 'leave me the fuck alone' did you not understand?"

"The part about why, if you really meant it, you'd answer the phone when I called."

"Because my other choice was sticking a fork in my eye. What do you want?"

"No, you do. The boyfriend? The 'usual time, usual place' guy with the burner phone? He works for Unilab as a pharma rep and his name is Manan Namboothiri."

"What the actual flying fuck?"

"We checked the Unilab website. He's for real." Because the last thing I'd wanted to do was give Church a false lead.

"Where did you get this?"

"From one of the many people you never talked to."

"Who?"

"Uh-uh. Go talk to Namboothiri. And let me know what he says."

"Why?"

"Really?"

I hung up, then texted her the spelling of the boyfriend's name and, for extra credit, his employer's.

"Is it wrong of me to never want to speak to that woman again?" I asked Bill when I was done.

"I think it's magnificently self-sacrificing, if that's how you feel, that you keep calling her to give *her* the pleasure of talking to *you*."

"No, it's actually completely selfish. The only thing I enjoy about it is knowing how much she hates me, too." We started walking up the block. "Do you think we can get anything more accomplished today?" I asked.

"That would depend on your definition of 'anything.'"

"On the case."

"No."

"Good. Because I'm hot and tired and hungry. I want dinner, a shower, and bed."

"I know where to find all those."

I tilted my head to look up at him. "You'll make pasta?"

"With pesto. And a side of broccoli rabe. And my cellar is well known for the finest Perrier in New York."

We got on the 6 train and headed downtown.

CHAPTER THIRTY-EIGHT

Bill's not a morning person. His bedroom is in the back of his apartment, its window about ten feet from the wall of the next building, with a heavy shade covering it. Which meant I'd showered, dressed, made tea, and called my mother from the easy chair by the time he staggered into the living room in a bathrobe.

"Coffee?" he said hoarsely.

"No, I'm Lydia. Please try to remember."

He moved past the counter and filled the kettle. "I have to do everything around here," he grumbled as he spooned grounds into the French press.

"It's your apartment," I pointed out.

"Oh." He made a show of looking around. He disappeared into the bathroom, then went back into the bedroom. When the water boiled I got up and poured it over the coffee. He came back out in jeans, a T-shirt, and bare feet. Glancing at the French press, he asked, "How long?"

"Four minutes, fourteen seconds."

On his way to the kitchen he detoured by the chair to kiss me. "You're a wonder."

"I wonder, too."

Coffee mug in hand, Bill ambled over to the couch and sat. The room was cool because it was air conditioned—silently, unlike my office—but the heat haze was already blurring the edges of the buildings I could see in the distance out the big front window.

"You know what would be funny?" I said.

"What?"

"See how the buildings get fuzzier as they get farther away? What if that was actually true, and we got up to the hospital and it was just one big smudge?"

He lit a cigarette. "Might as well be. Feels that way."

The night before, we'd called Cohen, putting her on speaker so Bill could talk to her and make pasta at the same time. She was all admiration.

"I'm going to call that other detective," she said. "Ahn? Just to get on his nerves. It seems to me like we're piling up enough reasonable doubt to fill a dump truck."

"Glad you're happy," Bill said. "Talk to you tomorrow."

Now, I gave Bill time to metabolize some caffeine and nicotine, then said, "I need to go home and change my clothes." The fiction we maintain for my mother—that I work a lot of nights, surveillance or protection, things like that—would be more difficult for her to pretend she believed if I kept a wardrobe at Bill's and showed up in the morning in a different outfit.

"After which?"

"I'll call Linus. Then we'll see."

Bill finished his cigarette, then his coffee, and vanished into the bedroom once more. He came out in brown slacks, a white linen shirt, and a tan linen jacket.

"Wow," I said. "Who're you trying to impress?"

"Yo mama."

"I'm dubious."

"I'm not trying to impress her with how good I look. I'm just hoping she'll be impressed that I'm trying to impress her."

We walked across Manhattan in the early heat to the Chinatown apartment my brothers and I were raised in, where I still live with my mother. The deal with my brothers is, they pay the rent, the groceries, etc., and I stay in the place to keep an eye on her. It's our plan that she'll eventually move to Queens and live with Ted and his family, but it's not her plan yet. "Queens, pah, so far away!" she says every time she gets in the Chinatown-to-Flushing van that takes twenty-five minutes to get her two blocks from her front door to two blocks from Ted's. It takes her longer to get to Elliott's, in upper Manhattan, but when you point that out she says she knows and that's why Elliott and his family need to move back to Chinatown. Meanwhile she saves face because she thinks she's secretly keeping an eye on me.

I'd called to tell her we'd be coming over so we wouldn't surprise her when we walked in. She acted surprised anyway, both to see me—"my too-skinny never-home daughter"—and to see Bill's sharp tailoring—"who is the white baboon pretending to be?"—both said in Chinese.

"Neih hou, Chin Tai-tai," Bill said, presenting her with a bag holding three large and perfect oranges.

She snorted, took the bag, peered inside, and handed it to me. In Chinese she said, "Does he think I can eat something so big? Do I look to him like I'm starving? Put these in the blue bowl."

Because my mother, to some degree, speaks English, Bill has learned not to ask me what she said when she's spoken in Chinese. He just beamed at her while I found the blue ceramic bowl and put it, with the oranges, in the living room. Ma bustled grumpily at the stove. "I'll make tea."

"We just had breakfast, Ma," I said, which wasn't true, but I didn't want to have to stay.

My mother doesn't lose, though. She turned to Bill and in English said, "You will have tea." In tone it was very like a loan shark saying, "Pay up or I'll cut your throat." Bill was smart enough to nod.

"Okay, you guys," I said as I went into my room. "Have fun." I peeled off my trousers, shirt, and jacket, all wilted from yesterday. I gave a brief, longing thought to a tank top and running shorts, but who knew who—whom?—we'd have to face today. Following Bill's fabric-choice lead I picked wide black linen pants and a swingy blue linen tunic. I was buttoning the tunic when I heard a commotion in the living room. Finishing off the top button as I went, I strode out there to see Bill grinning and my mother flushing bright red.

"No, you don't kiss me! You do again, I tell daughter shoot you!"

"What happened?" I asked.

"What happened? Your mother's a genius! She's so smart I got carried away and kissed her!" Bill said.

"Ma?"

My mother spoke in rapid Chinese. "The white baboon is crazy. He said something that made no sense so I said he speaks too much Greek. That's an expression in English, right? Your brother told me. I thought he would understand me and not be so crazy. But he got crazier! He kissed me!"

"He speaks too much—oh. The expression in English when you don't understand something is 'It's Greek to me.'"

"That was what I said."

Not quite, but okay. I turned to Bill, switching to English. "She said you spoke Greek, so you kissed her?"

He was still beaming. "Greek! Kanellopolous!"

I must have looked blank, because he went on, "Sophia Scott's name was Kanellopolous. She was Greek."

"We knew that."

"*The Odyssey*. Odysseus was trapped on an island. By a nymph named Calypso. It's not about music. It's about myth. Sophia Scott was Calypso."

I grabbed my mother and kissed her myself.

CHAPTER THIRTY-NINE

Bill and I picked up some red bean buns from M & W on Canal and went to sit in Columbus Park. We found a bench a little distance from the concentric circles of observers surrounding the concrete xiangqi and gin rummy tables. Some of the watchers had laid bets on the games' outcomes; this, by Chinatown tradition, gave them the right to complain, instruct, and demand as moves were made. A few benches down from us a trio of musicians were setting up with an erhu, a qinqin, and an accordion. Beyond them, despite the heat, two teams of kids whooped it up at soccer practice.

"Oh God," said Church when she answered the phone.

"Good morning," I said. "Found Manan Namboothiri yet?"

"I can't even spell Manan Namboothiri yet. He's not at home but his employer says he'll be at River Valley at ten trying to sell somebody something. I'll pick him up there. Anything else? Good, then goodbye."

"Something else," I said. "Calypso."

"What about him?" she demanded. "Don't tell me you found him, too."

"Yes. No. Not him. Her. Not found. But we think we know who it is. It's Scott."

"What are you talking about? And what's all that shrieking? I know. You're drunk at some goddamn all-night party that's just breaking up and you thought it would be funny as hell to call and piss me off."

"We're in the park."

"Again? Don't you people ever work?"

"Believe me, talking to you is work. Now listen." I laid Bill's logic out for her.

When I finished I heard a tune from the band and shouts from the soccer field, but silence from the phone at my ear. I was just about to ask if she was still there—I could imagine her hanging up on me mid-explanation—when she said, "*The Odyssey*. You're serious with this shit."

"Ask Namboothiri."

"You know what it means if you're right? It means both my potential witnesses are gone. Poof, vanished. One was killed yesterday and one was really the victim all along—not the killer like you were trying to sell me. And you know what *that* means? There's fewer people to say Kazarian didn't do it. Maybe even more motive for him, if he was obsessed with her and she was dating someone else."

A wild yell as a shot on goal was deflected by the diving goalie. Even the xiangqi kibbitzers looked up. "Oh my God," I said, "talk about obsessed. He didn't know her and he's gay, but whatever. I just gave you Scott's boyfriend. And if Scott really was Calypso, and she was in the hookup room at two thirty that day, you might have your killer. On your way to the hospital, learn to spell Namboothiri. It'll make it easier when you book him."

I lowered the phone and looked around the park. "Well," I said to Bill. "That was satisfying."

"For her, too?"

"No, I'm sure she's seething. That's one of the things that made it satisfying."

A breeze wiggled the leaves above our bench, but didn't seem to be interested in stirring the air down here. "Okay, I'm calling Linus," I said, smearing a rivulet of sweat that was running down my neck. "Then maybe we can find someplace to take an air-conditioned subway ride to." I pressed the Linus button on my phone.

"Cuz! Wassup?"

"The thermometer. How're things in the garage?"

"Nice and chill." Because of all the electronics it was always sweater weather in the Wong Security office. "I have more boring stuff for you."

"How do you know it's boring? Maybe I'll find it a thrill."

"Uh-huh."

"Hi, Lydia!" I heard Trella call from across the room. "Believe me, it's boring."

"Okay, shoot."

"Your man Albert Walsh," said Linus. "He's a lawyer. So's his wife. They live on Long Island and make piles of money. Two kids in private school. House is mortgaged but not heavily. Bank accounts, some joint, some separate. IRAs, 401(k)s. Stocks and bonds and pussycats. No, forget the pussycats. We can't see how much is in the accounts unless we—"

"Which you won't."

"Yeah, no, of course we won't. But no flurries of activity, which probably means no borrowing from one to shore up another, any of that. He looks pretty flush, steady, and like I say, boring, from here."

"Okay, send it on over, we'll have a look. Thanks, guys."

Smiles and frowns bloomed around the xiangqi table nearest us. Money passed from the hands of those frowning to the hands of the smilers. Two new players took their places at the board. Bill and I headed over to my office on the other end of Canal Street to check out all the boring stuff Linus had put in the Dropbox on Albert Walsh's finances. As incompetent as my air conditioning was, it was better than the park.

Or it would have been, if we'd stayed long enough.

We stuck our heads in the travel ladies' door and said our hellos. In my office, I switched the a/c on and opened Linus's Dropbox on my office computer. I detoured to the bathroom while Bill sat at my desk and scrolled through Linus's reports. As I exited the bathroom drying my hands, I heard "Whoa."

"Whoa what?"

"I think whoa. We've heard this before, no?" He pointed to a line on the screen.

"What am I looking at?"

"Walsh's stock buys over the past year."

"I—whoa." The line he pointed to read "High Point Nursing." "That's the travel nurse company the hospital's going to use if the nurses go out."

"That's what I thought. And Walsh"—Bill grabbed a pencil and paper and did a quick calculation—"bought a sixty percent share in it four months ago."

"The computer will do that for you, you know."

"Do what?"

"Math."

"I like to keep my hand in."

"Walsh owns the lion's share of High Point Nursing?"

"And that," Bill said, mic-dropping the pencil onto my desk, "is how you make money when nurses go on strike."

CHAPTER FORTY

The reason we didn't stay long enough for my air conditioning to actually do any good was because of something else we found in the summary of Walsh's stock-trading activity. Most of what we looked at was, as Linus and Trella had reported, dull and boring. They had no reason to think the High Point transaction was any different from any other, and so they had no reason to particularly pay attention when, three months after his buy—almost a month ago—he sold close to half his shares.

Bill did, though.

"I had no idea you could read these things," I said to Bill. "Financial reports like this. They make my eyes cross."

"Pretty good for a guy who never owned a share of anything in his life, huh? Actually, in 4H, when I was a kid, I owned a quarter of a heifer."

"So, Walsh sold half his shares." I ignored his heifer, not being exactly sure which kind of a cow a heifer was. "To who . . . m?"

"That's not info that's in this report. We could ask Linus to find out."

"Would it be legal?"

"I doubt it."

"Then let's go find out ourselves."

So we gave the a/c the rest of the day off and headed back up to River Valley.

I greeted the glacial air in the hospital lobby like an old friend. The sweet young man at the visitors' desk knew us by now and gave us badges to go up to Legal and see Albert Walsh. An elevator ride later we found ourselves facing the double glass doors with the etched logo, and a discreet buzz admitted us to the presence of the sleek, smiling, and slightly surprised Viola Lewis.

"It's Mr. Smith, isn't it?" she said. "And Ms. Chin? How are you today?"

"Couldn't be finer, Miz Lewis," said Bill. "We'd like to thank you for that little tip you gave us. It was helpful, it sure was. Now, this morning, we'd be grateful if we could have a few minutes with Mr. Albert Walsh."

"Mr. Walsh? Is he expecting you?"

"No, ma'am, but I suspect he'll see us. You might mention we'd like to discuss High Point Nursing."

Looking doubtful, Viola Lewis pressed some buttons and spoke into her headset. She listened, raised her eyebrows, and said, "Yes, Mr. Walsh." A beat, during which I assumed Walsh cut the call, and she said to us, "He'll be free in five minutes."

"Thank you, ma'am," Bill said. "We do appreciate it."

We went to sit among the magazines.

"Do you have any idea how hilarious that accent is?" I whispered to Bill.

"Accent? That's my authentic self being freed at last."

The magazines in a lawyer's waiting room are always boring, and I risked falling asleep before the action began if I started leafing through one of these medico-legal periodicals. So while Bill perused the latest issue of *The Quinnipiac Health Law Journal*, I drummed my fingers for the ten, not five, minutes it took before the door in the wall opened. As I'd suspected, Walsh was the type to play show-'em-who's-boss games. A pale young woman wearing a business suit and a cowed expression gestured us in and silently led us to a small conference room, windowless but lined with shelves of leather-bound law books. It occurred to me to wonder if anyone actually consulted these books anymore now that their contents were all online, and what lawyers were going to use to impress people with over the coming web-based decades.

Albert Walsh was on our heels, opening the conference room door almost as soon as the young woman had shut it. I stifled a laugh at my mental image of him peeking around the corner to see if we were in here yet. He stopped in the doorway and demanded, "Who the hell are you?"

"Bill Smith," Bill said, then pointed to me. "Lydia Chin. Private investigators working on the Sophia Scott homicide." The accent was gone, as was the affability.

"What the hell are you doing here?" Walsh made no move to proceed into the room, and because Bill and I hadn't had a chance to sit before he stalked in, we all three stayed standing in a knot at the entrance.

"We believe you have information pertinent to our investigation," Bill said.

"You're wrong."

I took it. "Interesting you say that, since you don't know yet what information we're talking about."

"I only knew Sophia Scott as a member of the nurses' negotiating team," Walsh said icily. "I have no idea why anyone would want to kill her, and if I did, I'd have spoken to the police about it, not to people like you."

Oh, the old "people like you" card.

"That second part might be true but the first isn't," I said. "You also knew her as your mole."

Walsh went pale from the crown of his bald head down to his shirt collar. After a few seconds a scarlet flush crept back up the other way. He didn't say anything, but the heat of his anger was probably raising the air-conditioning bill.

"Come on," I said. "Sit down." Without waiting for a response from the man whose conference room it actually was, I pulled out a chair. Bill went around the table and did the same. Walsh, when he belatedly responded, yanked out the chair at the head of the table. Not a good move, because it meant he'd have to keep swiveling his head if Bill and I played ping-pong with this interview.

So we did.

"You were paying Sophia Scott to be your pipeline into the nurses' deliberations," I said.

Bill picked it up. "We weren't sure why you would bother to do that, because you were the least conciliatory of the negotiators. But then we found out about High Point Nursing."

He gave it a beat, so I grabbed it. "You needed the information Scott was feeding you to make sure the nurses *didn't* get what they wanted. So they would go out on strike. So High Point Nursing could supply a hospital full of travel nurses."

"Were you also planning to undermine the negotiations once the strike started, to prolong it?"

"Not good for patients," I said, "or for River Valley's actual nurses. Or the orderlies and supervisors who have to pick up the slack. But nice for people with stock in High Point."

"That sounds to me like a conflict of interest, Mr. Walsh," Bill said.

Walsh's jaw clenched. "There's no professional-ethics problem with me owning stock in High Point."

"Oh, but it's not just stock, is it?" I said. "It's a controlling interest."

"Or it was," Bill said, "until you sold half your shares. And while what you said about owning stock might be true, I could make a hell of a case for ethics violations, and maybe even law violations, when you enlist a mole from the other side."

Walsh glared at Bill but his glare was thin and I saw fear behind it.

"So far we're the only ones who know about this," I said. "And we're not in the business of cleaning up messes all over this hospital."

"Though I sort of wish we were," Bill said, "because it could be lucrative. You're not the only guy with a nice little swindle going on." He sighed. "But we have a job to do."

"Yeah," I said. "It's not the same job as the cops are doing but it's related. So if you plan to keep puffing out your chest and telling us you had every right, etc., etc., then we'll just tell Detective Church about you and High Point and your mole and she can deal with you and we'll go on doing our job."

Walsh didn't answer. I stood.

A drop of sweat appeared on Walsh's temple.

Bill said, "Come on, Lydia, sit down. For Pete's sake. Give the guy a chance."

Walsh glared at Bill—nobody wants to be beholden—then at the polished tabletop. He looked up at me and growled, "I don't have time for this. What do you want to know?"

"The whole story," I said. "What came first, how you found Scott."

Bill added, "Did you take this job with this scam in mind?"

"It's not a scam. I told you. It's perfectly legal for me to own that stock."

"We're not the ones you're going to have to convince, but okay." I sat down again. "Did you take this job with this *plan* in mind?"

"No." Walsh shook his head. He paused a moment while he seemed to be looking for the right words. On guard, I warned myself. He's a lawyer, words are his weaponry. He sat back and said, "I'm a labor negotiator. Management side. That's my specialty and my experience and it's what they were looking for here nine months ago when I was headhunted. The nurses' contract was coming up and they wanted to get ahead of it."

"Is that normal? To hire a specialist so far in advance?"

"Seriously? You think nine months is far in advance? Any responsible organization starts labor discussions long before a deadline. That's what they were doing here." Absently he spun the signet ring on his finger. "When I started here I looked seriously at the nurses' demands. Tried to see what compromises management could make. I thought that was my job. But every time I met with Margaret—Margaret Weldon, she's head of the negotiating committee—and with people from Admin, it got more and more obvious that the hospital wasn't prepared to give up anything beyond the absolute minimum." He suddenly stopped twirling the ring and sat up straight, as though remembering what he'd been told about not showing nerves. He looked me straight in the eye—no doubt he'd been taught that, too—and said, "Nurses don't like to strike. They worry about their patients." Now he looked at Bill. "Or some of them have money problems, or visa problems." Visa problems. "The hospital was calculating they wouldn't walk out, and if they did, it wouldn't be for long. We were instructed to go through the motions, but there was to be no actual negotiating."

"Who gave that instruction?" Bill asked.

"Margaret. I assumed she got it from above."

"Did you know she hired a firm to investigate the nurses on the committee? To see exactly which ones had money or visa problems? That that was why Bacay quit the committee?"

He frowned. "Blackmail?"

"Sure sounds that way."

He shook his head. "You can see it, can't you? What a let-down this place is? I came to work here because I thought I could do some good." Boy, I thought, a lot of people in this hospital seemed to know how to sing that song. "Being the management guy—it's a niche, and it's interesting work, but you're not always the good guy. I was dumb enough to think that here, both sides were the good guys."

"Sad," Bill said. "Very sad. And when you realized you'd been played, you decided to get yours and to hell with both sides?"

"It wasn't exactly like that—"

"Stop!" I slapped my palm down on the table. "We don't care what it was exactly like. We're investigating a murder here and the trail's getting colder by the second as everybody in this goddamn hospital covers his own ass."

CHAPTER FORTY-ONE

Without a glance at me, probably so he wouldn't crack up, Bill said to Albert Walsh, "High Point Nursing. Tell us about that."

Walsh looked at Bill with narrowed eyes, and then at me. I kept a steady scowl going. I was getting a tremendous kick out of having usurped the bad cop role.

Walsh said, "High Point. Yeah." A silent moment, and then, "One day, early on, I had a meeting with Margaret Weldon and that chief admin, Dr. Gordon-Platt—you know her?"

"Yes."

"I went to the meeting armed with a memo. An offer I'd worked out, something management could do that would cover all the nurses' most-wanteds and wouldn't cost the hospital a fortune. The nurses would have to give up some things, which would make management look good, but they'd get a raise, better staffing ratios, one or two other things so their team could go back to the members and get them to ratify. It was stepped, over four years—for Christ's sake, it was perfect! It was exactly the kind of thing I was hired to do." Walsh's jaw hardened. "The kind of thing I *thought* I was hired to do. Dr. Gordon-Platt listened to my summary, didn't even read the memo. 'No,' she said. 'You're giving up far too much,' she said. 'They'll take a lot less. They won't strike.' And she got up and left." He looked daggers at the door. I wondered if that meeting had been held here in this room. "Margaret got up to leave, too. She smiled and said, 'Don't worry about it. You'll catch on.' Bitch. I just sat and stared at the door for a while after they were both gone."

"Sad," I echoed Bill. "Very sad."

"Listen—!" Walsh snapped.

"We're listening," I said. "We're hearing a lot of Oh Poor Me, and it's really not very interesting."

Walsh looked at me. I looked at the door and raised myself in my chair a few inches.

"Lydia," Bill warned.

I blew out a breath and sat.

Walsh watched me sit. "We had another couple of meetings in the weeks after that. Margaret was right, I did catch on. When negotiations actually started we got that instruction about going through the motions, but by then I didn't need it. I was pretty disgusted. I'd worked for some big corporations—"

"Spare us," I said. "Get to High Point."

We'd better finish this soon, I thought, or Walsh would pull a muscle in his jaw, clenching so hard for so long.

"I stopped for a drink after work one day. The TV had the Knicks game and some online gambling commercial came on. A couple of guys started saying there's always someone somewhere giving odds on anything. Like even the weather. One of them said that's one of the few things you can bet on because you can be sure the fix isn't in. I don't know, maybe it was the scotch, but I said, if I were you guys, I'd bet on a nurses' strike at River Valley Downstate. Management over there is acting like the immovable object. But I've been listening to the nurses.

I'm telling you, they're going out. One guy said, you sure? Sure as the weather? I said, well, not the weather, but close. They laughed and said forget it, then, and started talking about something else. But I kept thinking about it. I went home and started researching travel nurse companies. Management wasn't happy with the one they'd been using. That wasn't my lane but I'd heard it around the water cooler. So I looked at a couple of the publicly traded ones. High Point stock was cheap enough. I started buying it."

"And three months later you owned the company."

"I don't *own* the company," he sneered. "Just, like he said"—a jerk of the chin at Bill—"a controlling interest. Enough that I could set the terms of a potential contract with River Valley."

"And that's not a conflict of interest? Yeah, don't bother to explain why because I'm not going to believe you."

"Lydia?" Bill said. "Just let him go on."

"No," I said. "No, I'll go on. River Valley liked your terms, of course, because you'd found out around the water cooler what they didn't like about the company they'd used before. High Point management liked that the new owner"—okay, I did use the word just to annoy him—"was practically promising a strike. Oh, so many happy people. Do they know you're on the management negotiating team? Would they even care? So High Point and River Valley signed a contract and the hospital's been paying ever since to have a guaranteed pool of nurses sitting around waiting and you've been doing everything you can to make sure the nurses actually do strike including enlisting a mole and a go-between, and this isn't a hospital, it's a sewer." I tried to say "fucking sewer" but even Church-influenced me couldn't quite manage it.

"How's she doing?" Bill asked. "Sounded pretty right to me."

"The only question I have now," I said, "is what was in it for Bradley DeBreng."

Walsh had been staring at me through my entire rant and he didn't say anything now.

"Stock," said Bill. "That's where the other half of the stock went."

It was my turn to stare, and then I laughed. "Oh my God, you're right. He sweet-talked Bradley into investing his grandpa's money. That's why Bradley didn't want us to tell his dad. Because it was a stupid investment like the ones DeBreng Senior keeps saying Jordy makes. Bradley made one and he woke up with buyer's remorse and now he has to protect his stupid investment by making sure the nurses actually strike. How'd you do it, Mr. Walsh? Did you get him drunk? Took him to that bar you first had this idea in? You make half your investment back and now you have a partner in crime."

"It's not a crime—"

"Oh, stuff it. I bet Bradley was the front man with High Point." A glower from Walsh told me I'd hit my target. "Just in case anyone there might get queasy at the idea of a guy in your position owning a controlling interest."

"Bingo!" Bill said. "And a controlling interest in Bradley DeBreng, that's not a difficult acquisition, is it? He's used to being told what to do."

I grinned and sat back. "You know what?" I said to Bill. "Looks to me like we have two more people with motives to kill Sophia Scott." Bradley DeBreng also had an alibi, but I didn't mention that.

Walsh said, "What do you mean, motives? What the hell motive do you think I have?" He kept swiveling his head as though the ping-pong match were still going on.

So we played an extra inning.

Me: "Maybe she thought you were about to be busted and she was going to rat you out before you could sing."

Bill: "Or you found out she was a double agent and she was reporting on management to the nurses."

Me: "Or she wanted more money, or a cut of the stock deal."

Bill: "Or she was coming on to one of you and the other one was jealous."

Me: "Or her conscience was bothering her and she was sorry she'd let you talk her into it in the first place."

"Oh for God's sake, you people are insane!" Walsh threw up his hands. "None of that was true and you know it."

"I don't know it," I said.

"Me either," said Bill.

"She wasn't coming on to us and she wasn't a double agent and she didn't want out. Why would she? It was her idea."

I looked at Bill. "What was her idea?" I asked Walsh.

"She came to me. She never even knew about High Point. She offered me information on the nurses' discussions."

"For?"

"Money, of course."

"That's it?"

"What do you mean?"

"That was the only reason she got messed up in this?"

Walsh shifted uncomfortably. "What other reason?"

"It was convenient," I said, "that she found an unscrupulous member of the management team to sell information to. Notice I said 'unscrupulous,' not 'criminal.' Bill wants me to be nice."

Bill smiled benevolently while Walsh fumed.

"She watched you, in the first couple of sessions. She watched all the lawyers, and you were the one she chose."

He couldn't deny it, so he said nothing.

"So she came to you and made her offer," I went on. "But, see, she had more than money on her mind. She was determined the nurses wouldn't strike. I'm sure she was glad to double dip but what she was really there for was to give you info to use to undermine the nurses and keep the strike from happening. You say she never knew about High Point and I believe you." I turned to Bill. "Crazy, huh? I believe him." Back to Walsh: "But you must have been aware she didn't want a strike. That that was why she came to you in the first place. And we want to know why."

"Why what? Why she didn't want a strike? How should I know?"

"She never told you?"

"She never talked to me! It would've been crazy to be seen together. Even that first contact she made was risky. After that, everything went through DeBreng. Honestly, I thought all she wanted was money."

I regarded him. "Okay," I said to Bill. I stood. "I'm tired of this. At the risk of letting yet another pile of poop go undetected in this cesspool of a hospital, I suggest we move on to other things."

"What other things?" Walsh wanted to know.

"Sorry, Mr. Walsh, but that's none of your beeswax. Just keep your nose clean and hope we don't have to take this any further."

Bill stood up and walked around Walsh to follow me out the door.

CHAPTER FORTY-TWO

"I wonder if he's sitting there staring at the door the way he did when Gordon-Platt and Weldon walked out and left him stewing," I said as Bill and I threaded our way back through the corridors of the River Valley Downstate Legal department.

"I wonder if you'll ever be the same now that your inner Detective Church has been unleashed."

"I admit to regretting I couldn't thank him for the coffee."

We emerged into the reception area, where Bill slipped back into his Kentucky accent to tell Viola Lewis we appreciated her help. We all wished each other a great day. A lawyer in a navy suit was waiting for the elevator, so Bill and I waited silently with him, and we all rode down together, gathering up more passengers as we went. On the first floor we all went our separate ways. Bill and I returned to the bright and freezing lobby.

Bill said, "What now?"

"The bad cop gets to be the boss?"

"When it's you."

"It might be me from now on. I kind of liked it."

"We'll talk. We might have to arm wrestle for it."

"No problem." I flexed my biceps. "Meanwhile I find it incredibly interesting that Walsh says Scott came to him, not the other way around. You think that's true?"

Bill nodded. "Oh yeah. If he'd been the one to find her he'd have wanted us to know how smart he was, tracking down the one member of the nurses' committee who could be bent."

"I think you're right. So why did she do it?"

"She must have had a hell of a good reason because doing it put her in a dangerous position. If she got found out, the union would be screaming for her head. Management too, for making them look sleazy."

"And after she got fired, which she for sure would, the River Valley blackball machine would be working overtime. I mean, the supervisors might be in a different union but no member of any union would ignore that kind of a sell-out."

Bill looked across the lobby. "Unless."

I waited but nothing more was forthcoming. "Unless . . . ?"

"Unless I can go have a cigarette. I'm working on a theory."

"You realize that's extortion?"

He spread his hands to show me the lobby. "I'm just trying to follow the custom of the country."

The air outside was thick, not moving, almost difficult to push through. Still, I greeted the heat like an old friend the way I had the air conditioning. I wondered what that said about my ability to sustain lasting friendships.

Back across the street Bill lit a cigarette and pulled in smoke.

"Well?" I said. "I'm waiting. Or was this just a trick to get me to agree to stand here like a dope on this sweltering street corner?"

"I thought you liked the heat."

"I thought you had a theory."

He took another drag. "I do. It goes back to references. Brown and Delgado and all Quick Draw's basement guys got great references after they got fired because the scam was Quick Draw's. That was the deal. I'm raking in the dough, I pay you off and if you have to be the fall guys, don't worry about it, I'll make sure you get great new jobs. What if this is similar?"

"How?"

"Well, maybe the scam, whatever it is, belongs to the guy who'd be giving a reference."

"Scott's supervisor? O'Brien? But what kind of scam?"

Bill took one more draw and crushed the cigarette out. "Just half again," he pointed out, holding up the butt and then dropping it in a trash can. "As supervisor, O'Brien would be the one who signs the time sheets. He's also the only one who said Scott was cooperative and would step up if she was needed. That she'd work overtime."

I saw where he was going. "Not quite. Holcombe said that, too."

"Uh-huh. And he quit as soon as she was killed."

"Because he was creeped out, like he said? Or because he was scared on a much more mundane level?"

We looked at each other, then crossed the street again to greet my old friend, the air conditioning.

◆

Liam O'Brien, in his pink supervisor's scrubs, was surprised to see us. "How's the investigation coming?" he asked. "Something else you think I can help with?"

"Oh, yes," I said. "Can we go somewhere?"

The somewhere he led us to was the same storage-room-turned-lounge as the first time.

"What's up?" The aroma of burned coffee filled the air as O'Brien closed the door. He lifted the pot. "Want some?"

"No, thanks."

Bill accepted this time, which I figured was his own lookout.

"Mr. O'Brien," I said, "we've spoken to Marshall Holcombe and also to Albert Walsh."

He hesitated, covering the hesitation by saying, "Albert Walsh? I don't think I know who that is."

"Oh, sure you do. Sophia would have told you. And Holcombe, of course, you know."

"Well, sure, and I wish he still worked here. It's taking HR forever to replace him. The safe staffing levels the nurses are demanding—"

"Funny, I feel like you're trying to distract us. Scott joined the nurses' negotiating committee for a reason and Holcombe quit for a reason and we think the reasons were the same. We think you and they were padding their time sheets."

"What?" O'Brien knotted up his forehead the way you do when someone's speaking too quickly, or in a foreign language.

"Time sheets. Padding. Overtime they never worked. That you signed off on. Nobody works real hard and everyone goes home happy. Except finally Sophia Scott never goes home."

"You're nuts. I'm sorry but I don't have time for crazy theories. You need to go now. I have to get—"

"Back to work. Right. Scott never took an extra step in anyone's direction. She didn't offer anyone a hand and she didn't work overtime except on the time sheets you signed."

"That's why she was so against being transferred to Pediatrics for a couple of weeks," Bill said. "She was afraid OB/GYN would see a sudden drop in overtime hours and someone would begin to wonder why. Plus in Pediatrics she might actually have to work overtime, oh shit. You even called Pediatrics to say you couldn't do without her."

"That was a risk," I said. "Plus while she was gone you lost money yourself. All you had was your share of Holcombe's time and a half. Oh shit again. How long had you three been running this scam?"

The coffee cup in O'Brien's hand suddenly imploded, gushing coffee out of its broken bottom. He'd squeezed it to bursting. We all stared at the brown splotches on his white nurse shoes.

He looked up at us. "You don't—"

"Know what we're talking about, we have no idea, Scott and Holcombe both worked that overtime, and no one gets paid enough at this hospital anyway, uh-huh stop. You understand the police can get those time sheets? A little forensic accounting and there you go. Or even, they might not need that because Holcombe has two little kids and I bet he'd flip in a minute in exchange for no jail time."

O'Brien went as white as his shoes used to be.

"But wait." Bill took it up. "The police don't know about this scam yet, do they?" He looked to me.

"One of so many at this place they're ignorant of," I confirmed.

"Correct me if I'm wrong," he said, still talking to me, "but all we're being paid to care about is getting Jordy Kazarian off the hook for a murder he didn't commit, right?"

"That's right."

"Then if we get the information we need from Mr. O'Brien here, we might not need to tell the police anything about this."

"You know, you might be right. Not that we could guarantee they'd never find out."

"But it wouldn't be from us."

In unison we turned expectant looks to Liam O'Brien.

"Goddamn you," he breathed.

"I'm sure," Bill responded. "But meanwhile . . . ?"

O'Brien walked to the coffee table, picked up some paper towels and wiped his hands and the floor. He threw the towels away and poured another cup. "Yeah. Yeah, okay, you're right. Happy?" He dumped in milk and took a slurp.

"Not at all," I said. "I might get a little happier if I had the details."

"And you want to make her as happy as possible," Bill said. "She can be really mean."

O'Brien sat heavily on one of the chairs. I perched on the arm of the other and looked pointedly at my watch.

He took another gulp. "Yeah. Ah, shit. No one does get paid enough around here, especially not nurses." He glanced up. If he was looking for any sign of sympathy, he didn't see it. His lip curled but he went on. "Holcombe was first. He wasn't hard to persuade, raising two little kids in New York. Sophia, I don't know what the hell she needed the money for. Actually I think she didn't—need it, I mean. She just liked getting away with things."

"How long?" I asked.

He looked away. "Three years, give or take."

"In all that time, no one asked questions?"

He shrugged.

"The secret to a long-term hustle," Bill said, "is not to get too greedy. Not to think just because you got away with something you can get away with more. Small and steady. That's how you did it, right? I congratulate you. Most hustlers can't hold themselves back. But I can see how a strike would've been a problem."

"Like you said." O'Brien sighed. "I get travel nurses in here, it gets to be obvious we don't need all that overtime. I can fake it for a while, say I'm only having them do critical tasks, letting other things go, but any strike would be a risk and a long one could've been a disaster."

"So you decided the solution was for Sophia to join the negotiating committee and make sure a strike didn't happen."

"She did. It was her idea."

"But you liked it?"

"Of course I did. So did Holcombe."

"And you knew part of doing that was she sold info to management?"

He shrugged again, drank more coffee. "I thought that was a bad idea. She said it was insurance. Make sure management held all the cards. It's not like I was in a position to tell her what to do. I wanted to stay as far from that shit as possible."

"I'm sure. So many people staying far away from so much shit around here, and yet it's everywhere. Who else knew?"

"About the overtime? No one."

"Holcombe didn't tell his wife? Scott didn't whisper it to her boyfriend?"

"I have no idea. If they did, they didn't tell me."

"Any other nurses involved?"

"Two was enough. Like he said"—he pointed his coffee cup at Bill—"don't get greedy."

"Yeah," I said, "right." I looked around the coffee-smelling scruffy storeroom. "Well, like *I* said, we'll keep this to ourselves unless it materially affects the Scott investigation. If it does, we'll have to turn it over to the cops. Otherwise it's our little secret. But you know what it would be called if you start it up again with other nurses, don't you?"

Before O'Brien could answer, Bill said, "Getting greedy."

CHAPTER FORTY-THREE

"Come on," Bill said, down in the lobby once more. "I'll buy you lunch."

"Great idea. Where?"

"Mexican restaurant near here. Fish tacos, good for the brain."

The restaurant was called Conmigo and it had more kinds of tacos than I'd ever seen. My brain did need a little help, though, so as tempting as the acorn squash tacos were, I ordered grilled fish, Bill ordered breaded and deep-fried fish, and we got a side of yucca with achiote and pickled onions on the theory that when the mouth's happy the brain works better.

"You know," I said as we waited for our food, "if we were being paid per lawbreaker or ethics violator we found on this case, we'd be rich."

"But no closer to finding out who killed Sophia Scott."

"We wouldn't have to care. We'd be rich."

His beer and my Mexican coffee arrived. I love Mexican food but they're thin on tea.

"Seriously," I said, sipping the cinnamony froth off my mug, "I've never seen so many people doing so many nefarious things. It's a little disheartening. No, it's a lot disheartening. A hospital? Isn't it a thing that medical people are supposed to at least do no harm?"

Bill shrugged. "I always thought so."

"And with all this going on, are we any closer to finding out what actually happened to Scott? I hate to utter these words, but Church is right."

Bill's eyebrows went up.

"Well, if Scott was Calypso, and since Sivek is dead, there go our potential witnesses. Sivek may have killed Scott, but then who killed Sivek? If Sivek didn't kill Scott, who did and why, and still, who killed Sivek? Or do we not care who killed Sivek because it was probably a crazed ex or something and it has nothing to do with Scott?"

"You're babbling."

"I know. It helps me think."

"You should take up smoking."

"You had a cigarette on the way over. Where's your brilliant idea from that?"

A pierced and tattooed waitress appeared with our lunch on heavy Mexican crockery. She asked if there was anything else she could get us, but since I didn't think she had a solution to the hospital crime wave, I shook my head.

"Well, at least this taco is great," I said after a bite. "Now I'm waiting to see the effect on my brain."

"I'm waiting, too."

"Are we really not going to turn O'Brien in?"

Bill didn't answer.

"Yeah," I said. "Those kids of Holcombe's were seriously cute."

"Also," Bill said, "think how unhappy Church would be. It's just another thing she'd have to investigate."

"Well, God knows we don't want to make Church unhappy. But listen, what if it *is* relevant? Like, suppose Scott wanted out and one of them killed her because they were afraid she'd expose them?"

"I guess it's possible. Though if she did she'd expose herself, too. She could just get out and keep her mouth shut. And why would she want out? Also, she sounds to me like the kind of person who, if she wanted out, you could just offer her a bigger cut. Let's keep it to ourselves for now."

"You're just a big mush ball, you know."

"Well, if Church—"

On cue, my phone rang with the cathedral bells. Bill and I shared a look, and then I answered.

"I don't believe it," I said. "You're calling me? Or is this a butt dial?"

"There's an asshole joke in there but I don't have time to find it."

"I don't think it's fair for you to call to insult me," I said. "You have to at least wait until I call you."

"Jesus Christ," Church said. "Is anything ever easy with you?"

"I hope not. What's up?"

She sounded like she was talking through gritted teeth. "I interviewed the boyfriend."

"Namboothiri?"

"No, some other damn boyfriend. Of course Namboothiri."

"And that's what you called to tell me?" I said, when she didn't go on. I sipped some coffee.

"Shut up and listen. Those texts on Scott's phone to and from a prepaid burner? I was sure the burner was Kazarian's. But now Namboothiri says it's his. And also that he threw it in the East River as soon as he heard about the murder."

"I love a sentimental man."

"Uh-huh. If you're about to ask me if I'm going to send divers down there, I'll have you taken up as an EDP. Right now I'm taking his word for it, though I don't completely believe him."

"Don't believe him about what? Throwing away the phone? Sending the texts? What?"

"Maybe he's covering for Kazarian for some reason. Maybe they're really the item and Scott was the beard and the texts are to and from Kazarian."

"Oh my God, you're nuts. And why would Jordy have been texting Scott?"

"He was selling her drugs?"

"Boy, there's a reach. You have anything at all on that? Jordy as a dealer?"

"No. But believe it or not, I didn't call to tell you my theories."

"Good, because I hate them."

"Remind me to give a shit. The texts say 'same time, same place.' With a date. Namboothiri says they were for setting up hookups. One of them would text and the other would send a yes or no. Occasionally, a different time. According to him, if something worked for them both, she'd go and sign up on the hookup room sheet. Then at the time and day, he'd meet her there." She added, "You were right, by the way. She was Calypso."

In my head I said, *You're welcome*, but to the phone I just said, "Okay."

"Yeah. So, the reason I called is, the last text on her phone, the one from the day before the homicide, which may have set up the hookup that turned into the homicide. He says he didn't send it."

"Well, of course he does."

"Right, but in this case on the day of the homicide he was at a training at his company's home office. In Morristown. New Jersey. Not only is that a hundred-and-fifty-person alibi, but the training was scheduled months in advance. He says he wouldn't have suggested that date."

"But it was from his phone. Which you're not sending divers for."

"In the goddamn East River? Jesus, listen—it was from his *number*. That doesn't mean his phone."

I met Bill's eyes. He'd finished his taco and almost all of the yucca and I could see he was practically jumping out of his skin.

"A spoof?" I said. "Is that what they call it? Someone fakes your phone number?"

"Right."

I grabbed a piece of yucca with my fingers. "All right," I said. "I admit this is all really interesting but why are you calling me? If you were someone else I'd think you were gloating, or someone else else I'd think you were politely keeping me updated, but you wouldn't bother with either, so why?" I popped the yucca in my mouth.

"Because it's a goddamn loose end. There could be a dozen explanations for it, but we have twice that many cases hanging fire over here."

It took me a minute. "Oh my God. You want us to look into it for you."

"I have a suspect in custody and no other suspects who don't have alibis. I sent this to Cyber to get them to trace it back to the real number but they hit a wall. I'm being told to forget it and move on. I'd be happy to move on, but . . ."

"But what?"

"I don't like loose ends." She took a long breath. "It could be Kazarian sent Scott that spoof text to get her there and kill her, but he says he didn't, and if he did, it's not on his phone. Sure, maybe he has a burner. If he does we didn't find it. Maybe it's in the East River with everyone else's. But how would he have known about the texts in the first place? Listen, I still think I have the right guy. I think the DA can indict and convict on what I have and Kazarian can go away where he belongs. But I don't like loose ends."

I paused. There was no way we weren't looking into this, but there was something else I wanted and I was more likely to get it if she thought I needed more persuading. "If this loose end," I said carefully, "unravels your whole case—"

"Then it does. From where I stand I have a solid case against Kazarian. If I don't, I want to know it before I go to the DA and make an ass of myself."

"Okay. We'll check it out, but there's a trade I want."

"Jesus."

"You thought there wouldn't be?"

"Just tell me what it is."

I reached for another piece of yucca. "Your witnesses. The ones who claim to have seen Jordy with Scott, the ones you're so sure of. Who are they?"

"Shit. All right, but—"

"No witness tampering, uh-huh. I'm not even going to bother to be insulted. Who?"

"One's a barista, a corroborating witness we found after we talked to the first. The first, that's Kazarian's father."

CHAPTER FORTY-FOUR

I alternated between devouring my now-soggy fish taco and telling Bill about Church's two bombshells.

"She doesn't seem to think Namboothiri denying the text is a bombshell," he said.

I licked my fingers and sent them toward the last piece of yucca. "She sort of can't," I said. "It would screw up her airtight case. Which I'm sure Cohen can stick all kinds of holes in, but Church needs to get it off her desk." I swallowed the yucca and wiped my fingers as the finale to a great meal. "You know, I hate the idea that Jordy's whole future is a case file piling up with two dozen others on an overworked detective's desk."

"I'm detecting a faint note of sympathy for Church."

I picked up my coffee. It was cold, too, but it was still quite tasty. "She said she doesn't want to make an ass of herself. But I think the real reason is she believes Jordy's her guy, but in case this really does mean something, she wants her conscience clear."

"You're accusing her of actually trying to do the right thing?"

I shrugged and finished my coffee. While Bill paid the check, I made another call.

"Cuz! How you holding up?" Linus shouted into the speakerphone over crashing guitars and a heavy backbeat.

"I'm melting."

"All my beautiful wickedness!" he screeched. The music was turned down and in a normal voice he added, "*The Wizard of Oz*. The original, you know?"

"Hi, Lydia," I heard Trella call from across the garage.

"Hey," I said. "Trella, I just had some of the world's best coffee."

"No kidding. Where?"

"Conmigo on the east side. You have to try it. Listen, you guys, how hard is it to spoof a phone number?"

Linus said, "By spoof, you mean—?"

"You get a text from me, so you reply but it's not me. Isn't that a spoof?"

"Just checking because there are lots of kinds of spoofing. If that's what you mean it's pretty easy."

"What about covering your tracks so if NYPD cyber experts try to find the real number behind it, they can't?"

"How long did they try?"

"I'm not sure. A couple of hours, maybe half a day?"

I heard surprise as he asked, "Did they give up? That's not real long."

"Political realities. Does that mean the spoofer covered his tracks really well?"

Trella spoke up. "It means he was at least good. Maybe great, but maybe not. The NYPD Cyber squad, I bet they had other cases to work on at the same time, right?"

"That's the impression I was given."

"You have to really focus on that kind of thing," she said.

This from someone in a garage with blacked-out windows, pounding music, endless blinking lights on countless machines, files open on half a dozen screens, new and modified devices in various stages of development on every surface, a boyfriend across the room, and a big yellow dog on the floor.

"Meaning you could do it?" I asked. "Find the real number?"

"Just shoot us the spoof, cuz," Linus said.

Church had given me the numbers of Namboothiri's burner and Scott's cell phone, but I hesitated. "Is it legal?"

"Cuz," he said patiently, "spoofing isn't legal. You can't catch a fish without getting wet."

"Maybe not, but you don't have to hold your nose and cannonball into the lake."

Nevertheless, I held my own nose and gave him both numbers.

When Bill paid the check, he'd left a big cash tip prominently on the table, which accounted for the waitstaff at Conmigo not kicking us out while I talked on the phone. For the third phone call, though, we thanked them—Bill in Spanish—and left, because it was going to be a short enough call to make from the street while we walked. I employed the same subterfuge I'd used to find out whether Bradley DeBreng had been in his office, and the answer was the same: yes. So Bill and I set out to see Bradley and Jordy's father, Dr. Irwin DeBreng.

CHAPTER FORTY-FIVE

As befitted River Valley Downstate Medical Center's chief of medicine, the office suite of Dr. Irwin DeBreng was in the administration tower, though on the floor below Elizabeth Gordon-Platt's. When we reached the lobby elevator I called the office and gave the receptionist my name and the message that we were on our way up to discuss Dr. DeBreng's son.

"Please hold," then some classical music Bill identified, when I held the phone for him, as Vivaldi's *Four Seasons*.

"'Summer,'" Bill added.

"Of course, 'Summer.' Only someone with a sense of humor would be playing 'Winter' now."

Just when I was getting fond of Vivaldi the receptionist returned. "I'm sorry," she said. "Dr. DeBreng has nothing to say to you about Jordan."

"Oh, was I not clear? It's not Jordy we want to talk about. It's Bradley."

The elevator opened and we got in without waiting for an answer.

As striking as the physical resemblance was between the brothers, even more impressive was the temperamental one between father and elder son, unmistakable as we walked through to DeBreng's executive office.

"What the hell do you people think you're doing?" DeBreng demanded as soon as the receptionist had shut the door. He didn't sit, just stood glowering by the window in his unbuttoned white coat. I wondered if he actually wore it while he was administrating or if he'd put it on to intimidate us. He stood silhouetted, as I'm sure he knew, against the bright East River.

I walked past him and sat in one of the guest chairs facing the desk and waited for him there. Bill followed. DeBreng was left furious but glaring at our backs, so he strode over and sat in the giant ergonomic leather chair behind the desk.

"That's better," I said pleasantly. "I hate to squint. I guess everyone does." Bill smiled and nodded. "Dr. DeBreng, we're here to do you a favor and keep you from looking like a complete jerk in court."

"What?"

"You told the police you saw Jordy having coffee with Sophia Scott when you know perfectly well it was Bradley. We don't want you to have to tell that lie under oath."

He jumped up, fists on his desk, and thundered, "Get out!"

"Oh, please." I crossed my legs. "Here's what you were thinking: Bradley must be having some cliched midlife crisis. He'd taken up with Sophia Scott. Something went wrong because with Bradley something always goes wrong, which is why you constantly have to swoop in and save the day. Of course Bradley's always appropriately grateful and tries even harder to be a mini you. That must be satisfying and it's something Jordy has never done. Anyway, something went wrong and Bradley killed Sophia, and now you want to make sure everyone thinks it was Jordy who knew her, not Bradley. You'd chuck Jordy right over a cliff if you thought doing it could save Bradley a hangnail."

DeBreng leaned forward on his knuckles. "You arrogant little bitch!"

Now Bill stood to face DeBreng. I put my hand out as if to stop him from whatever violence he was considering committing to avenge the insult to my honor.

Keeping an eye on Bill, DeBreng said, "There's another witness who saw the same thing I did."

"No," I said. "There's a witness who, when shown Jordy's and Scott's pictures, and asked if she'd seen them together, said yes. She wasn't shown Bradley's picture. Now would you both please sit down?"

Bill and DeBreng did the testosterone thing of who'd back down first, but it was Bill because, after all, he was only faking. DeBreng also sat, on the edge of his fancy chair, his legs poised no doubt for another spring.

"Now," I said, "it's like this. You saw Bradley having an intense discussion with Scott at that café with the back mezzanine. You didn't know what to make of it at the time—though you couldn't have approved, because you knew her reputation for taking a run at doctors—but after she was killed you jumped to the ridiculous conclusion that they were having an affair and that Bradley had killed her. This was a Pavlov thing because of how many times you'd had to pull Bradley's, er, chestnuts out of the fire before. You just assumed it was time to do it again. Your own son, and that's the assumption you made."

DeBreng started to show his teeth like a dog giving a warning. Well, I was the one who'd invoked Pavlov.

Bill said, "Or maybe he hadn't killed her, but if their affair became public knowledge Bradley would be in the NYPD crosshairs anyway, and his marriage could be in trouble."

I said, "Not good for Bradley's rep or your little Happy Valley up there in Scarsdale. But luckily for you, you have a spare son. He's useless anyway because he'll never make you proud. In fact, he embarrasses you. And he's already been arrested once for this crime. Plus, they look alike, your offspring. A brilliant solution comes to you! You call Detective Church and act the reluctant dad whose conscience nevertheless demands he tell a damning truth. The rest is history."

A gritted-teeth pause. "If you people aren't out of here in the next ten seconds—"

"You'll what, call the police? Go ahead. You'll have to call them anyway to tell them you've thought it over and you were mistaken. Don't worry about it, though. Bradley's passionate focus on Sophia Scott had nothing to do with sex. It was about money."

DeBreng's forehead folded into a frown. "What are you talking about?"

I gave myself a moment to enjoy the idea of saying something like *Well, Bill, I guess we've been kicked out, so we'd better leave now.* But fun wasn't why we were here. "Sophia Scott was a management mole," I said. "Bradley was her handler. Those meetings were debriefings."

DeBreng stared in disbelief. "Bradley?"

"Seems unlikely, doesn't it? Such initiative. But there you are."

"I—that's absurd. Why would he do something like that?"

"Ah. I'm afraid you'll have to take that up with him. He didn't want us to tell you."

"Tell me what?"

"Any of this. He said if we did he'd get you to send the flying monkeys after us, or something. But you see, Bill and I feel like we have a job to do here, which is to try to keep Jordy from spending the rest of his life in prison. That would be a lot easier if his own father hadn't manufactured this stupid story and sold it to an overextended cop. You can talk to Bradley or not, we don't care, but you should know this. We're on our way from here to the café to talk to the barista. You know, your corroborating witness? We have both Jordy's and Bradley's photos. And you'd better believe Jordy's lawyer almost hopes the case does go to court because she can't wait to call out both the great Dr. DeBreng and his son, the lesser Dr. DeBreng, as collaborating perjurers."

"What—Bradley doesn't know anything about this."

"Well." I stood. "You might want to tell him. Have a nice day."

Bill threw DeBreng a raised-eyebrow smile and followed me out of the office.

As soon as the elevator doors closed behind us Bill laughed. "Chestnuts? Who *are* you?"

"The successful private investigator will be capable of adopting many and varied personas, as the situation demands," I intoned.

"Sherlock Holmes's PI Handbook again?"

"Don't be ridiculous. The Michael Group Trainee's Instruction Manual, by Darius Georges."

"Seriously?"

"Were you serious about Sherlock Holmes? Pretty good, though, right? Appropriately corporate and boring? But it's true anyway, so teach it to your apprentice, Juarez. We do have to go see the barista now, right?"

"We sure do, before it occurs to DeBreng to run over there and bribe her. How did Juarez get to be mine?"

"You're the one who keeps encouraging her."

As we walked over to the Puerto Rican café, I swore I could see heat rays rippling up from the sidewalks like in a cartoon. The air conditioning inside the place wasn't as useless as in my office but it wasn't River Valley's fridge, either. The conversations in the space mingled with some kind of romantic guitar-and-vocal music. I got us a table and Bill went up to order at the counter. I followed him with my eyes as he talked to the barista.

"She'll bring it," he said, returning. "She's the one, right?"

"Blue hair, nose ring. According to Church, yes."

We waited, not long, for his coffee and my mint tea. When the smiling blue-haired young woman put our two steaming mugs down on the table I said, "Kayla, right?"

"Uh-huh." She tilted her head. In addition to a silver ring in her nose she had a couple dozen tiny rings and studs parading up her ears, three silver rings in her right eyebrow, and a stud below her lower lip. "Do we know each other?"

"No. I'm Lydia, this is Bill. We're investigators. I'd like to show you a couple of photos. I know you already talked to a detective but it would be great if you could take another look."

She raised the undecorated eyebrow. "About that nurse that was killed at the hospital?"

"That's right."

She shrugged. "Sure. But I only saw her once. Her and that guy."

"Is this the woman you saw?" I showed her Scott's photo.

"Yeah. Like I said, just that once."

"With this man?" I clicked on a photo of Bradley DeBreng.

She nodded.

"You're sure?"

"I told the other detective."

"Yes, but what you said was you'd seen her with this man." Now it was Jordy's photo.

Kayla gave me a puzzled look, which pulled the eyebrow rings closer together. "Right. Him."

"They're two different men."

"No way."

I switched to Bradley and then back to Jordy. "Brothers."

"No way," she said again, peering down at my screen. "Twins?"

"No, a couple of years apart."

"Can I?"

I gave her the phone. She swiped and swiped again. "Wow."

"Now that you see them both, can you say for sure which one you saw in here with the nurse?"

She glanced at me, swiped back and forth a couple more times, and said, "No. I guess I can't." She looked at the screen once more and said, "Did I mess something up? I don't want to get anyone in trouble."

"Oh, no, no. We know which one it was. Everything's good."

She handed me back the phone with a wry grin. "I wonder how much trouble they got each other in when they were kids. 'It wasn't me, it was him.'"

Thinking of my brothers and me when we were kids, I grinned with her. We'd never tried to blame each other for our misdeeds. Partly, it didn't seem sporting. Partly, our parents always had a supernatural ability to know who was actually guilty anyway.

"Are we cool?" she asked. "I gotta get back to work."

"Yes. Yes, go ahead. Thanks."

I picked up my mint tea. I was glad for the warmth; the air conditioning in here was stealthily better than I'd first thought.

"Well," I said, "another one of Church's theories shot full of holes."

Bill drank his coffee and didn't answer.

"But it leaves us no closer to knowing what actually happened than we were, isn't that what you were about to say?"

"Yup. That's why I said nothing."

I sipped my tea. "I'm tired of this."

"Of . . . ?"

"So many scams and grifts, so much lying and covering up, so many motives for this murder, and Jordy's still in jail and nobody seems to care who actually did kill Scott." I gazed across the room at a photomural of people picking coffee beans. "I have an idea. Let's move to Puerto Rico and open a coffee shop."

He nodded. "I can always count on you to arrive at the perfect solution."

"Yeah," I said glumly. "Just not to the crime."

And speaking of crime, my phone blared out "Bad Boys."

"Linus." In spite of myself, hope leapt in my heart. I switched the phone to speaker so Bill could listen. We leaned over the table, and I was grateful for the café's island music, masking our words. "You have something?"

"Good news and bad news."

"Why does no one ever have good news and good news?"

"Then it would just be good news. Trella found your spoofer phone."

"What? That's great news! Trella? You on here? You're a genius!"

"Maybe not so much," Trella said. "I found it, but that's the bad news. It's a prepaid burner."

The hope in my heart sank slowly back down. "Oh. Do you have any idea—"

"None. Sorry."

"Nuts," I said. "Nuts, nuts, nuts!"

"Whose is it?" Linus asked.

"What do you mean? That's what you were supposed to find out."

"No, I mean, the number that got spoofed. Whose is that?"

"Oh. Sorry. It's the boyfriend's. The nurse who got killed, that was how they set up their hookups, by text. That number texted her to set one up but we think it was really the killer setting her up to be murdered." The music changed, insistent drums now under an urgent singer. I knew how he felt. "I hoped we could find out who it was. All this proves is it wasn't the boyfriend. The cops will say it could've been Jordy."

"Eyegor, you mean?"

"Right."

"And he didn't do it?"

"We think he didn't, no."

"Well, then, I have an idea."

CHAPTER FORTY-SIX

I called Church, didn't get her, left a message. Then I called Linus back. "I couldn't reach the detective," I said. "I think we should just do it."

"All *right*! Doing it! Trella, hit it before she changes her mind."

"'Same time, same place, today,'" Trella said. "That's the text?"

"That's it."

That's what Linus's idea had been: send the hookup text to the burner phone, from a spoof of Sophia Scott's number. Which then, after unpeeling many onion layers, would be traceable back to me.

"We'll set it up so it looks like you're not nearly as good as he is at hiding stuff," Linus had said. "Probably he'd show up anyway, without the PS, just to show you how smart he is."

Possible. But we'd added the PS to the text anyway: NO ONE ELSE KNOWS ABOUT U, NOT EVEN MY PARTNER—YET. WE CAN KEEP IT THAT WAY IF U LIKE.

Of course, we didn't know who "he" was yet, or even if "he" was a he. Or if "he" still had the burner phone, or would fall for this. But no one had any other suggestions.

Including, half an hour later, Church. Bill and I were still in the café, where we'd ordered more coffee and tea to fuel us for the coming afternoon. When my phone bonged out the cathedral bells I offered a friendly "Good afternoon, Detective."

"You're crazy. You and your cyber guy both. And where the hell are you? Another park, with a salsa band?"

"A café."

"Oh, how nice." I was surprised her sarcasm didn't drip out of the phone and melt my ear. "Have a macchiato for me. I'm too busy to sit around cafés in the middle of the day."

I almost said, *You know this place. It's where Jordy Kazarian didn't meet with Sophia Scott the way his lying father said he did.* But that would have taken us down a whole different road and we could get into that later. I asked Church, "Do you have any other bright ideas?"

"I don't need bright ideas. I have a suspect in custody."

"You're the one who asked me to find the spoofer."

"You found a burner. That spoofed another burner. Great. Any reason it couldn't have been Kazarian's?"

"Because he's innocent?"

"So give me something real. Don't give me burner phones."

"We're trying."

"Go ahead and try, I have work to do."

"On some other case."

Church's voice darkened. "Scott's homicide is the only case worth investigating?"

"I didn't mean that."

"Yeah, you did. Lucky you with only one thing on your desk. I get chewed out for shit like that. Three other people were killed in this precinct in the last few days, in case you didn't know."

"And one was killed in the Nineteenth, as I recall."

"Jesus. So go bother Ahn and leave me alone."

"We said in the text, *same time, same place*, and we added, *today*."

"Said? Christ in a crap game, you did it already?"

"Was there a reason not to?"

"What if I wanted our cyber guys to do it from here?"

"You just said it was crazy."

"It's also police business. Maybe I'd have taken it to my captain, who doesn't know how crazy you are."

"And admit you'd asked us to find the phone when your guys couldn't? And we did? Anyway, I called you when we came up with it and said it all in the message and you didn't call back until now."

"Because I was working."

"And so are we. Same time, same place, today, that's a little over two hours from now in the hookup room. Be there or be square." I clicked off.

"She's not happy?" Bill asked.

"Oh my God. Can we please solve this case so I can get her out of my life?"

"Funny, I bet she feels the same."

I narrowed my eyes at him and went back to my tea. We worked out the plan as we drank and the music played. Then it was time to go.

◆

Linus had said anyone with the chops to trace the message back to my number could do it in about an hour. If they couldn't trace it, I was hoping they'd come anyway; the blackmail threat was clear and we'd mentioned my partner to give a big clue. And an unused basement, what better place to get rid of a dumb chick PI would-be blackmailer? Leaving now would get Bill and me to the hookup room extremely early. But naturally, if the spoofer came at all, he'd be very early, too.

We still had our ID passes, which got us as far as the elevator bank. There, as we'd arranged in the phone call I'd made between the other two calls, we met Juarez. Her lanky frame was in uniform and she gave us her easy grin.

"Hey, Boss. And Boss Two. What are we doing today?"

"You're getting us into the east basement and then going back to work," I said. The east basement being now more secure than it used to be, Bill and I figured Jordy's route would end abruptly at a locked door somewhere along it. We needed Juarez's keys, so I'd called her, but we didn't need her to be along when we confronted a killer, so as we headed for the elevator that would take us to the basement, I told her a little fib. "We need to double-check some things."

"What things?"

"Measurements. For the lawyer."

She cocked her head. "Measurements?"

"You've seen those charts in court. So many feet from this door to that one, hallway this wide, that kind of thing."

She gave me some side-eye. "How come you needed me? Sergeant Montero's in charge now. He'd have let you in, being this is legit."

"It's legit if the DA does it. They have no obligation to let in anyone working for the defense until after Jordy's indicted."

"But Montero would. He likes you."

"But we're persona non grata in a lot of this hospital," Bill said. "Montero would log our visit and someone might get their panties all in a twist."

"Ah. So really, you're sneaking in."

"You're sneaking us in. Then you're going back to work."

"My shift doesn't start for an hour. I could help, like hold the measuring tape or something."

"We're going to use the measuring app on the phone," he said. "Doesn't take two people, even. You're already breaking enough regulations getting us down here. Thanks, and go back to work."

We'd been right about the locked doors into the hallway maze. She unlocked the last one and said, "You trying to get rid of me?"

"Yes. We're trying to keep you out of trouble. Goodbye." I closed the door in her face. Of course she was the one with the key, so the gesture was only symbolic. She opened it a second later and stuck her head in.

"Okay, I get the message. See you later, Boss and Boss Two." She winked and pulled the door shut again.

The east basement hallways hadn't improved over the last couple of days. The moldy smell, the odd sharp shadows, the skittery noises that made you jump. Or maybe it wasn't the noises.

"Nervous?" Bill said.

"Yeah, a little. Who told you the phone had a measuring app?"

"I made that up. It does?"

That seemed like a cue for an eyeroll, but he'd already gone around the corner.

The plan was for me to hang out in the once-again-off-limits hookup room, waiting for Sophia Scott's killer to come. All we needed from him or her was a couple of sentences that would make it clear on the phone's recording app, which of course I was running, that their appearance here was because of my text and not a coincidence. We weren't expecting or even hoping for a confession. I had full faith that Church could extract that, possibly even from an innocent man if she promised to never speak to him again.

We were, of course, expecting that Scott's killer would be planning to kill me, too, after finding out what I knew and whether it was true I hadn't told anybody. Bill, who'd be hidden in the shadows at the dark end of the hallway, was supposed to prevent that.

◆

Back in the café, we'd exchanged theories on who it was we'd invited to this party. My money was on either of the DeBrengs, though I didn't think Bradley had the know-how to spoof a phone number. He did have a twelve-year-old kid, though.

"Do you have a sleeper?" Bill asked, reaching for a french fry.

"Elizabeth Gordon-Platt. She has no motive I can see and I cannot believe she'd get her hands personally dirty but I love the idea. What about you?"

"I'm hoping for Quick Draw," he said. "Maybe Scott had found out about the stolen-goods scheme and she was blackmailing him."

"Sivek and six guards were involved in that, too. Maybe she was blackmailing one of them. Or all of them. Wow, could be a big party."

"And my sleeper is Margaret Weldon. She has the same things working against her as Gordon-Platt but she'd be as satisfying."

We discussed the other possibilities among the known players. Bill suggested Venturino, to stop Scott from undermining the nurses' new contract. I said, "That's ridiculous."

"Why, because you like her?"

"Come on, you only suggested Weldon because you have a soft spot for Bacay because he's Filipino."

"I bet he can cook. Mmm, adobo, lumpia, sinigang . . ."

"I can't believe you can dream about food so soon after those tacos. What about Walsh?"

"Motive?"

"A desperate, hidden, hopeless passion for Scott?"

Bill laughed.

"Probably, though," I said, wiping my fingers, "it's something as boring as some doctor cheating on his wife with her and he suddenly got cold feet."

"You know," Bill said, as the music changed again, to ringing, rhythmic steel drums, "it's impressive to be a person in a position to do so much damage that more than a dozen other people have motives to kill you."

As it turned out, when our company finally showed up, it was no one we'd expected, and the damage had long since been done.

CHAPTER FORTY-SEVEN

"How're you doing?" That was Bill whispering in my earbud.

I whispered back, "I don't know if I'm more creeped out that I'm waiting for a killer or that I'm doing it in this skanky place."

The air I was breathing carried the odors of stale perfume and a forlorn whiff of pine cleanser. The red gauze draped on the single overhead light was supposed to make the hookup room romantic but Cupid was the farthest thing from my mind. Except maybe if he brought me his bow and arrows. Bill and I had decided not to carry at the beginning of this case; it's almost impossible to legitimately get a weapon into a hospital and highly illegal to smuggle one in, no matter how licensed you are. We didn't trust our guest to be observing the niceties, but we were gambling that their need to be sure of how much I actually knew and whether I'd told anyone else would be enough to keep them from bursting in here with guns blazing.

"Where are you?"

"In the corner near the chair contraption."

"Not on it?"

"Eeww."

"Sure you want to stand? It could be a while."

"I'll take that chance. Besides, so are you. Aren't you? Ready to spring into action?"

"I'm leaning on the wall."

"Gross."

That was enough conversation. It was still an hour before "same time" but if I were meeting a dumb chick PI would-be blackmailer, I'd want to show up early to get the drop on her.

And a few minutes later, he did.

A shadow slipped into the room from the dim hallway. Then the red-shrouded light went out.

In that instant I dropped behind the chair. The door quietly pushed shut behind my visitor. Bill had taped the lock, though, so I wasn't worried about being trapped in a small room with a murderer.

Okay, maybe I was, just a little.

A piercing white beam swept around, strobing shards of mattress, swing, and walls.

I crept to my right and chucked a piece of something I found on the floor—again, eeww—to my left. The light swung there immediately.

The door burst open.

Oh, for Pete's sake, Bill, I thought. *It's too soon. He hasn't said a word yet.*

But it wasn't Bill.

The light beam soared, swooped wildly, and went out. Churning shapes in the doorway resolved into limbs flailing, bodies tangling. Before I could come around from behind the chair I heard Bill's shouting voice and his running footsteps. The red light came back on, with Bill's hand on the switch.

"Stop!" A man's loud shout, not Bill's.

Bill stopped. I stopped.

The tangling bodies stopped, resolving into Juarez in front, not moving, a gun held to her head by the man behind her, Darius Georges.

Talk about a sleeper.

"Smith, get in the room, close the door. Chin, you better be in here or I'm shooting these two before I come find you."

"That's a very odd threat," I said, moving out from behind the chair but staying, as much as I could, in the shadows. Bill stepped in and shut the door. "If I weren't here, how would I know you'd made it?"

"I didn't think you weren't here." I could hear the smirk in his voice. "I thought you might be chicken enough to stay hidden. But nice that you're stupid, I mean brave, for your friends here. Throw down your weapons, both of you."

"Don't have one," I said. "You know how hard it is to get a gun into a hospital?"

"I seem to have managed. Chin, hands behind your head and don't move. Smith, take off your jacket and turn around."

We both did as he said, and Bill pulled up the bottoms of his jeans to prove he had no ankle holster. Then we reversed roles. I had no jacket, but lifted my tunic enough to prove I had no gun in my waistband. As I did the same for my pants legs I said, "Why did you kill her?"

"I haven't killed her yet. She's right here. Keep your hands behind your heads and kneel."

"Not Juarez." Bill and I did as told. I could see Juarez, gun at her temple and Georges's arm around her throat, give me a wide-eyed *Hey, come on* look. I said, "Scott."

"My God, you people are punks. Is this where I confess because I've got the upper hand, only it turns out there are a dozen cops outside? Well, damn, you forgot the cops. And really, no weapons? You set a trap unarmed? I'd fire an operative who did this. And this is your backup?" He yanked on Juarez's neck. "I knew you'd have him"—a nod at Bill—"but I have to admit I didn't expect her." A push of the gun into Juarez's temple.

"We didn't either."

"Not a deep bench you have here. Handy, though. I came to apprehend this woman, Sophia's killer"—he tightened his arm on Juarez's neck—"and you stupid people interfered. It was awful. You wouldn't stop and listen. I lost hold of my gun in the fight and someone started shooting. In the end, you were all dead. Awful."

"Nobody will believe that."

"Of course they will. She and Sophia were having an affair and Sophia was going to out her, so she murdered her."

"You're—"

Juarez shoved off backward. She didn't have much force but it was enough to stagger Georges. From my position on my knees I lunged for his ankle. I was too far away and missed. Bill tried the same move at the same time, managed to grab onto Georges's pant leg but a kick in the face tossed him backward.

I leapt to my feet. Juarez twisted, trying to pull free. Georges shoved her stumbling into me.

A bang, a flash, and a bullet whining through the skanky red air. Metal shrieked, glass tinkled.

Bill yelled, "Shit!"

I threw Juarez aside and dove for Georges's knees. His second shot went where he expected me to come from, higher up; I heard it scream over my head. I brought him down and was wrestling him for the gun when the door slammed open and a voice I knew yelled, "Everyone stop *now* or I'm going to shoot every fucker in here until you all stop moving."

It seemed we hadn't forgotten the cops after all.

CHAPTER FORTY-EIGHT

I froze where I was, half buried under Georges with my fingers clamped on his wrist. Church was framed in the doorway, her gun held two-handed and perfectly steady. I'd bet she was an ace at the range. Behind her were two River Valley security guards.

"Don't move, Juarez," I said. "She'll do it. Bill, you okay?"

"I'm good. Yo, Detective."

"You're a cop?" said Georges. "Thank God. I'm Darius Georges. I'm a security consultant. I—"

"He's not security here!" Juarez barked, though she didn't move. "I am. I'm—"

"All of you just shut the fuck up. I'm taking everyone in and you can all tell your stories at the precinct." Speaking into the radio at her shoulder, she gave her location and asked for backup. To the security guys behind her she said, "Stay back." To us: "You two, George or whatever your name is, and Chin. Separate, slowly. But do not stand up. God, this red light, what the fuck? If there are any weapons here they'd better hit the floor in two seconds. One, two."

My fingers sprang off Georges's wrist. He put the gun down.

"That's it? Four assholes, one gun?"

"You know," I said, "this may be hard to believe but I'm glad to see you, Detective. I was pretty sure you weren't coming."

"I was pretty sure you weren't stupid enough to really do this. Then I thought about it and decided you were."

From the floor beside me, Georges said, "Detective—that's right, isn't it? You're Detective Church? We spoke. I'm Darius Georges from The Michael Group. I—"

"Oh, yeah, the Chicago cop, I remember."

"Yes, well, I—"

"Ohmigod!" I burst out. "Oh my God. The Chicago cop."

Georges whipped his head around to me and I knew I was right.

"Shut up, Chin," said Church.

"The Chicago cop," said Bill from the shadows in the corner of the room. "The one with the son."

"My family is none of your business," Georges snapped.

"You just shot me, so yeah, it is."

"You got hit?" I started to scramble to my feet.

"Chin, sit *down*. Smith, you okay for now?"

"Yeah. I'm sure they can fix me up upstairs. His son did a year because Sophia Scott dropped a dime on his drug-dealing ass."

I saw what he was doing and picked it up. "His son," I said softly, "was in love with her. She left him holding the bag. She promised she'd wait for him and then she split." I added, "What a bitch. I'm sorry."

"Oh, come on," Bill said. "Sophia was a bitch, sure, but how stupid was the kid to fall for someone like her? I'm pretty sure he was stoned all the time anyway. No great loss."

"Go to hell!" Georges roared.

The elevator dinged in the distance and footsteps hurried down the hallway. "All right," Church said, "everyone just shut up again. We'll deal with this one by one."

"My son," Georges said, and I was surprised to hear his voice break, "sold weed. A little weed. In prison he found heroin. He's been in rehab three times and he lives in my basement. Back then, he was pre-med at Northwestern. He was going to be a doctor."

The room filled with cops and they hauled us out, one by one.

CHAPTER FORTY-NINE

The sparkling-river, gleaming-cloud view from the Admin fancy conference room was even better than it had been the first time Bill and I had gone up to breathe the rarefied air. For our part, we looked better, too, all scrubbed and well turned out because there were no more basements to crawl around in and my brother Elliot was taking us, Jordy, and Cohen out to lunch. We had to wait for Elizabeth Gordon-Platt, but we'd come without an appointment, after all, just some more of that "we won't take much of her time but trust me, she really will want to see us" stuff I'd gotten to be so good at working this case.

Gordon-Platt walked in as Bill was expounding to me on the various shapes and roles of the tugboats on the East River. It was actually kind of interesting, and I was a little sorry to see Gordon-Platt's navy-suit-clad, ghostly reflection in the window glass.

She stopped right inside the door and as we turned she said icily, "I have been on the phone all night and this morning with my donors and my board trying to explain gunfire, a police intervention I was not made aware of in advance, and four people—including you two—taken out of here in handcuffs."

"You're welcome," I said, flopping into a chair on the window side of the table. "Sit down."

Gordon-Platt made a strangled noise, but she stalked around to the head of the table and sat. "I want you out of here as soon as you say what you came to say. And say it all so you don't have to come back."

"Oh, don't worry," I said as Bill sat beside me. "We don't want to spend another second in this hospital if we don't have to. Except maybe in the Emergency Department with my brother. Bill was there yesterday getting his neck bandaged. Before the handcuffs, I mean."

Bill pulled on his shirt collar so Gordon-Platt could see the bandage over the place Georges's bullet had torn the flesh but missed the artery. He grinned affably and straightened his tie.

"We brought you something, though." I lifted a folder out of my shoulder bag and slid it along the table to her. "You don't have to read it now. We just pulled everything together in one document for your convenience."

She didn't touch the folder, but said, "Everything?" as if the word described a gross disease.

"All the scams and grifts going on in this hospital."

"Well, no," said Bill. "Just the ones we know about."

"Oh, right, good point." I took a breath. "We were hired to keep Jordy Kazarian out of prison. Trying to do that took us through the underbelly of your hospital, and I don't mean the basement. And what we found out was it all comes back to you."

That was the conclusion Bill and I had come to when we finally sat together at Shorty's after a couple of hours at the 23rd Precinct and some triumphal time on the phone with Cohen explaining why Jordy's charges were being dropped.

◆

Church had interrogated each of us herself, separately, a uniform standing by in each room in case we got rowdy. She came and went multiple times. When she was finally satisfied our stories matched, she told Juarez, Bill, and me that we could go.

"Georges called his lawyer." She was standing with the three of us near her desk in the detective squad room. "I can't talk to him again until she gets here. But it's pretty clear. His firm has been working with the hospital a long time. That's how he knew the layout of the basement and the codes to the outer doors—he'd come himself for the security walk-through."

Which Quick Draw, I realized, had told us. *Prick in a three-piece suit came here*, he'd said. *George somebody, no, I think George was his last name. Darius Georges.*

"And he spotted Sophia Scott then?" I asked. "Hell of an unlucky break for her."

"No, no. He had no idea she was there—not even that she'd become a nurse—until they were hired to do backgrounds on the negotiating committee. As managing partner he was giving the reports a quick once-over before they went to the client. Almost not paying attention—and there she was. The girl who'd ruined his son's life. On a committee to demand more money. His son had apparently just checked into rehab for the third time."

"So, what? He snapped?"

Church nodded. "And decided he'd kill her with what had destroyed his kid."

"He told you that?"

"I said it to him and he didn't deny it. In fact"—she looked away, as if she were embarrassed, though until then I wouldn't have said that was an emotion Church was capable of—"he started to cry."

◆

"No, don't interrupt," I said to Gordon-Platt now, when she opened her mouth. "We'll be out of here faster if you just let me go on. The man who killed Sophia Scott found her because your legal department hired his firm to do background checks on the nurses' negotiating committee for dirt to blackmail them with. That background check/blackmail scheme was Margaret Weldon's but you clearly encourage that at this hospital because you tried it on me with my brother. Then Georges killed Sivek because, since the east basement had no security because you were too cheap, Sivek was running an illegal business down there. He saw the murder, tried to blackmail Georges, and was way out of his depth. What Georges didn't know, though it might not have mattered, was that Sophia Scott didn't join the committee to get more money. She joined it to stop the strike because if there was a strike and travel nurses came in, it would become clear OB/GYN nurses didn't really need to work all the overtime she was getting paid for and *that* scam would be exposed. And meanwhile your man Albert Walsh was doing everything he could to get the nurses to strike so the travel nurse company he and Bradley DeBreng own could clean up."

Elizabeth Gordon-Platt's face was its usual unmoving mask, except now it was chalk white.

I turned to Bill. "What's that instruction to medical people?"

He smiled. "Primum non nocere. First, do no harm. That's the Latin translation from the original Greek. Hippocrates, *Of the Epidemics*."

Sometimes his brain full of stuff is quite useful. "It seems to me," I said, "that that's not what's been going on around here."

We both watched Elizabeth Gordon-Platt struggle to keep from exploding. Just when I thought her top was ready to blow, I said, "Some of this, of course, the police already have. Some of it we didn't tell them because it wasn't part of our case, and believe me, they'd rather not have anything to do with this place anymore. But it's all documented here. So this is what you're going to do."

"You can't—"

"Oh, I can, and I will. You're going to settle with the nurses. Their demands are reasonable and good for your patients, who I don't see a lot of people worrying about on these top floors here. Whom? Okay. You're going to back off Alon Bacay. We're keeping an eye on him and if he gets fired or doesn't get his citizenship . . ." I tapped the report.

"I can't do anything about his citizenship."

"They'll look for recommendations from his job." I gave her a thin smile, though not as thin as her lips were right then. "And finally, you'll let my brother set the terms for Seymour Larson's gift. Toilet paper, elevator repairs—whatever Elliott wants, as long as Larson agrees you'll smile and thank Larson in as flashy a news conference as you want to hold." I stood. "Here. You can keep this."

Bill stood, too, and we walked to the door. He pulled it open and held it for me. I walked through, turned, and though there hadn't been any, I said, "Thanks for the coffee."

We left, heading for the restaurant where we were meeting Elliott, Cohen, and Jordy. After that I had to go home and change.

This evening Elliott was going to take me back to the airfield for a sunset parachute jump.

ACKNOWLEDGMENTS

Josh Getzler
Jillian Schelzi
Yuri Simon, MD
Lorena Vivas, CCRN
Steve Blier, Hillary Brown, Susan Chin, Monty Freeman, Charles McKinney, Max Rudin, Jim Russell, Amy Schatz, Sylvia Smith
Barb Shoup
Chris Chiang
Cheryl Tan
Patricia Chao
Vicki Hendricks
The New York Society Library
The New York State Nurses Association